Journey to Kokoroe

By

Laura L. Comfort

Essence of Galenia: Journey to Kokoroe

By Laura L. Comfort

Copyright 2013 by Laura L. Comfort

Illustrations copyright 2013 by Laura L. Comfort

ISBN: 978-0-9920792-0-8

ACKNOWLEDGEMENTS

I would like to offer a special thanks to my fellow writers particularly Richard Ankers for his great feedback and encouragement, and Jennifer Bogart for her helpful tips on publishing.

Kelley Stark, my editor, for asking me tough questions and providing sound advice.

My husband's tough questions, sound logic and scientific know-how that helped me create a plausible world.

And finally my children, Sydney and Keaton, for being a patient and encouraging audience – thank you for sharing this fantasy world with me and contributing your wonderful ideas.

Laura L. Comfort
November, 2013

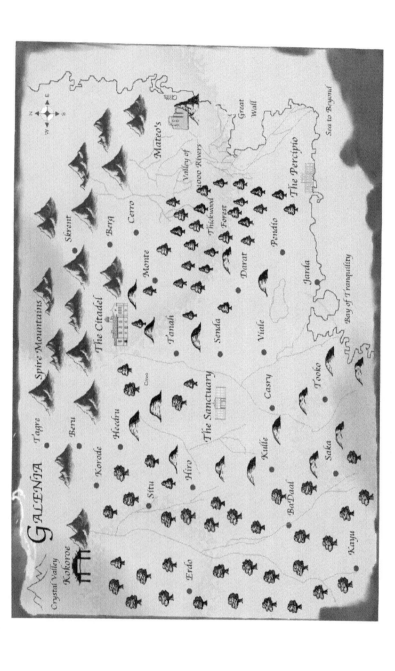

This book is dedicated to my family; thanks for

putting up with my obsession.

Table of Contents

PROLOGUE

The head wound was still bleeding.

Although Cardea was not the town healer, she had years of experience tending to minor injuries. On more than one occasion, she'd helped set bones and cleaned up various wounds of the Jagare who were at risk of such things while on the hunt or protecting the village. This was different. She had just finished replacing the bloodied dressing with a clean one when Hamlin, her husband, returned with the healer, Leader Chieo, who was also the Juro of the village.

Cardea rushed to the door bowing quickly as she greeted the new arrivals.

"Thank goodness you've come!" She beckoned them with the bloodied cloth she still held in her hand, "It looked like a simple cut at first, but other symptoms have appeared and the bleeding won't stop."

As Cardea quickly explained the girl's symptoms, Leader Chieo rushed over to the cot where the girl still lay unconscious. He could tell right away that the head wound was only part of the problem. The girl was extremely pale and beads of sweat were trickling down her face. Her breathing was constricted as though there was a great weight on her chest.

Chieo closed his eyes and placed his hands above the girls' chest. He was still for a moment and then slowly moved his hands, hovering above her body. When he had passed completely from head to toe, he sighed and opened his eyes.

PROLOGUE

"The girl has no Essence in her at all," Chieo said solemnly. "This would explain her symptoms and that would make her Kameil."

Seeing the fearful look on the faces throughout the room, Cardea rushed to the girl's side as if to protect her.

"She's just a child!" cried Cardea. "Surely we must treat her."

"Older than a child I would think," Leader Chieo replied. Seeing the maternal instinct in Cardea, he quickly added, "Of course, she is still too young to be a threat and we should therefore treat her."

Reaching into his bag, Chieo pulled out a mask and fit it over the girl's mouth. A small pouch was connected to the mask and when he opened the valve the girl inhaled the contents of the bag. Each breath was deeper and stronger than the last until she finally began to breathe easily.

He turned to Cardea, "The gas will help her breathing for now, but she will need another bag in an hour or so. In the meantime, we can address the wound. You say you used powdered Tossu plant to try and clot it?"

She nodded.

"That typically would be enough. I think if we mix some powdered Essence to the plant she will respond better. We will apply it heavily, then bandage it."

Cardea rushed to get her bowl of Tossu powder while Chieo pulled a small jar of light pink powdered Essence from his bag. Using a small spoon, he added a portion of the shimmering substance to the Tossu powder, blending them together.

Once he tended the girl, Chieo approached Hamlin. Until that moment, Hamlin had stood quietly in the corner, where he could observe what occurred without interfering.

Hamlin bowed to Leader Chieo as he approached.

"Hamlin, what are your thoughts?"

Hamlin knew Chieo was concerned how the village would respond to having treated a Kameil and the burden Chieo had placed on Cardea and Hamlin since the girl was in their care.

"She is a young enough that, I think, it will prevent anyone from casting her out too quickly. Plus she is still unconscious; I think that will allow enough time for Cardea to plead her case."

Chieo nodded. "Yes, I agree. Would you arrange for a town meeting then? Say, in an hour's time?"

"Thank you, Leader Chieo." Hamlin bowed again and left quietly.

Chieo addressed Cardea. "She should improve enough so you can leave her while you are attending the meeting."

Cardea reached out and grabbed the girl's hand. She was reluctant to leave her at all, but she was more fearful of the town's reaction to discovering a Kameil in their town. She nodded her agreement.

"One hour," Chieo said, closing the door gently behind him.

CHAPTER ONE

Cause and Concern

The room was crowded.

Most of the town showed up for the meeting and were sitting on wooden risers that formed a semi-circle. Three ornate chairs with high backs had been placed on a dais in front of the steps providing all in attendance a clear view. Leader Chieo was seated in the centre chair, Cardea occupied the one on his right, and the tall, muscular Jagare leader named Kaine dominated the seat on the left.

Once most people were settled, Kaine rose and spoke to the crowd.

"Greetings our good people. Thank you for coming on such short notice. Leader Chieo and our dear friend Cardea have a serious matter to discuss and a decision is required." He inclined his head toward Cardea. "If you will be so kind?"

Kaine returned to his seat as Cardea stood. "Thank you, Leader Kaine." She bowed slightly in Kaine's direction and then turned her attention to the crowded room. Pacing a little as she spoke and wringing her hands, she told her story.

"I was in the woods gathering some needed supplies; I was running low on Mugwort, Skullcap and Bloodroot. I had just filled my basket and was about to return home when I heard a voice in the distance calling out. I'm not sure what was said, but when I turned I saw someone lying on the ground a short way off." Cardea paused, then continued somewhat exasperated. "Well, I dropped my basket and ran to see what had happened. I found this young girl. It took me no time at all to realize she must have tripped over the root by her feet. The girl had landed poorly and smashed her head on a sharp rock. Of course I didn't hesitate, I just picked her right up and carried her home. I did have my cart with me so I was able to wheel her most of the way." Cardea began wringing her hands as she paced.

"Once we arrived at my cottage, I cleaned her up and treated the wound. I have no idea where she came from. She's obviously not from our village, so I sent Hamlin to get Leader Cheio straight away. It was a good thing I did, too, as the poor thing was getting worse even after I dressed the cut."

The villagers quietly listened to Cardea's tale, concern on their faces and questions on their lips. Cardea glanced at Leader Cheio before she continued. He nodded his head and again she addressed the people. She made sure to look them in the eyes as she talked hoping to gain their empathy. When she finally disclosed the detail the girl was Kameil there was an audible intake of breath from the crowd.

"I implore you to remember, she is a child first and foremost. Being Kameil, though important, need not be the only factor to determine her fate."

Whispers quickly became animated rumbling, which in turn, became raised voices full of fear.

"We must protect her!"

"She can't stay here, they will come looking for her!"

"Yes, we must think of our own younglings!"

"Heal her, then let her go!"

Chieo stood and raised his hands, promptly the silence resumed.

"I hear your concerns and the struggle within you. Yes, we must heal her. To do otherwise is to condemn her to death – we are not murderers."

He had the full of attention of the room; no sound could be heard.

CAUSE AND CONCERN

"Before a decision is made, I recommend we hear what the child has to say. Since she is currently unconscious, I think we postpone any drastic measures. What say you?"

An older man stepped forward; although he was hunched and seemingly unsteady on his feet his voice was strong and carried throughout the room.

"Thank you for your wise council, Leader Chieo. I agree that we should heal her, and then send her away as soon as she's fit. I think increasing guard duty is essential to our safety."

"Hear, hear!" echoed across the room.

Chieo said, "Agreed, thank you for your wise council Leader Nyack. Another meeting will be called when we have more information from the child. Cardea, will you continue to watch over her?" Cardea bowed and looked please at the charge she was given. Chieo continued. "Please let me know when the girl wakes up. Thank you all for coming. Be well."

The assembly resumed their discussions as they slowly made their way out the door. Cardea, eager to return home, led the way.

* * *

Hanna took in a deep breath. She could smell flowers and freshly cut grass. Imagining she must have fallen asleep in the woods behind her house, she was surprised when she opened her eyes and saw a peculiar ceiling above her. Often she had lain on her living room floor staring up at the ceiling, imagining shapes in the stucco. This ceiling, however, had thick wooden beams and wood slats across them. She caught movement out of the corner of her eye and turned her head.

6

"You are awake! Thank goodness. You must be very thirsty; lie still for a moment and I will get you some water."

Hanna was puzzled. She had never met this person before yet she spoke to her like a concerned parent. As she watched her pour water from a jug, Hanna tried to think where she'd seen this lady before. Her hair was curly and her face had a pinkish hue. Confused and unsure where she was, Hanna tried to think of the last thing she could remember.

She recalled having another typical day at school, of noisy hallways and bright fluorescent lights that left her with yet another migraine to end her day. Following the nauseating bus ride home, the smell of sweat mixed in with perfumes and cologne, she had escaped civilization by hiding in the woods behind her house. She gazed up at the canopy of the trees as she lay on a bed of greenery. Taking in the refreshing smell of moss and pinecones, she twirled her hair around her fingers, unconcerned of the dried leaves and twigs that became entangled in it. Her daydreams were interrupted by a cracking sound, like a person walking on branches. She jumped to her feet and glanced around; perhaps twenty feet away, she saw her. Completely taken by surprise, Hanna was more curious than worried. She had never seen anyone in the woods before; today was the first. A lady with a kind face that had a pinkish hue was meandering through the bushes.

'That's it!' Hanna thought. She recalled watching the woman taking cuttings off the bushes, then pick up a basket and begin walking in the opposite direction. Aside from being in the usually vacant woods, something seemed strange about this woman, but Hanna couldn't really explain what it was. Her clothing was simple and dated looking, and although filling a basket with plants may not have been typical it wasn't odd enough to warrant suspicion.

Still, Hanna was unable to contain her curiosity and followed her. The woman disappeared behind a tree. Hanna quietly moved in closer. When she peered around the tree there was no sign of the lady. Hanna scampered in a little further. She wondered how she could have lost her so easily. When there was still no sign of her, Hanna's curiosity increased. She desperately wanted to talk with her and find out who she was; when her headache's didn't get the best of her, she tended to be a social creature.

Hanna caught a glimpse of her, only to lose her again behind another tree. Feeling as if she was being pulled, Hanna ran calling out to get the lady's attention and proceeded to trip on the protruding root of a rather large tree. She flew into the air and, as luck would have it, hit her head on a rock. That was the last thing she remembered.

"You're the lady I saw in the woods. I was trying to catch up with you, but..." Hanna put her hand to her head and winced in pain.

Although taller than Hanna, the woman would be considered short by most adults. She was rather plump, but not terribly so. Her soft curly hair was held back out of her eyes by a blue ribbon. Her long skirt was covered in smudges of dirt.

"You must have tripped. You banged your head on a rock, which gave you a nasty cut. When I found you, you were unconscious so I brought you to my home so I could tend to you. My name is Cardea. Let me help you sit up, slowly, dear."

Hanna hadn't expected to be so weak or dizzy as Cardea put her arms around her and gently pulled her to a sitting position. She adjusted the pillows and propped her so that she was able to drink without spilling. She took a sip of the tepid water which was so refreshing it actually made her feel a little better as it trickled down her throat.

"I'm Hanna," she said, wiping the drips of water from her chin.

Cardea looked at Hanna warmly. She sat on a stool that was beside the bed. As intrigued as she was about the girl, she held off on peppering her with questions and instead concentrated on getting her steady and fit to talk to Leader Chieo.

"Do you think you can eat a little, Hanna? It is well past dinner; I'm sure you must be starving."

"Yes please, but I was wondering, if I just banged my head, why am I so weak? What time is it? How long have I been here? Where is here and do you have a phone? My mom will be worried."

"Let me get you some bread and preserves and then we can see about getting you some answers." Cardea stood up and made her way across the room.

Hanna looked around and was surprised by her surroundings. She was in a large, dimly lit room. Directly across from her there was a wooden table with benches. In one corner was a large fireplace with a few chairs covered in blankets and pillows. Cardea was working at a counter against a wall, which had an island in front of it. The walls were lined with shelves full of jars and bottles. Throughout the room, hanging from the ceiling and attached to each of the four large pillars, hung dried flowers and grasses. She realized these were why the room smelled like the woods. There was a set of stairs leading up most likely to a bedroom, Hanna figured. In front of the door was a large mat and coats hung on the wall. Her little cot looked out of place; she wondered if it had been placed there temporarily, just for her. Several hanging lanterns flickered giving the room an eerie glow. This cottage was just the thing she would dream up when wandering in the woods. Was it possible she was still asleep? It was like being in a medieval herbalist cottage or maybe a witch's. Hanna laughed in spite of herself.

Cardea came back from around the counter with a tray holding bread and jelly, some cold meat and a few slices of cheese. She placed it on the table beside the cot and used her apron to wipe her hands.

"Do you think you can help yourself?" she inquired with concern in her eyes.

Hanna flashed her a reassuring smile, nodded her head and took a piece of cheese. Her mouth was watering; she suddenly realized she was famished! She took a bite of the cheese with much appreciation. Unsure if it was just from the hunger, it was the best cheese she could remember tasting.

She exclaimed, "Delicious! Thanks so much."

Once Cardea saw that Hanna was quite able to eat on her own she put a shawl over her shoulders.

"I need to step out for just a minute. Will you be all right?"

Hanna nodded again, chuckling at the concern Cardea was showing. She was like a mother fussing over a small child. Normally, had it been Hanna's mother, she would have been incensed to be treated this way. She would have rolled her eyes and reminded her mother that she was fourteen and did not need to be coddled; having Cardea fret over her though, made her feel safe.

When Cardea slipped out the door Hanna continued devouring the plate of food left for her. Everything tasted wonderful and each bite renewed her strength. Thinking about her unanswered questions, she realized it was unlikely there would be a phone in this place. With no sign of electricity, a cell phone appeared to be the only chance for making a call; however, Hanna had the impression that Cardea was someone who was unlikely to own one and neither did Hanna.

Just as Hanna was finished eating the last morsel on her plate the door opened. Suddenly the room was full of people. Hanna was unsettled and fear began to grip her. Seeing the panic in Hanna's face, Cardea quickly made her way over to the girl.

"No one's going to hurt you. We just want you to get better and help you find your way home." Cardea leaned over and gave Hanna a comforting hug. She felt a little better, yet was still full of trepidation.

"Let me introduce everyone to you. This is Hamlin my husband."

The gentleman in the back quietly stepped forward. He gave a gentle smile, "How do you do?" and then returned to the corner behind the rest.

"This is Leader Chieo the town healer."

Hanna was most interested in meeting this person. He was only three feet tall and had a grey beard that reached down to his chest. His face showed age, yet was smooth and pinker in hue than Cardea's. Instead of typical pants and shirt, he had on a tawny coloured robe with a golden braided belt. He held an intricately designed staff with a pink crystal on the top that was held in place by what looked like wooden ribbons crisscrossing over top of it.

"May I check if your fever has gone down?" he asked.

She nodded and he reached over and placed his hands on the sides of her face. He felt her forehead and the back of her neck. Hanna expected some sort of a thermometer from a Healer; this technique was the kind of thing she would expect her mother to use. He poured her another glass of water from the pitcher on the table and handed it to her.

Turning to the others he said, "Her fever has been greatly reduced. Only a little heat from the wound seems to be present."

He returned to the door and quietly spoke to the two men there.

"Cardea," Hanna said softly, "who is the other man Leader Chieo is speaking with?"

The individual Hanna spoke of was the most intimidating person in the room. He was the tallest one there. He had brood shoulders and was very muscular.

11

This Hanna knew because his shirt had no sleeves. In fact, he was wearing thick, leather armour on his chest and bands over his forearms. He wore leather pants and his boots went up to his knees. Once again Hanna felt like she was in a dream, one that took place in medieval times.

"Oh my apologies, how could I overlook Leader Kaine?" Hanna got the feeling that Cardea had not forgotten to introduce Kaine, and instead was hoping to avoid bringing attention to his presence, which was somewhat absurd seeing how he stood at least a foot taller than everyone else in the room; more than three feet taller than Leader Chieo. Leader Kaine stayed where he was and nodded. He didn't smile yet he didn't come across as unkind.

"Well that's everyone and this is Hanna," she said gesturing to Hanna. "I will make some tea while we all get better acquainted."

Cardea turned and went back to the counter while Hamlin prepared the fire.

Leader Chieo moved closer to Hanna. "Hanna, do you know where you are?"

Hanna shook her head. She could feel the tension leave the room as the others acknowledged her ignorance. Now she really felt anxious. Why would they be relieved that she didn't know where she was?

"You are in Kayu." Chieo stated.

When Hanna stared blankly at him he added, "A small village in the southeastern quadrant."

Chieo obviously assumed this cleared things up as he changed the subject.

"Where do you live Hanna?"

"Oh, my house was just ten minutes in the opposite direction that Cardea was heading..." She left out the rest of the sentence which was 'when I started chasing her' as that didn't seem to be the best statement to make at this time.

"Does anyone know you were out this way?"

Again panic must have shown on Hanna's face as he added, "Will they know where to start looking for you? We hope to help you find your family as soon as we can."

Hanna thought for a moment. It was Tuesday and that meant her mom would be home late, as she would be going straight to her exercise class from work. Her brother wouldn't know she was gone as he most likely wasn't yet home himself. Her father was out of town at a conference so the fact that she was missing wouldn't be noticed until bedtime. Even then, there was a good chance her mom would assume she had just gone to bed with another one of her migraines when Hanna wasn't at the door to greet her. She may not notice her missing until school the next morning.

She was unsure as to the motives of this strange assembly of people and was not ready to tell them that no one was looking for her. Normally she had so much to say, but at this moment panic had rendered her silent. Tears began to well up in her eyes.

"Don't worry child, we will find them." Leader Chieo placed his hand on her shoulder, which warmed her and calmed her.

"On another matter, it is clear to us that you are Kameil as you are completely void of Essence, what do you normally use as your source? Is this why you collapsed in the forest, because you were running low?"

Hanna shook her head, "I'm sorry, I don't understand what you are asking me. Did I run out of what? It's clear that I'm who?"

Now it was Chieo's turn to be taken aback. He thought these were fairly clear questions and would be the easiest to start with. Perhaps she was still a little foggy.

"You are Kameil."

"Never heard of her. My name is Hanna Taylor."

"Kameil is not a name, it is your race, is it not?"

"Um, no. I'm Caucasian."

Everyone exchanged glances. This was turning out to be a bigger mystery than they originally thought. Chieo was worried and thought perhaps there was another question he had better ask.

"Have you ever heard of Mateo?" The others in the room gasped.

"No, who is Mateo?"

It was Hamlin who answered the question as he set out mugs on the table. Without looking up he said, "A ghost story people whisper around the fire to try to explain what they don't fully know."

Chieo sat back. The most pressing dangers had been addressed and now it appeared they had an even bigger puzzle on their hands.

"I feel like I'm dreaming. This place is very odd to me. Your names and even the way you look – well it's not usual where I live. Do you guys have cell phones or WIFI or something? Heck, even a map and I could show you where my house is."

Chieo chuckled, "My dear, now I do not understand what you are asking me. A map, however, is something we can provide. Leader Kaine would you mind bring your maps?" Kaine nodded and quickly left the cottage.

Cardea invited everyone to sit and have tea. Hanna found she had the strength to get up and they helped her to a chair by the fire. Hanna had become confident that no one had any intentions of harming her and she began to relax.

Kaine returned in short order with a couple rolls of parchment under his arm. He unrolled the smaller of the two and showed it to Hanna.

Chieo explained, "This shows only the southeastern quadrant. Since you walked only a short distance from home you could point out the area you live."

As far as Chieo knew, Kameil didn't have any large towns, but rather lived in small encampments that often

14

moved around. Even though the girl claimed not to be Kameil he assumed she must live as one.

"This here is Kayu, the largest village this far south."

Noticing that Hanna looked puzzled Cardea pointed to the woods. "Here is where I was gathering herbs and here is where I found you."

Hanna figured these people must have given up all ties with the modern world and that was why their map looked hand-drawn and lacked any streets or places she'd even heard of. She thought it bizarre though that they wouldn't include the major cities or even the province names.

"Thanks Cardea. That should put my house just past the edge of the trees, I guess where your map ends."

Everyone was exchanging glances again. Hanna felt like she was from an alien planet as no one showed signs of understanding what she was saying.

"Don't you have a larger map? One of the city or even the province?"

Kaine picked up the other rolled map from the floor where he had placed it. It was much larger and Hamlin helped hold it up.

For the first time Kaine spoke. "This is the map of the world. It may be harder to pinpoint where your camp is. Perhaps you got turned around in the woods? Do you recognize any of the town names that may be close to where you live?"

Hanna was dumbfounded. This map was very similar to the previous one except there were many more towns and less detail of walking paths and names of hills that the other one had.

"Wow! I didn't realize there was so many places this far North. I thought there were roads and another subdivision right over here. This is weird. Anyway, my house is still below where your map shows. Don't you have one that goes further south?"

"I'm afraid we do not Hanna. You see there is nothing further south. Past the trees are mountains and they go on and on. They come back out here." Chieo pointed to the top of the map. "That is where Tagre is located. Do you live in the mountains?"

Hanna laughed. "I wish! But no, I live on a long cement street surrounded by houses just like everyone else in suburbia."

"This is a puzzle!" Chieo glanced at the confused faces around him; the girl seemed to be speaking nonsense. "Well, it is too dark tonight to journey through the woods; I myself am likely to get lost." Chieo winked at Hanna. "I'm sorry to cause concern to your family, but I think we best wait until the morning to try to find your home. Besides, I think you could do with a little more rest first."

Hanna agreed.

"Cardea, I think we will take our leave of you. Hanna, do you mind staying here for the night? I know Cardea and Hamlin will make your stay comfortable."

"Sure thing. I hope I'm not putting anyone through too much trouble."

Cardea chuckled and gave Hanna another hug. Kaine rolled his maps and then the three men left the cottage leaving Cardea alone with Hanna.

"Won't Hamlin be staying too?" Hanna asked.

"He will return. He has business he must attend to before he turns in for the night. More tea? I also have some pie that would hit the spot, don't you think?"

The town was assembled again to hear the information Leader Chieo had gathered. With Cardea absent from the meeting, Hamlin sat in her empty seat, although, he looked like he would rather be anywhere else.

Chieo explained that the village was safe for now and they would be taking the girl home in the morning. He confided that she was not Kameil with hopes that it would diminish their fears; nevertheless, it was agreed between

Hamlin and Kaine that leaving everyone with more questions and fewer answers may just bring about a renewed sense of panic. For now he told them their plans were to seek out her home in the morning and they acknowledged this as an acceptable decision.

CHAPTER TWO

Hide and Seek

Hanna was enthusiastic.

She had slept well and since she'd had such a positive reception from everyone the previous night, was looking forward to the adventure of the day. After sharing a delicious breakfast with Cardea and Hamlin, Hanna was less anxious to go home and more eager to look around outside of the cottage. Before she could begin her adventure, Chieo arrived with Kaine.

"Hanna, may I have a word before we venture out the door?" Chieo said.

"Good morning Leader Chieo! Of course we can talk."

Hanna was filled with curiosity as Chieo led her to the corner to speak.

"I thought it prudent to give you some idea of what to expect. You may not be accustomed to a village the size of ours...there will be rather a lot of people outside wanting to get a glimpse of you. We don't get many visitors our way. So please do not mind our curiosity." Chieo said. "Now, did Cardea give you another inhale of medicine this morning?"

"Yes. She said it would help me breathe more easily? That I was having troubles last night when I was unconscious?"

"That is right. That should do you until you get home. One more thing, if you find yourself in conversation with someone other than our little group of friends," he motioned to those in the room, "I would appreciate it if you would refrain from divulging details of your home. It may cause more confusion and questions than we can handle at the moment."

"Oh sure, no problem. Do you mind if I ask questions?" Hanna looked at Chieo with such excitement he had a hard time denying her request.

"All right, but perhaps you could ask one of us."

Again he signaled to the four of them in the cottage. Hanna smiled and nodded, accepting his terms. With that settled they went out the door to greet the sun shining day. Hanna had braced herself for the paparazzi. She realized this was a little far-fetched as she was not a movie star, but her imagination sometimes got carried away. What she saw, though, surprised and delighted her more than she had anticipated. Leader Chieo's idea of rather a lot of people was less than a crowded movie theatre.

She was pleased to find that instead of looking out onto a concrete world, she was surrounded by wooden houses and shops, grass and trees, benches and even a large, stone fountain. It reminded her of a Christmas village she had seen in a store window one December. There was a crowd of people and judging by what she could make out of the town, it was probably most of the people who lived there. Some were close by and greeted her with a smile while others pretended to be busy. More than ever Hanna wanted to walk around the village and explore each building, but she knew the responsible thing to do was make her way home. Her family would most definitely be worried by now.

Chieo led the way and people bowed as he went by. They passed the fountain and chose a path that went between two cottages and vanished into the woods. Some of the villagers followed them just beyond the buildings and then watched them disappear into the trees. Hanna noticed that the trees appeared a little thicker and somewhat taller at this end of the woods. She wasn't sure if her eyes were fuzzy, as she noticed that everything appeared to have a slightly pink tone. She thought, perhaps, this was worth mentioning to Leader Chieo.

"Leader Chieo, why is everything pink?"

Chieo stopped suddenly. Hanna had been following so closely, she almost bumped into him. She was sure that if she had, she would have rolled right over top of him, which probably wouldn't be the best incident to test their new found friendship. She made a mental note to stay a few more paces back once they resumed walking.

"You did not mention this before. Did you notice it last night?"

Hanna thought a moment. "Well, I suppose I did, but I thought it had something to do with the lighting in the room. I'm usually surrounded with bright white fluorescents all day; the lanterns gave off a much nicer, softer glow. So I guessed it was just from that."

"Hanna, you continue to amaze me. Please, walk beside me so we can talk some more." They continued walking down the path; it became less and less worn as they moved on. "Tell me, does everything have the same intensity of pink to you? Is there anything that appears brighter or perhaps, a darker shade?"

Hanna looked around. "Yes. The trees are darker than the bushes and grass. The colour in the air is barely detectable."

Chieo tilted his head as he listened, fascinated as she spoke. "I wonder...would you look at us and tell me if you notice any differences there?"

Everyone stopped walking so Hanna could carefully look them over. As she gazed from one to another her smile broadened across her face.

"What do you know? Now that I stop to look, it seems very clear to me! First of all, you are all much brighter than the trees. I remember thinking Cardea had a pinkish face, but now I see that her hands, arms and what I can see of her legs, are all the same colour. Hamlin has the same shading, but he looks like he has slightly darker skin.

Sort of like a pink blush over a suntan. Leader Kaines' face is not so pink, but his arms are, almost like he's had a bit of sunburn. And...Leader Chieo! Now that I see you out in the sun, your head is positively glowing! It's still a soft shade of pink, mind you, but even the air above your head looks a bit brighter. I wonder why I never really noticed it until now?"

Chieo glanced at the others whose faces were full of shock and surprise except for Kaine, who kept his emotions hidden behind an impassive expression. They resumed walking. "It is not surprising you did not notice sooner. It does require a certain concentration to detect. What is surprising though, is that you can see the Essence at all. A rare gift indeed! Cardea, if you would be so kind to take the lead as I believe we will soon be heading off the beaten trail?"

"Oh yes, of course!" Cardea scampered up to the front, happy to lead the way.

Hanna said, "You mentioned something about Essence last night. What is Essence?"

"I am starting to think, child, that you are not from Galenia!" Chieo chuckled, as did everyone else. "You see our world revolves around the Essence. It is our life source, it is the very air we breathe. Every living thing on Galenia, be it an animal, a tree or a person, contains some of the Essence. Without it, they die. The exceptions to this rule are the Kameil. They are completely lacking Essence. Look at your arms and hands. What shade of pink do you see there?"

Hanna obediently pulled up her sleeves to look at her arms. They were white, as always. Even in the summer her arms were very pale compared to most people, as she didn't spend much time in the sun, preferring to stick to the shade.

"No pink other than the air around them." Hanna paused, "That's why you think I'm Kameil."

Chieo nodded.

"But if I'm Kameil and don't have any Essence, how can I survive? You just said without it, you die."

Chieo took a moment before he continued the discussion, carefully choosing the words he next spoke. "There are other ways to attain Essence. One of which is to inhale it in its gas form, like you have been doing. One of the reasons you were struggling with your breathing was due to your lack of Essence. It is also why you were getting increasingly ill. If we had not given you the gas it would have only been a matter of days before you were... beyond recovery..." He intentionally refrained from saying dead.

Even so, what little colour Hanna had was completely drained from her face. It suddenly dawned on her why everyone had appeared so serious and Cardea so caring and protective of her. She felt extra grateful for their help, but then it dawned on her, her whole life she had survived without this so-called Essence.

"So why now?" she said thinking out loud. Noticing his confusion she explained, "I never needed it before so why now?"

"Why indeed. I am most curious how you survived without it."

"Leader Chieo, the more we talk, the more I think that perhaps I am from another planet, but how on earth did I get here?" Hanna couldn't help but chuckle at her pun; no one else caught her joke.

"I'm not sure I get your meaning, but yes, it's another riddle for us to solve. For the time being, let us pretend you are not from Galenia, as at this moment we are as unfamiliar with each other's ways as possible. This may be the easiest way to converse since we do not have any common ground."

"Excellent, what fun! My planet is called Earth."

"We even have different names for the world! You are certainly far removed from us! So, there is no Essence or need for Essence on your world?"

"Right. You said it was rare to be able to see the Essence. If it's everywhere and in everything, why would it surprise you that I can see it?"

"Well most in our society, our world as we know it, can't. Only Juro have The Sight and you are clearly not Juro."

"Cool I have a special talent! But what's a Juro and why is it clear that I'm not one?"

With a chuckle Chieo explained, "First of all, the Juro are one of the three main races. Second, Juro have not in recorded history been any taller than a Wendalbrush, which is a shrub roughly my height. You are clearly much taller than that! Thirdly, we have Essence most predominantly in our brains which is why it appears my head is, how did you say it, positively glowing?"

"Interesting. Okay, so then what are the other two races?"

"They are the Jivan and the Jagare. The Jivan have an even distribution of the Essence and the Jagare have the most concentration in their muscles and deep in their bones."

"So if I were to guess, that means Kaine is Jagare and Cardea and Hamlin are Jivan?" Chieo nodded his agreement "So are all Jagare over six feet tall and all Jivan the size and shape as Cardea?"

"For the most part yes, however describing someone's height by how many feet tall they are is rather peculiar."

Hanna laughed. She had never really thought how odd that sounded.

"Do they have special powers too, similar to seeing the Essence, since they have the Essence elsewhere?"

"Yes I suppose you could call them powers. We would refer to them as talents or skills. The Jagare are strong, exceptional hunters and therefore are our protectors. As for the Jivan, they specialize in nurturing, harvesting and many other valued and needed skills. As for my own race, we use our gifts to be scholars and manipulators of the Essence."

To help her understand his meaning, he extended his hand and a small pinecone from the ground rose up and landed in his palm.

"You're kidding me!" Hanna exclaimed with a jump in her step.

Chieo looked somewhat startled at the accusation, unclear what Hanna meant.

"Okay, now I know I'm dreaming. And to think, this whole time I've been talking to a wizard!"

Confused by this term, Chieo had decided they had talked enough for the time being and kept his focus on where they were headed. He could tell by the girl's jubilant outburst she had not meant to offend, but for now he preferred to reflect on what he had discovered about her thus far instead of further pursuing their conversation.

Hanna sensed Chieo's change in mood and didn't press on with her multitude of questions. Instead she bounded ahead to walk with Cardea. They walked on in silence for another ten minutes. Hanna spent the time thinking over all that Leader Chieo had said. She would have thought he had made it all up just to amuse her except for how serious everyone seemed. Also, there was that whole 'near death' situation that caused it to be much more real than any words could have conveyed. Sometimes she had dreams that felt so real and seemed so believable that it wasn't until she was fully awake that she realized how far-fetched they were. She thought that she must be in a deep sleep, maybe even passed out and this was the world she had created. When she reached the spot where she fell down she was sure she would wake up.

Cardea stopped. "Here we are."

She pointed to the rock stained with Hanna's blood.

Hanna looked around and began walking toward where her house should be. She was convinced she would wake up at any moment. The others continued to follow, but remained behind her at a bit of a distance. She thought they would eventually fade away and she would be alone as she emerged out of the woods because she had just imagined them, for it all seem too unreal. Solemnly she marched on, sad to leave this adventure behind her. She glanced over her shoulder expecting no one to be there, but her eclectic ensemble still shadowed her.

Then something dawned on her. She should have reached the tree she had been lying under by now. She expected to see it any second, peeking out from behind every tree. She knew the spot very well as she sat there often and had made her own little comfy nest, clear of rocks and sticks with extra moss to sit on. Another thing she noticed was that the air was still pink and she knew it was not pink when she sat under the tree. The trees should be getting thinner and hints of civilization should be popping up, a car horn in the distance or a dog barking, the edge of a fence visible through the trees or a plastic bag stuck in a piece of brush. But the woods were as unfamiliar to her at this point as Cardea's cottage had been.

For the second time in the last twenty-four hours fear gripped her.

"It should be here. It should be right here! I'm positive we would have come across my tree and I should be able to see my house."

The more she thought about it, the more frenzied she became. She was about to burst into a run as panic set in when Cardea appeared beside her and took her hand. Hanna squeezed her hand as she choked back her tears and to prevent herself from taking off. Kaine spoke quietly to Chieo.

"I will scout ahead and return shortly."

Chieo nodded and said, "Come, let us sit and rest our feet. If your home lies anywhere near here, Kaine will find it."

HIDE AND SEEK

Hanna was glad to let someone else run and search for her. She realized she did feel somewhat weak again and her head was starting to hurt.

"Hanna, I have been thinking, I want you to prepare yourself in case Kaine comes back without news of our destination. I want you to consider, for a moment, that something unnatural has happened here and perhaps you may need to stay with us for a time."

Hanna shivered as she tried to get her fear under control. She thought about the little village they had left behind and was intrigued at the prospect of going back and exploring it. She felt a little guilty though; while she was having this great adventure her parents would be worried sick. Hamlin placed his rucksack on the ground and pulled out some dried fruit, buns and a few mugs. He then took out a canteen and poured water into the mugs and handed them out.

Making a show of eating, she nibbled on a bun, as she feigned interest in the discussion about the weather and the names of the plants nearby. Cardea talked about the uses of the plants and the best way to store them. She told Hanna she was the town Herbalist. It was her duty to collect different plants and herbs and make all sorts of useful medicines, potions and preserves.

After half an hour Kaine jogged back into view and slowed as he approached the little picnic. Kneeling down he placed a hand on Hanna's shoulder.

"I have travelled through the trees and came across nothing other than mountains. There are no signs of villages or people to be found. If your home is nearby, it is truly hidden from us. I am sorry."

Hanna stared blankly at Chieo, not sure what to do.

"Hanna, you will stay with us until your family is found. I sense some sort of enchantment has touched this place. We will get to the bottom of this mystery. Leave your worries behind you – your parents are safe and you are safe and there is nothing more we can do at this

26

moment. I suggest for now, we enjoy each other's company and see where this opportunity takes us."

Hanna nodded, feeling numb. With little choice she accepted Chieo's guidance. Suppressing her fear she focused her energy on learning everything she could about these people and this place.

CHAPTER THREE

Houses and Homes

Hanna dragged her feet.

She was incredibly weak by the time they made their way back to the village. She was dizzy and her breathing was much more forced. Barely aware of the concerned look on the villager's faces when she reentered town, she went straight to the cottage.

Hamlin helped her to the cot while Cardea got out the Essence gas mask and then placed it over Hanna's nose and mouth for her to inhale. Turning to Chieo, she stated "We need to address her lack of Essence if she's going to stay here. Relying on gas alone is too risky."

"I agree. I think a crystal would be the best solution," Chieo agreed, "however, first we will need to call one more meeting." To Hanna he said, "We must take our leave of you Hanna for just a little while. When Cardea or Hamlin returns you may choose to explore the village. For now, I think you would benefit from some rest?"

"Leader Chieo, if it's okay with you I'd like to stay and make sure recovers," Cardea said.

Leader Chieo bowed his head. "A good precaution, thank you."

Hanna could barely make out what they were saying; it was as if she were under water. She thought they were telling her to rest and she was relieved at the suggestion, as she had been trying very hard not to collapse. Cardea fussed over Hanna, taking off her shoes and laying a blanket over her before pulling up her own chair.

As it turned out, a town meeting did not need to be called as most everyone had gathered outside the cottage waiting for an explanation about the return of the girl.

Chieo explained that Hanna was not just an outsider from the town, but possibly from Galenia. He had no definite answers. What he knew for certain was that the girl was not a threat. She was lost, scared and far from home. It was unlikely anyone would come looking for her so Leader Kaine suggested that the search for her home should continue.

"Leader Kaine has requested a meeting of the Jagare to discuss this matter further. In the meantime, I need a volunteer to be Hanna's companion while she is here as Cardea and Hamlin have graciously offered much of their time already and need to return to their work. They have, nonetheless, offered to continue providing Hanna lodging."

A brown haired boy with freckles stepped forward. He wore simple homespun pants and shirt. The twinkle in his eyes and the infectious grin he wore added a whimsical touch to his plain clothing.

"Leader Chieo," he said with confidence, "I will be Hanna's companion and teach her the ways of our village, if you please."

"Ah, Kazi thank you. Your help is most welcome." he said to the boy then turned his attention back to the crowd. "One other matter, although it has been confirmed that Hanna is definitely not Kameil, she is still void of Essence."

There were murmurings through the crowd and Chieo knew he needed to gain their trust in order to persuade them to give her the use of a crystal.

"She is unique and has abilities...she has the gift of The Sight." He paused while the weight of his statement took hold over the crowd. Being able to see the Essence was unheard of outside of the Juro race. It was a powerful gift that was key to their survival. Chieo saw that any hesitation he may have encountered only moments before had been completely dismissed after his last statement.

"In order for her to survive here she will need a crystal. What say you?"

"Hear, hear!" Rippled throughout the village along with a few "Keep her safe!" and "Protect the child!"

Chieo turned to Cardea "I will go obtain the crystal, and then, I too, need to return to my duties. Kazi, please accompany me."

Leader Kaine raised his voice to be heard above the chatter that had broken out amongst the crowd. "All Jagare, please meet me in the hall."

The crowd dispersed as everyone began to make their way back to their responsibilities and to share the news with those unable to partake in the meeting.

Kazi tagged along beside Chieo as they made their way to Chieo's cottage. Chieo filled him in on everything he knew about the girl. He wanted to prepare him and coach him a little on what was the best way for them to spend their time together. He knew that Kazi would be a great companion for Hanna. Aside from their similar age, Kazi was one of the most knowledgeable youths in the village and could answer most questions Hanna asked. He also knew that Kazi would be heading to school soon; Chieo thought he might, perhaps, have a travel companion.

When they exited his cottage Nyack, the Jivan leader was waiting.

"Leader Nyack. Thank you for waiting. I assume you were intending to request a meeting between the Leaders?"

"Yes Leader Chieo," Nyack said, "shall I arrange for one this evening? My cottage is available."

"Yes, yes. That would be splendid. Would you be so kind as to pass this information on to Leader Kaine?"

"Very good. Thank you for your time Leader Chieo."

With a quick bow Nyack turned and headed to the hall to inform Kaine.

Chieo and Kazi went to Cardea's cottage. Gently he knocked on the door and then let himself in. Hanna was still sleeping and Cardea was gathering supplies, getting ready to head out the door. Chieo handed Kazi an ornate wooden box.

"You know what to do when she awakens." Chieo bowed to Cardea and then went out the door.

Talking to Kazi in hushed tones Cardea said, "Do make yourself at home; there is a basket of fruit on the table. I'm sure you will have a lovely day." She squeezed his shoulder and with one last glance at Hanna, left the cottage.

Kazi grabbed an apple then went and sat in one of the chairs by the fire to wait.

When Hanna woke, she stretched and sighed, enjoying waking up in the cottage again. She sat up slowly in case she was still dizzy.

"Hello." Kazi stood up and took a few steps toward her. "My name is Kazi. Leader Chieo has asked me to show you around, that is, if you are interested."

Hanna was thrilled. "Nice to meet you, I'm Hanna, which you probably already know. I would love a tour! I've been dying to check out this place."

"I have something that will address that too. Leader Chieo asked me to give you this. It will prevent you from losing strength."

She carefully rose, crossed the room and took the box that Kazi held out. The wood was highly polished and there were detailed carvings on the lid. When she opened it, her jaw dropped. On a blue cotton pillow rested a beautiful pink gem about half the size of an egg. Carefully she picked it up to examine it closer. It was warm and as she held it she felt the warmth spread through her. One side of the gem was flat and smooth, the other resembled a diamond. A long leather cord had been attached to it. Like a necklace, she lifted it over her head and let it hang against her chest.

HOUSES AND HOMES

"The Crystal needs to be touching your skin." Kazi informed her.

Hanna tucked the crystal down the front of her shirt. The warmth against her chest was more intense than when she was holding it.

"But now you can't see it when it's under my shirt." Hanna protested as she liked the idea of proudly displaying her new jewelry, it seemed a shame to tuck it away.

Kazi said, "That is a good thing. It is much safer to hide such a valuable treasure."

"Hide it? Whatever for? I want to show it off! I'm grateful to be allowed to wear it."

"If you truly are grateful, then drawing as little attention to it as possible would be the best way to show it. The villagers understand you are wearing it; however it is a very precious item. If someone outside our village saw it or even heard of it..."

"Okay, I don't want to know. Let's not give me something new to stress about. Hidden from view is a compliment? Then I will do my best to keep it that way." Noticing the bowl of fruit on the table, she walked over and pulled out an apple.

"Okay Kazi, where to?"

* * *

As they walked out the door, they nearly tripped. There, in front of the cottage, were dozens of packages and baskets. Hanna bent down and peeked inside one of the baskets; it was full of food. A bundle of clothing tied with a string was next to it.

"What do you suppose all this is about Kazi?"

"I think the villagers are welcoming you and thought they would help by offering items you may need while you stay."

"Cool! If you don't mind, I think I will try these on."
She picked up a bundle of clothes and said, "I've been
wearing the same clothes for two days; I could use a
change." Kazi chuckled as Hanna went upstairs looking
for somewhere private to put on the new clothes. She
ducked into the first room which she assumed must be
Cardea's and Hamlin's based on the size of bed and the
large wardrobe it included. While waiting for her return,
he brought in the other parcels and left them on the table.

"Now Hanna, you look like a true Jivan! You're even
less pale than you use to be."

Hanna looked at her arms and noticed she did indeed
have a bit of pink starting to appear there.

"Sweet! I like this gem, I feel better than I have in a
long time. Okay Kazi, lead the way!"

As Kazi took her through town, visiting such shops as
the bakery and a clothing store, he explained a little about
how the town worked.

"The main floor of each shop is where the home
owner does their trade and the upstairs is where they sleep.
The exception to this of course is the Nursery. What a
hassle that would be carrying babies up and down the
stairs. Not to mention the safety issues that would create."

"Is the nursery like a daycare centre?"

"Oh no, it's full time care, day or night. That would be
silly to have to move the Hatchlings. I'll give you a tour of
the nursery when we get there as long as Havard approves;
he's the guardian of the Younglings."

Even though this confused her, Hanna just let it pass
as she had other things on her mind.

"I've noticed that the villagers seem to treat me like
I'm famous or something. Are all your guests greeted this
way?"

"No, but then we don't get many guests. If we did
they would be treated with the same kindness as everyone
else. You, however, are different, special." Kazi hesitated.
"We've heard you have The Sight?" It was more of a

question than a statement. Not that Kazi didn't believe Leader Chieo it's just that it was a unique situation.

"What's The Sight?" she asked.

"It's the ability to see Essence."

"Oh ya right, my special talent. Although, Leader Chieo said that all the Juro can do this as well and I know I'm not a Juro, but it's not like it's rare."

Kazi stopped walking. He placed a hand on Hanna's shoulder, turned her to face him and looked straight into her sage green eyes.

"This ability makes the Juro essential to our way of life. With it they can heal us, lead us to Essence sources and guide us in many other important tasks. Though they're long lived, their numbers are fewer than any other race which is why only one or two live in any village and a handful more in the cities. They are valuable to us. Although everyone gets a voice in the village, Leader Chieo's opinion counts for much. You have The Sight, which may be the limit to your abilities; however, even that much has value. One day you could prove to be as capable as any Juro, so you are honoured. I apologize if I have not shown you enough respect." Kazi lowered his eyes as he said this feeling foolish to have been so cavalier with Hanna.

Hanna bent her head upside down to look into Kazi's eyes.

"Don't be silly, I'm just a little odd, I always have been." Kazi laughed at this. "I would prefer if you just treat me like any other normal person, okay?"

Kazi said, "Done." They resumed walking until they came to a long, single story building.

"This is the Nursery."

Kazi knocked on the door. Instead of the door opening though, a peek hole slid open and a pair of eyes appeared.

"Good day. What can I do for you Kazi, son of Krigare?"

34

"Hello Havard. I was wondering if I would be allowed to show Hanna our Nursery?" Havard paused and then said, "No safer place for her in the whole village. Please come in."

With a few clicks, the door creaked open. It was an incredibly thick door with large hinges and Hanna could see multiple locks as they passed into the room. Hanna didn't really know what to expect when she came in, but was intrigued by what she saw. A group of children sat on the floor, listening intently to a women sitting in a large armchair telling a story. Some kids were sitting at a long table with beads on boards doing what she thought looked like math. One child was painting and a few were reading loose pages. A man was roaming between each area offering suggestions or answering questions. It was obviously a sort of school, yet it was unlike any classroom she'd been in. For one thing, it was much quieter.

"Nice to meet you Hanna. You are most welcome here." Havard bowed to her. Feeling awkward, Hanna bowed back. From what Chieo told her, she knew he must be Jagare. He had the same muscular look as Kaine and wore the same leather armour. He was tall with the same colour in his arms. The main differences between the two were that Kaine's hair was dark, almost black where Havard's was light brown. Also, something about Havard's eyes gave him a softer appearance.

"Thank you. So, this is a school?"

"No, no. These are the Younglings. Only Kazi will be going to school this year."

"Really?"

Kazi added, "Yes, I will be leaving in a few weeks. I have just finished my basics here and came of age last month."

"You're the only one old enough to go? "

Kazi nodded. "We are a pretty small village. Last year three people got to go and next year there are five, but it's just me this year."

"Okay." Hanna asked, "So, what were the basics you learned?"

"Oh you know, a little reading and writing and beginner math. I even have some map skills as my father is a map maker."

Hanna laughed.

"Okay two questions. If that's the basics, how come this isn't considered school and then what do they teach you at school?"

"The basics are passed on by the Nurturers of the village. They provide us with what we need to know so we are prepared for school. At the school they teach us what we need to know for our life skill."

"Oh. That sounds like the colleges or universities where I'm from. We don't go to those until twelve years of 'basic' school which happens when we are around 18."

"Wow. By 18 I hope to be confirmed in a town and working. We go to our schools at age thirteen. I can't wait to see it!"

"What do you mean 'confirmed in a town'? Do you plan on leaving this village?"

"I'm not sure. It depends what skill I choose and where there is an opening."

"Oh yes, I understand that."

"Anyway come on, I want to show the rest of the place." Kazi waved to Havard as they crossed the room to a hallway with several doors. He pushed open a few doors as they walked by. One was a large kitchen with a fireplace; another was full of tables and benches. It was the last door at the end of the hall, however, that was their destination.

"Okay, we need to be quiet in case any Younglings are asleep."

Hanna tiptoed when they walked into the room. Cradles lined the walls and large fluffy rugs covered the centre of the room. There was a sizeable fireplace in the corner and rocking chairs all around. Several people sat in the chairs feeding babies. Above each cradle a soft pink glow hovered. Kazi motioned for Hanna to follow as they headed for a look closer. He pointed to the babies being fed.

"They are a few weeks old." Motioning towards the closest bed he explained, "but she will be hatching any day now."

Hanna was caught by surprise. She looked in the crib and instead of seeing a baby she saw what looked like a pink egg the size of a small football. Instead of a hard shell, it seemed to be made out of a stretchy substance for as she watched she could see a foot push against it causing it to rise. She could see right through it and sure enough there was a baby inside.

"Why are they in that? How do they breathe?"

"You've never seen a Hatchling before?"

Kazi was as surprised as Hanna, but for different reasons.

"No, but who put them in those...things and why?" Hanna was nervous and worried that the babies would suffocate.

Kazi chuckled. "Well, no one silly, they were laid that way."

"Okay, please explain and please tell me they are safe. Babies where I'm from are born differently. Where I'm from only birds lay eggs, well, and reptiles. Either way, people don't."

"Of course they're safe. Our birds lay eggs, but so does every creature here – including us. The eggs start out much smaller than this though. Come over here."

They walked to the other side of the room where the cradles were tinier than Hanna initially thought. Inside were smaller versions of the pink egg she first saw, but it was a darker rose colour and the 'shell' was much denser; she couldn't see into it. She continued to follow Kazi as he spoke and looked into each crib he showed her.

"So they start small and, as you can see, their casing is much tougher. As the baby grows, the casing stretches. It's filled with special liquid, which is where they get their nourishment. You see some of these have crystals placed on them? That way the Essence can be absorbed right into them. We used to keep Hatchlings in nesting grounds next to the crystal pockets. Unfortunately, with the random invasions it wasn't safe anymore. This works well though and it's much easier to protect them in here."

Hanna wasn't sure if he was talking about the babies or the crystals.

"What's a crystal pocket?"

"Sorry, I keep forgetting how much you don't know. The pockets are caves full of crystals in every colour; black, blue, purple, red and of course, pink. Only the pink ones contain enough Essence to be of real value, but there are far less of them than the others. Keeping the Hatchlings close to the cave would be enough for them to absorb the amount of Essence they need.

"Anyhow, babies stay in their casing for seven months and when they are strong enough they break open and begin to breathe the air and drink milk. Understand?"

"Yes, I suppose it's not that different than back home. It's just that our babies grow inside us instead of hatching."

Kazi looked intrigued. "I can see how that would be beneficial. Your young would be more protected in a way. Although, you couldn't share taking of care of the child until after they were born."

Hanna nodded and thought of another question. "So, I thought that every living thing on the planet contained Essence. Why do the babies need more?"

"We are all created with it, just not with enough. We can survive, but are healthier and stronger if we have more. Most creatures choose their nesting grounds close to a crystal pocket for this reason. But like I said, for us, it is no longer safe." Whispering, he walked out of the room. "We best not disturb them anymore."

"Kazi I still have a few more questions. Why aren't the crystal pockets safe?"

"You've heard of the Kameil?" When Hanna nodded he continued. "Since they have no Essence, they are in constant danger of dying. The best chance they have for survival is the crystals. It seems though, that they have become...well, addicted or something because they are constantly trying to get more than they need. The crystals take hundreds, even thousands, of years to form and if too many are consumed all creatures will be in danger. We protect the crystal pockets so that they are not depleted. We never used to take the crystals out, but too many of our Hatchlings have been killed over the raids, so for their protection, we needed to keep them in the villages. Fortunately, crystals don't lose their Essence that quickly. One crystal can last for many years and be used for many generations of Hatchlings."

"If that's the case then why do the Kameil take so many?"

"We don't know for sure; that's part of the problem. What was your other question?"

"You said the Nursery is night and day. Don't the parents want to be with their babies? Do all those other kids stay here too?"

"Yes of course parents want to be with their little ones. They visit their Hatchling daily. Some may even stay in the sleeping quarters overnight. When the Younglings reach age two they live both here and with their parents.

Sometimes they are with their parents for a few nights or weeks and sometimes they stay here; this happens often if the parents' work takes them away from the village for a while. Sometimes new parents will switch their duties, for a time, so they can be at the Nursery working and then they can spend more time with their Youngling. That sort of thing." Hanna was trying to make sense of all that Kazi had been telling her.

He noticed she was deep in thought. He put his hand on her shoulder and softly said, "We all look out for each other; it's how we survive. In a sense, each Hatchling and every Youngling has many parents and is loved equally between them."

Hanna could understand the benefits of this type of community. She wondered if the kids or "Younglings" preferred this sort of group living or cherished the times they got to be alone at home. From what she could tell, they seemed to be enjoying themselves.

Kazi led Hanna back down the hall through the main room and back outside. They had gone through most of the buildings that circled the fountain.

"Hanna, do you have horses where you're from?"

Hanna exclaimed, "Yes we do! I haven't had many opportunities to spend with them though. I went on a trail ride once with camp a couple years ago."

"Excellent, so you know how to ride?"

"Not really. Someone lifted me on the horse and then the horse did the rest. I just held on and hoped the horse didn't decide to take off. I've always wanted to learn though. It's just, I'm a little scared of them; they're so big..."

"I understand how you feel. I was intimidated when I first started working with them. I can teach you to ride if you want. Come on, let's go to the stables."

Hanna was giddy with excitement. They took a path between the cottages in the opposite direction of the woods where she had come from. There were a few more buildings scattered here and there. She spotted the stables a short distance ahead and an empty field, to the left of the stables, with a fence around it. When they reached the stables, Kazi opened up the big wooden doors. Instantly Hanna was hit by a strong odour of hay and horses.

"The horses will be out back right now. How about I show you where we keep everything and then we will go find them?"

Kazi pointed out the stalls where they kept the horses overnight. Between the stalls was the tack room where the saddles were and on the wall hung bridles and buckets full of brushes and picks for grooming. He gave Hanna a handful of treats to give to the horses and instructed her how to keep her thumb tucked in so it didn't get chomped on. She wasn't feeling very confident with that piece of advice. They went out the back door to where additional pens were as well as a pasture where they could see a few horses while others were further into the trees.

"We don't have too many horses here as not many people travel out this far. We usually have about ten."

Kazi opened the gate and let Hanna through before closing it behind them then he whistled. A few horses walked towards them, the others just perked their ears and watched. Kazi patted a horse that had sauntered up to him and offered his hand with the treats. He placed a bridal over its head and then walked to where Hanna was. He helped her give treats to another horse while he was being nuzzled by the first.

"We will start lessons tomorrow. For now let's just get you comfortable being around them. Let's give these two a good brushing."

Kazi showed her how to put on the bridle and they walked the horses out the gate. She learned how to tie the horse up properly, brush it and clean its' hooves. At first she was nervous walking around the large animal, but her confidence grew as she worked with it. It surprised her how the chestnut fur that looked shiny and smooth from a distance was actually rough in places where the dirt clung to it from when it had rolled in the mud. The silky looking mane was coarse, not smooth like she expected. Anxious to be riding, she tried to be patient with just getting to know this horse. She never realized what personalities they could have. She already found she was getting attached to this creature.

They returned the horses to the field and started making their way back to Cardea's cottage.

"Hanna, Chieo said he didn't know how long you are able to stay with us. While you are here perhaps you would be interested in helping out in some way?"

Hanna nodded. "Absolutely. I'm grateful for everyone's kindness. What can I do to help?"

"How about with the stables? They need to be swept and kept clean. Also, the horses all need to be groomed, fed and ridden. I have been helping out with that for the last couple of weeks – I could always use an extra pair of hands."

Hanna was excited. She had really enjoyed her short time with the horses so far. Of all the places they'd been to, that was where she wanted to go again the most.

"That would be great! I'd love to help. Thanks Kazi."

"Okay. We'll start first thing tomorrow. I'd better get you back to Cardea's; it's close to dinner time – I'm sure she'd appreciate your help at the moment, especially with all those packages we left on her table. I'll come and get you in the morning."

Kazi was so easy going and fun to be around Hanna didn't think twice about giving him a hug. "Thanks for everything today. It was fun. I think I need to keep a journal so I don't forget everything you've told me! See ya tomorrow."

Cardea was busy stoking the fire when she came in.

"Hi Cardea, I've had such a great day! I still can't believe all the gifts that came. What should I do with them?"

"I'm glad you had a good day Hanna. Why don't you start by sorting them out? Any food, dishes and such can go on the counter. All the personal items you can take up to your room."

"My room?" Hanna looked around and for the first time noticed the cot was missing.

"Yes, Hamlin moved your bed back upstairs. We have an extra room up there where our son use to stay. He's got a cottage of his own now," she added with a tone of pride in her voice.

"We just brought the cot down temporarily when you were so badly hurt, much easier to keep an eye on you down here."

Hanna ran up the stairs to check out her new room. In addition to the bed, there was a side table, a chest and a small desk. She peeked in the drawers and found paper and some old fashioned writing tools, perfect for journaling. The trunk had an extra blanket in it. The two drawers by the bed were empty, providing a place to put her clothes. A quick peek out the small window revealed a view of the town with its quaint little cottages and the fountain with its melodic trickle as the water splashed into its basin. She took a deep breath of fresh air and smiled to herself. She knew she should be worried about finding her way home, but this was turning out to be a great adventure. The thought of missing school and instead learning how to ride horses helped ease any anxiety she may have felt. Besides, she told herself, it's only for a little while.

CHAPTER FOUR

Lost and Alone

Nandin's life was lacking.

Raised in the small village of Pendio, the highlight of his life was the time he went to the Citadel when he was thirteen. School itself was not overly thrilling, but he enjoyed meeting new people and making friends. Prior to leaving for school, Nandin had helped the village farmers bring in the seasons crops. He was quick to learn and the villagers thought he would make a great farmer so when he went to school he took up the trade. It provided little in the way of excitement, however, he didn't mind the hard work and he was rather good at it.

In-between schools, at the age of sixteen, he came home for a visit. When one of the local farmers died he stayed to help and never returned to finish his studies. At first Nandin was proud of the fact he was able to assume the responsibility the town had given him, but it didn't take long to realize what he had sacrificed. He never got the chance to say goodbye to his school friends, or the girl he was sweet on. On top of that, they were spread out all over Galenia and that meant there was little chance of ever seeing them again. These facts alone may have been tolerable, but with no peers in his village he became lonely and felt somewhat separate. The local girls were either too young or too old for him; six years difference may not be considered much, but at eighteen the gap felt immense.

Farming for these two years left him feeling old before his time. After a long, hard day's work in the fields he would come home, exhausted, eat supper, wash up and often collapsed on his bed for the night. When catching a glimpse of his reflection he thought he even looked old. His face and muscular arms were set in a permanent tan from spending his day outdoors. His ash blond hair often had the impression of being darker than it was due to the dirt that constantly settled there.

Home was the same little cottage he grew up in. His dad had died when he was very young and it had just been Nandin and his mother for as long as he could remember. His mother was the village Spinster; she spent her days spinning yarn and spent her nights quietly reading or knitting. Always thoughtful of her son, she prepared his dinner and had it ready for him when he came in. Nandin couldn't help, but feel sorry for his mother, as she was so isolated and alone. Whatever spark that may have once filled her had faded as she contented herself to the mundane routine of her life. Replete with sullenness, Nandin was aware of the similarities between his mother and himself.

He diligently worked hard and took pride in his efforts, but so far the reward had been spending his days sweating and his nights alone in his room. He wouldn't have minded it so much if he came home to a wife; someone he could laugh with, someone to share a life with. Instead he came home to his mother who just let life pass her by, like all the best years were behind her. Nandin felt he was regrettably doing the same thing with little hope of escaping.

* * *

It was a particularly hot day for spring. After sweltering in the fields for most of the day, Nandin decided to break early for a change. He returned home to find his mother gone, probably picking up some supplies in the village. He washed up and, with the rumbling of his stomach, figured he would drop by the inn and see about getting an early meal as well as something cool to drink.

When he wandered into the inn he was somewhat disappointed to notice the common room was empty, although, he was not all together surprised due to the time of day. He settled in hoping others would stop by soon; he was in the mood for companionship. The innkeeper approached Nandin carrying a cup of ale.

"Hot one today, eh Nandin?" he said as he placed the mug on the table in front of him.

"That it is. I know it's a little early for dinner, but do you have anything I can munch on?"

The innkeeper nodded. "I'll see what I can come up with."

As he disappeared into the kitchen the bell above the entrance jingled as a man entered the inn. He stood still as he looked around the space allowing his eyes a chance to adapt to the dim room after being out in the bright light of the day. He was either tall for a Jivan or short for Jagare leaving Nandin unsure what the man's race was, although his confidence of travelling alone leaned toward Jagare.

"Afternoon stranger," Nandin called out, "it's a little barren in here at this time of day, but you are most welcome to join me if you care for company."

The highlight of Nandin's life lately was on the rare occasions when people passed through town. He always made a point of seeking them out to learn what went on in the world outside his little community. To Nandin's delight the man made his way over to his table.

"Thank you. I think I would like that. My name's Nean." Nean bowed, causing his long dark hair to dangle before he tucked his hair behind his ears then pulled out a chair and took a seat at Nandin's table. How different the two of them must have looked Nandin thought, as he unconsciously ran a hand through his own close-cropped hair.

"Pleased to meet you, I'm Nandin. So tell me Nean, what great adventure brought you to our humble town?"

The innkeeper popped his head around the door to see who else had entered the inn. Nandin held up two fingers and Stephan returned to the kitchen to prepare an extra meal.

Nean was enthusiastic as he explained. "I'm meeting up with some friends. We're planning to meet in the forest for a few days of good fun."

Nandin had heard of reunions. Even though people went to the same schools it was seldom that they would end up in the same town or city as their classmates. After the end of the term many graduates had made it tradition to come together periodically over the years – with Nandin's early dismissal he never learned when or if his group would meet. He sighed.

"What's the problem?" Nean asked.

Nandin shook his head, coming out of his reverie.

"Sorry, it just sounds...fun."

Nean laughed. "You make it sound like that is a foreign concept for you."

"I guess it is. I don't have many opportunities for that sort of thing."

"Well then this is your lucky day my friend! You are most welcome to come with me – I guarantee you will have a great time. It's bound to be an unforgettable party."

Nandin's heart skipped a beat. He wanted to leap at the invitation Nean just put before him, but he had responsibilities here and besides, he thought, even though it already felt like he and Nean were close companions they had only just met. He was about to make this observation when the innkeeper arrived with their meal and placed it before them.

"Thanks Stephan." Nandin said.

"I will bring your guest here something to drink. What will it be? Wine? Ale?"

"You know," Nean replied, "I would really just like some water. Thank you sir."

Stephan smiled. "Water it is."

Nandin took a large bite of the chicken sandwich that Stephan had brought while waiting for him to return with the water. Once he had delivered Nean's drink and replenished Nandin's he disappeared again into the kitchen. Nean was the first to resume their conversation.

"Well Nandin, what do you think? You want to come along with me for a couple days?"

Nandin smiled nervously. "It sounds like a good time but I have work to do..."

"Of course you do but then, won't you always? When's the last time you took a day off? Surely the world won't fall apart if you're gone a few days. If you were sick wouldn't someone help out?"

"I suppose...but I never get sick."

Nean slapped his hand on the table.

"There you see! No vacation. No sick days. You deserve a little fun!"

Nandin chuckled. He was starting to warm up to the idea. Why shouldn't he have a 'little fun'?

"You hardly know me Nean. Why would you want me tagging along?"

Nean grinned. "I'm an excellent judge of character. From the moment you invited me to sit with you I knew we'd get along just fine and the more I chat with you, Nandin, the more I'm convinced you are just what this little gathering needs."

Nandin shook his head; Nean's exuberance was infectious.

"Won't your friends mind?"

"Of course not! The more the merrier. Besides, they're likely to bring friends of their own – I'm sure they'd be disappointed if I show up alone."

Another thought occurred to Nandin. "Are they likely to be bringing any girls?"

Nean's eyes sparkled. "Wouldn't that be swell? I don't know about you, but I'm looking forward to finding out!"

With that thought in mind Nandin agreed a few days off was just what he needed. Perhaps this was one of those moments where life would take a happy turn in his favour and he was not about to let it pass him by.

CHAPTER FIVE

Dreams and Destinies

Nandin was plagued with guilt.

After their meal at the inn Nean was ready to continue on his journey so Nandin returned home to pack a few things and leave a note for his mother. He was glad she wasn't there when he left, as he knew she would disapprove of him leaving. He didn't think he would be able to go through with it if he had to confront her so, like a thief in the night, he quickly gathered his necessities and disappeared into the woods. As they made their way deeper into the woods, Nean noticed Nandin's dour expression and understood that his new companion needed reassurance else he may turn around and go right back home.

"So Nandin are you in your first year of your trade?" Nean knew that turning the discussion back to Nandin's home may seem the wrong approach to maintaining Nandin's resolve; however, he knew more about Nandin than he had let on; he had been studying him for some time now. He was confident he knew just what to say.

Nandin grimaced. "No, I've been farming for two years now."

"Two years?" Nean laughed. "You look young for your age, I would have put you around eighteen, nineteen at most."

Nandin smiled. For someone who felt like an old man so early in his youth this was a sure way to lift his spirits. "I am eighteen. I left school early since old man Turner died and the village was short a man to help bring in the crops."

Nean cocked his head to one side as he asked another question he already knew the answer to. "So you never got to attend the Percipio?"

Nandin lowered his head.

"No. I didn't think much of it at the time, I mean what's the point in a farmer learning numbers and studying how the world works? I count myself lucky to be able to read and write, but even that is put to little use."

"Hmm...I suppose, but hey who goes to school to learn anyway? I for one thought it an excellent chance to get to know people – especially ones of the prettier gender."

Nandin laughed in spite of himself. "Don't remind me. I can't help but regret that missed opportunity."

"Not to worry my good man. I happen to have met enough for both of us – I'll find a way to introduce you to a few."

"That sounds like a great offer to me, but I won't hold you to it – I have little opportunity to be out and about, wandering the world meeting pretty girls."

"Well then I guess I will just have to bring them to you!"

Nandin considered the idea. "Nean you haven't told me what is it that you do. What kind of trade allows you this sort of freedom to be such a man of the world?"

A mischievous look crossed Nean's face. "Oh, it's highly specialized. I get all sorts of perks; the current gathering included."

"If I had known there was a trade like that, I think I may not have been so easily persuaded into taking up farming." Nandin sighed. "Too bad I can't turn back time."

"Why would you need to do that? No offence Nandin, but farmers aren't exactly a rare breed, it would be easy enough for your village to replace you if they needed to."

Now that Nean had planted that thought in Nandin's mind he thought it best to steer the conversation to more immediate issues; he needed to hook Nandin without going into too many details.

"So how about you set up that tent I brought while I get the fire going and perhaps conjure up a little something to eat before we call it a night?"

* * *

Even though Nandin was exhausted by the time he slid into his blankets for the night, sleep eluded him. The phrase 'farmers aren't rare' kept rolling around in his mind. It never occurred to him that he could change the course his life had taken, but then he had never questioned it before either. He liked his village, they were his family and when they had a need he could meet, he just did. He had been raised to think about his community first, but that didn't mean he had no choice; he just never considered it. Now the consequences of his lack of considering left him in a life where, he conceded, he was unhappy. If the people of Pendio knew he felt this way they would never expect him to continue on, would they? But then, what would he do? Surely it was too late for him to return to school. So what was Nean implying? Did he think Nandin had a chance to pursue...what? Now he thought about it he still had no idea what Nean did, let alone if he himself could do it.

As morning broke Nandin was quick to dress and start the fire. He felt the need to prepare a hearty meal before they were again off on their walk through the woods, partially because he felt indebted to Nean for bringing him along and partially because he was rather hungry. When Nean emerged from the tent, rubbing tired eyes and stretching, he eagerly took a seat around the fire.

"You're an early riser," Nean said.

Nandin shrugged. "It's just a habit, I always have to get an early jump on the day; besides, I couldn't sleep."

"Ah, not used to roughing it? Nandin has farming made you soft?"

Nandin chuckled at the irony of the remark.

"I think it was more from the sudden change of my situation...this is all a little out of character for me."

"From what I can tell Nandin, this seems very much in character for you. I think you've been living someone else's life...maybe it's time to find your own. By the way, these eggs are delicious. I didn't even know I had packed any or the bacon for that matter."

Nandin replied, "You didn't. I grabbed them from home. You can never underestimate the value of a good meal when you're out on an adventure."

"See, that's what I'm talking about! I'd be glad to take you on all my travels."

"Ah, so you think perhaps I should have been a chef?"

Nean grinned and he began to devour his meal in earnest. After they finished up, they dismantled their camp and were on their way. Nean seemed to bounce as they walked deeper into the woods and he rattled on about all sorts of inconsequential things. Nandin barely had a chance to get a word in edgewise. So prone to spending the days quietly in his fields, this constant chatter was hard for Nandin to process; he was scarcely able to form an opinion before Nean was off on a new tangent. What he didn't realize was that Nean was doing it intentionally.

As for Nean, he had always possessed the gift for gab, but by the evening meal even he was running out of useless things to talk about. He knew, eventually, Nandin would start asking the deeper questions he had yet to answer. The first of these didn't come up until they sat around the fire later that night; Nean figured his talking must have worn Nandin out and was grateful for the silence.

DREAMS AND DESTINIES

"So Nean, what 'highly-specialized job' it you do?"

"It's a difficult question to answer as I'm a man of many trades. I employ whatever talent is required in any given situation. But it's not really what I do that matters; it's why I do it."

"Okay, I'm hooked. Why do you do whatever it is you do?"

"I do it because I believe in choice. For example, I believe you have the choice whether or not you are a farmer."

Nandin shrugged. "Well of course I had the choice, it's not like anyone forced me into it..."

"Perhaps but that's not always the case. Some people would make different choices if they had the option. Sometimes it seems we have more choice than we actually do; it's just that we are so used to the restrictions that surround us we start to forget they are there."

Nandin knitted his eyebrows together as he considered what Nean was saying.

"I'm not sure I get your meaning."

Nean nodded. "By the time you meet some of my friends I think you will."

"I have a feeling you're not going to be any clearer about your trade are you?"

"In time, but at the moment I think I'd only confuse you further. Besides, it's late. I'm heading off to bed."

Nandin yawned. "I suppose that's a good idea. I'm sure tomorrow will be a late night with all the fun and games you've told me about."

* * *

"How long before we meet up with your friends?" Nandin asked the next morning while wrapping up the camp.

"I think we'll get there close to noon."

Nandin cleared his throat. "This little trip is taking a bit longer than you implied. I sort of thought we would have arrived yesterday."

Nean grinned sheepishly. "Well I thought if I told you, you might not come. I'm convinced you won't regret it."

"Maybe not today but when I get back home I'm going to have a lot of long days of hard work to make up for this lost time."

"Nandin that's just the wrong way to think of things." Nean stuffed the last of the morning dishes in his pack, brushed off his hands on his pants and led the way further into the forest. "Maybe you'll win some rounds of dice and instead of coins you could collect labour. Heck, maybe you will come out of this with a work force and you could take the summer off!"

"I didn't bring any coins. I didn't realize there would be gambling."

Nean shook his head.

"I think you worry too much my friend. Whatever gambling there will be it will be of no real value; we're just playing friendly games. If you want to play you could simply offer doing the night's dishes or preparing the supper – I know I'd take that wager!"

They encountered a sentry as they approached the clearing. Nean greeted him by name and explained to Nandin that the man was keeping a watch out for any Beasts. One minute they were in a dense forest following a narrow game trail and then the trees stopped and they stepped into a large clearing. Nandin was surprised at the size of it. Over a dozen small tents were set up in a haphazard fashion. Smoke rose from multiple fire pits; the closest Nandin could see had a large roast on a spit being turned over while it cooked. The largest tent at the far end of the clearing was much more impressive than the rest. Not only was it four times the size, but the plain beige canvas had wide vertical black stripes around the base and the top had black triangular edging dangling all along the rim. A flag with a castle in silver embroidery was attached to the top of the main supporting pole.

Something struck Nandin as odd about the camp. He could hear a few voices and see one or two men as they made their way through the camp or tended to the cooking fire, but for the most part the place seemed...empty.

"Nean, where is everyone?" he asked.

"They're coming. Looks like we made great time. Come on, I'll introduce you to a few lads I know are here."

Nean led Nandin between smaller tents until he came to one slightly bigger. He pulled back the flap and motioned for Nandin to enter. Inside was a round table with four men sitting around it. They each held a cup in front of them that rattled as they shook and then upended them to dump the contents on the table. When they lifted the cups, they revealed dice. One man laughed as he collected the round clay chips that were piled in the middle of the table.

"Good day gentlemen!" Nean said with enthusiasm. "Hodon I hope you're not cleaning out all our guests this soon, we'll have no one left when the party starts in earnest!"

The man named Hodon chuckled again and stood up as he bowed to Nean and Nandin.

"Wonderful! Boys let me introduce you to Nean and..."

Nean put a hand on Nandin's shoulder. "This here is Nandin. I found him in Pendio."

"Excellent. Nandin pull up a chair."

One of the men stood up. "He can take my spot. I'll go see about getting us some lunch and perhaps a round of ale." The man was tall, clearly a Jagare, but Nandin thought something about him seemed off; like he was stretched or worn thin.

Hodon slapped his hand on the table as he resumed his seat. "That's an even better idea. Thanks Sadul. Come Nandin, sit, sit!"

Nandin hesitated then sat in the proffered seat. "I didn't bring any coins..."

Hodon replied, "That's okay, we'll take village credits..."

Nean frowned and opened his mouth to object when Hodon waved him away.

"Oh Nean, you know I'm just pulling his leg. This is just a friendly game Nandin. We all start out with fifty chips. Whoever wins them all, or has the most when we call it quits, gets a free ride for the day."

Nean added, "In other words, they don't have to help with any of the work. You know, cooking or cutting the wood. All right, well I think you're in good hands here. I'll see you in a bit." Nean turned and quickly left the tent. Nandin leaped up and followed.

"Wait! Aren't you staying?" Nandin asked feeling a little uncomfortable at being left with a bunch of people he'd never met before.

Nean's brow wrinkled. "Oh, didn't I tell you? I have a few friends I'm supposed to meet up with and bring here."

Nandin shook his head. "Why didn't we just pick them up on the way?"

"Would have done if it was on the way. I figured since we would be passing by here anyway I'd just drop you off. I thought you'd rather hang out and get to know a few of the guys before everyone else gets here. Besides, I'm used to travelling. Just stay and have some fun. I'll see you soon."

Nandin considered it for a minute then conceded to stay. Nean shooed him back to the tent. Reluctantly Nandin backed in and rejoined the men at the table. He observed his fellow gamers. Hodon was a Jivan like himself, but lacked the muscular physique that Nandin acquired from hours of working on the farm. He had dark hair and his eyes kept darting about as if he didn't know where to look. Across from him sat a large fellow, obviously Jagare, with a sour expression on his face. He was clean-shaven and kept his hair tied back. The last man at the table was roughly the same size as Nandin, but was without the tougher features and bulk of someone used to hard labour.

"So Nandin," Hodon began, "This serious looking fellow here is Jon, he's from Darat. And Kal here is from...Jarda was it?"

Kal said, "Yep that's right. I got here last night and Jon arrived about an hour ago. So, to the game, right now we're just playing high roll gets the pot. Rules are simple – make your bid and roll your dice. Maybe after lunch we'll play something a bit more challenging."

"You mind just picking up where Sadul left off? He still has forty coins." Hodon asked.

"Sure." Nandin said

They played for another half an hour when Sadul finally returned and beckoned them to get some food over by the cooking tent. When Kal noticed Nandin still had his travel pack he offered to show him to a tent where he can put his stuff.

"Jon and I took this one here; you can take the one next to us if you want. I think they are saving the tents on this side of the camp for guests and the other ones are for our hosts. It should be good fun when everyone gets here I think."

"How many people do you suppose are coming?" Nandin asked.

Kal shrugged. "Not sure but the tents can fit two men comfortably so my guess is up to twenty guests and there are about ten or fifteen men running this show."

Nandin looked around as if expecting the fifteen men to suddenly materialize out of nowhere.

"Where are they then? I mean I've only seen two others aside from Hodon and Sadul."

58

Kal nodded. "Word came that there was a Wolcott in the area so they are guarding the camp. They're making sure they are ready to take him down if the Beast gets too close. Plus some of the others have gone off to bring more people like your friend Nean did."

"I've never been to anything like this before, is this...normal?"

Nandin and Kal didn't notice that Jon had come up from behind them.

"I don't think so," Jon whispered. "Nothing about this seems very normal to me. I for one don't trust them. Something weird is going on."

Kal laughed. "Ya, we've all snuck off to have a party. My parents would flip if they knew I was here."

Nandin was taken off guard by that comment. "Your parents don't know you're here either?"

Kal grinned. "You kidding? I just got back from the Percipio. After being gone for two years you think they'd just let me take off to gamble and play games? Nah, I told them I was supposed to go to Pendio actually. Left a note saying that I had a message for a previous classmate and I didn't want to wait for a Messenger to come and take it. Now that I've met you Nandin, you're the classmate I was supposed to meet."

Kal's grin widened as if they should all be amazed at his cleverness; however Nandin felt a knot in his stomach.

"So neither of you has met anyone here before?" Nandin asked, uncertain of whether or not he wanted an answer.

"No..." Jon began to say when Hodon spotted them.

He waved and hollered at them. "Come on, while the food's hot and there is some left. You don't know Sadul's appetite."

Jon eyed Nandin and said under his breath. "Be alert. We'll talk later."

As they made their way to the cooking tent Nandin asked, "Hodon, what's the big tent for?"

"Ah, that's set aside for our honoured hosts as well as our guest speaker – when he arrives."

That comment got Jon's attention. "Who would that be?"

Hodon smiled. "You will have to wait and see. I don't want to spoil the surprise."

"Okay," Jon replied knowing he wouldn't get any more details on that issue, "can you at least tell us who the 'honoured hosts' are?"

"Of course. You've already met some of them. Jon I believe Mayon invited you, Nandin came in with Nean and Kal arrived with Sim. The two you haven't met are Plyral and Thanlin."

"What makes them the honoured hosts?" Nandin asked.

Hodon handed them each a wooden plate as they walked into the cook tent and then grabbed one for himself.

"Well, it's their party, they're the ones who've invited everyone."

"So you and Sadul are guests too?"

Hodon chuckled. "No of course not. We're here to help run things. Someone needs to cook the food and keep up the camp while the hosts are out gathering..."

Sadul interrupted. "Right, a lot of help you do Hodon. Nandin did you lose all my coin to this lay about?"

Nandin chuckled. "Actually I managed to lower his supply a little."

"Good, keep it up. I think he could handle a little time scrubbing pots. He seems far too cheerful."

Jon had the impression Sadul was preventing Hodon from saying too much. Perhaps there was something he didn't want Hodon to share.

* * *

JOURNEY TO KOKOROE

Over the next two days more men arrived from different villages and cities. Nandin never found out any further details on the guest speaker or the whereabouts of Nean, but he hardly had the time to think about it. The dice games continued and different varieties were introduced. For those interested in more active games, an area had been allotted for horseshoe tossing as well as a game of keep-away. The latter consisted of a ball constructed from a piece of animal hide and stuffed with wool, then sewn shut. The ball was passed from player to player, who remained in the same spot. The opposing team could move and tried to snatch the ball while it was being thrown. If they caught it their team was then rooted to where they stood and the other team could move. In addition to the games, some of the workers even played instruments to keep the men entertained. To Nandin's disappointment no ladies had joined them.

On the fourth day the guests totaled twenty men. Rumour had it that everyone who was coming had arrived. Nean made an appearance for a few hours and then disappeared again; Nandin had no idea where. Unusual activity began in the early afternoon when several of the hosts' assistants assembled a raised platform; completed, it stood above the heads of the men and was large enough to fit two or three people on it. Another peculiar development was that two men had taken posts outside the large tent, flanking either side of the door as if guarding it. They were dressed in black from head to toe with only their eyes uncovered. They held long polished wooden staffs. These unusual items piqued the guests' curiosity, as typically only Juro were known to carry staffs.

They settled down to eat an enjoyable lunch when three more men dressed in black arrived. They entered the tent briefly then went and stood in front of the platform holding their hands in front of them, staring straight ahead. They never looked at or acknowledged anyone in the camp. Hodon mounted the stairs to the platform, carefully testing each one to ensure its stability. When he finally reached the top and seemed convinced the whole thing wouldn't collapse he clapped his hands.

"May I have everyone's attention? The moment we have been waiting for has arrived! Our guest of honour, Master Mateo, has graced us with his presence and is prepared to speak with you."

A hush spread across the clearing. Everyone had heard of Mateo. Stories were told around campfires, many of which seemed exaggerated. Growing up, most kids came to think of Mateo as someone adults had made up to scare them into behaving. He was a ghost or perhaps just a legend. Stories were told of disappearances connected to Mateo and most believed he was responsible for the creation of the abominations that were known as the Kameil. The crowd was filled with a mixture of fear and curiosity.

The guards by the tent pulled back the flaps and a tall figure emerged. There was an audible intake of breath as this impressive figure made his way to the platform followed by the two men in black. He wore a bright blue robe made of a shimmering material with long black pants of the same cloth. Neither the colour nor the texture of the fabric had been seen by any of the guests before. Another attribute that made this figure impressive was the fact the he was the tallest person anyone had ever seen; he was a good head taller than any Jagare. Facing away from the onlookers as he headed to the platform they could see his wavy hair, long and black with a few beads braided into it. He walked with purpose. Hodon hurried down the stairs and jumped out of the way just before Mateo was about to begin climbing. Mateo bowed to Hodon then headed up the stairs. Hodon seemed to stand taller at the courtesy, as brief as it was, and stood beside one of the guards in black who had joined the others in front of the platform while still holding the odd staffs.

"Welcome my brothers!"

As he spoke he raised his hands above his head and his robe fell open to reveal a muscular chest adorned with several gold chains that hung around his neck. His skin was like polished wood and there was a pink aura around him, which no one could believe they could see, as there was not one Juro among them. The only explanation was that he had been infused with a vast amount of Essence. This was unheard of for everyone knew that too much Essence was fatal. This being in front of them was full of conundrums and mystery. He had their undivided attention.

"What you see before you is a man with a vision."

His voice easily carried to everyone in the clearing.

"Unity! Equality! Choice! This is what I strive for. We are all of this world! We all deserve the same privileges and opportunities. I stand before you as proof that this vision is possible! I have the strength of the Jagare, my body is infused with the Essence as any Jivan and I can work the Essence as any Juro!"

To prove his point he closed his eyes and moved his hand in front of him in a circular motion. Dust rose into the air to form a small spinning cloud that grew until it was the size of a man. He opened his eyes and lifted the dust funnel to his platform. He reached in and the funnel dispersed back to the ground. In his hand he held a flower freshly plucked from the ground.

Nandin's jaw dropped open and everyone in the clearing was filled with awe. In the history of their civilization, no being had ever been able to contain the gifts of all three races. The very idea would change all they had ever known. Mateo seemed god-like but at this point, most still felt fear for he was unnatural in the extreme.

"I sense your hesitation, I understand your fear. For generations you have been brainwashed into dreading change, to reject it. I will work hard to gain your trust. I only want to help you reach your potential."

Someone broke from his reverie and shouted, "What about the Kameil? They are sick and dangerous! Are you not responsible for them?"

Nandin couldn't believe the courage his fellow comrade had. He had been surprised though that instead of an angry response, Mateo looked somewhat saddened.

"Yes. You are right. I am responsible. They are proof of failed attempts to make this vision a reality. If only the Juro helped it could have been avoided. So many innocent lives being altered so unjustly. In my isolation I had little concern for their fate, but this is something I am trying to remedy."

He motioned with his hand, "Look around you. The brave men that have assisted and guarded the camp are all Kameil. They are strong and healthy. I believe I have done right by them."

The men he referred to raised their arms in a cheer. Mateo beamed from the praise. The guests were shocked at this new development and looked nervously at the men around them.

"The greater news is this," he continued, "at last I have found the way! Before you are my Yaru." He indicated the men in black.

"Once they were they like you, but now they are more like me. Stronger, faster, smarter! Yaru, a demonstration if you will."

The figures in black began to spread out in a circle. Those up front where ushered back by Hodon and they moved until they formed a ring. Two Yaru entered the ring flipping as they went. Upon landing they began a style of open hand fighting yet it was faster and more intense than any the guests had seen. They continued flipping and rolling, crouching low and springing up incredibly high. The others joined in. It was a blur of acrobatics that astonished those watching. Their efforts were met with applause and three of the Yaru stepped back as the remaining two picked up the staffs they had laid on the ground. They began attacking and defending with incredible speed using their staffs as weapons. When contact with the staff was made a hollow clunk vibrated throughout the clearing. They jumped over, rolled under, and bent backwards without falling. Everyone was mesmerized. It was clear by the looks on their faces that the Kameil had also never witnessed the talents of the Yaru like this before.

When the Yaru finished, they calmly returned to their posts beneath the platform giving no indication that they had just preformed a near impossible display. Another round of applause erupted from everyone including Mateo. When the clapping died down Mateo spoke again.

"This, my friends, is what I'm offering you. Your presence here is no coincidence; you were chosen for you are the future of Galenia! You possess the key in your very core to become Yaru. I have discovered that not everyone was born with this potential so understand how privileged you are. My Kameil brothers are welcome to join us in our vision, as are any who would walk our path to freedom. I will train you, feed you, clothe you, and teach you. You will be a new race: stronger, more capable and with the freedom of choice; a choice that was taken from you the day you were conceived. A choice beyond that given to the race you were born to. Join me, if only for a time, to discover if what I say is true and then you can make up your own mind. If then, you don't share this vision, you are free to return to the life you knew before you came here. You have an hour to decide and then we make for the valley."

He descended from the dais and made his way back to the tent, joined by his five Yaru. The hum of those around Nandin grew in intensity as everyone tried to reason out what to do. Nandin was shaken to his core. Even though the clearing had been filled with at least twenty other Yaru potentials, Nandin felt as if Mateo had spoken directly to him. It was as if he had seen into his soul and knew the very ache that resided within. He never had a dream or plan before; he had always just drifted along with the wind. Leaving his destiny in the hands of other people, his choices too limited to be worthy of his intervention. It had left him empty. Now Mateo gave him a vision. And it was grand, complex. One that would change the world, fill it with hope and dreams like he had never had. He suddenly realized that Jon and Kal had been speaking to him.

"Can we trust him? I mean, why not just come to the village and tell us this, why lure us with this party?" Jon asked his new friends.

"Why do you think?" Kal retorted "I mean, if he just walked into my village he'd probably get stoned to death before he had a chance to speak, you know how fearful people are of him. One thing is for sure; he knows how to throw a good party. These last few days have been a riot. Maybe we should give him a chance. Why don't we go with him for a while and if we have any doubts, we'll just go back home? If we get the feeling he won't let us leave we'll just wait until he thinks we are committed to his cause. We can sneak away when he's unsuspecting."

Jon replied, "I agree. I think we need to find out what he's up to and report back to the Sanctuary. He wants to make us into these Yaru, but for what purpose? What exactly will we be doing?"

Nandin's eyes were focused on the large tent where he saw Nean emerge, still wearing the black attire of the Yaru. Nandin grinned and said, "I know one thing for sure; it will be highly specialized."

Jon and Kal exchanged glances wondering what it was they missed out on.

Kal said, "Ooookaay...does that mean you like my idea? You want to scope it out, then high tale it out of there if it gets weird?"

Nandin hesitated. Mateo's proposal sounded easy and kind of a no brainer; who wouldn't want the incredible speed and agility that the Yaru just displayed along with the freedom of choice that's been promised? But it meant leaving his home, his mother. And it meant trusting someone whom he had been taught to fear his whole life. He watched Nean as he casually made his way through the crowd, greeting friends along the way. When he spotted Nandin he waved as he made his way over.

"So Nandin," he said as he joined the small group, "you ready for another adventure?"

He glanced at Jon and Kal who were still waiting for his answer and shrugged. "You know, I think I am?"

CHAPTER SIX

Settling and Departing

Routine set in.

The following two weeks passed by quickly. Every day Hanna and Kazi would tend to the horses. Despite barely standing as high as a horse's back, Kazi was able to easily swing the saddles onto the horse and into place. Hanna still required his help as she could barely lift the saddle. Once the horses were tacked though Hanna proved to be a capable student. As she became more adept at riding, they joined Kaine, who made the trek daily back to where Hanna had fallen. Still, no sign of her home appeared. Occasionally they would come across animals that had died for no apparent reason and were completely void of any Essence. Leader Cheio explained that even the dead should have some traces remaining. It was another question without an answer.

In spite of not being able to go home, Hanna was enjoying herself. She had formed a rather strong attachment with a horse named Jade. It was the same horse she had groomed on the first day she went to the stables. He had a chestnut-coloured coat with a black mane and tail. When she clucked, he would trot across the field to greet her at the gate. Hanna was comfortable riding him as he wasn't too large around the middle like some of the others she'd ridden. He responded easily to her commands and guidance. One time, when she was first learning to lope, she had begun to slip. Instead of leaning back like

Kazi told her to, she tried to grab around Jade's neck. He slowed as much as he could and she gently slid off, rolling when she hit the ground. Jade made his way back to her to check if she was all right. The next few times she rode him, the horse picked up on her hesitation and slowed down whenever he sensed her losing her seating.

Kazi reminded her he would be leaving for school soon; she was not looking forward to his departure. Her friendship with Kazi was engaging. She felt so at ease with him, like she didn't have to prove herself the way she did with her peers back home. Unlike her other friends, he didn't care if she wore name brand clothes nor was he interested in her popularity. It made her wonder about the value of those other friendships. Instead of being preoccupied with what tomorrow would bring he was content with the here and now, ever ready to answer her questions and ask a few of his own. It was nice to be able to share her knowledge; even the mundane intrigued him. Hanna felt a kinship with Kazi that she hadn't felt in a long time.

Aside from her riding lessons, he filled her in about the comings and goings of everyday life in the village. She was fascinated about their routines on Galenia. She thought that this is what it must have been like in medieval times. Aside from the housing, they also traded goods instead of money. The village took care of one another like one large family. They made decisions together and worked for what they needed. Once a week they had a day off from their routines. They would play games similar to soccer or ultimate Frisbee and then come together for a village feast instead of eating in their own cottages. In the evening they would have a bonfire where they told stories or tales; some true and some were just for entertainment.

Hanna felt great comfort in her temporary home. Cardea and Hamlin were always kind and gracious and she was grateful to have her own space to retreat to at the end of the day. She spent those few moments of solitude filling a journal with the things Kazi told her. The personal touches she added to her room, such as the vase of fresh flowers and the gifts from the villagers of beautiful handmade quilts for the bed and decorations for the walls really made her feel at home. She was able to add to her wardrobe since the work she did in the stables allowed her to acquire clothing and anything else she may need. Often she chuckled to herself when she thought that if anyone here were to visit her actual home they would think it a mansion compared to the modest dwelling she was staying in. It reminded her of camping and at as much as she missed her own family, she was thoroughly enjoying her stay.

* * *

"It's been two weeks Chieo and still no sign of her home." Kaine seated himself on a stool next to the fire in Leader Chieo's cottage.

"I think we should reconsider her story," Nyack pronounced as he paced the room, "maybe her memories have been damaged from when she hit her head."

Chieo sat across from Kaine, listening to his fellow leaders. He knew they needed answers that he couldn't provide.

"Nyack, I have considered her story, and I have to admit it is hard to believe, but believe her I do. I fear though that we will not be able to solve this mystery on our own. I think we need to send her to Master Juro."

Nyack grabbed a chair and joined the other two by the fire. "Yes, that would be best. He'll know what to do. When can we send her?"

Kaine cocked his head to one side.

"So anxious to be rid of our guest? I didn't know you disliked her so much Nyack."

"No, no. I think she is a wonderful girl, she seems to be fitting in just fine; however, I have this foreboding. Something is wrong here and she plays a part."

Chieo said, "Yes I feel it too; something is not right in the woods where she claims to have come from. I fear it's a bad omen. I think Master Juro will want to see the girl himself. I have had Kazi giving her riding lessons in case it came to this. The journey to Kokoroe will be long and dangerous, but she needed to be healed and fit for travel. I think she is almost ready."

"What is your plan?" Kaine asked.

"I think Hanna will be hesitant to leave. If she has a friend along it would be easier. Kazi leaves for school in two weeks' time. He is starting his education at Kokoroe and can therefore go with her; I think he is also enjoying Hanna's company. Kazi's father should be back in a day or two and will travel with them. Kaine, do you think we can spare a Jagare to escort them? I know Kazi and Krigare have travelled much on their own, but with that crystal around Hanna's neck I fear for their safety."

"I will make arrangements between the Jagare. We will need to shuffle around some schedules, but it can be done in short order. I know a few candidates who would be interested in volunteering."

"Excellent. Let us plan the departure for two weeks' time. I will see if we can ease Hanna into the idea before then."

* * *

Hanna was thrilled. She had just come back from taking Jade out for a ride.

"Kazi that was great! I actually got to gallop! It was amazing; I felt so free."

"You're a natural Hanna. I have to admit, it took me a lot longer to get the courage to gallop."

71

SETTLING AND DEPARTING

"Sure, but you said you learned to ride when you were eight. I doubt I would even be able to trot and stay on if I was still that young."

Kazi laughed. They walked their horses into the stable where they proceeded to remove the saddles and brush them down. When they were done, they made their way back to the main village for a midday snack as riding always made them hungry.

Just as they rounded the corner they heard shouting.

"Attack! Kameil are attacking!"

Kazi grabbed Hanna by the hand. They ran to the Nursery and banged on the door.

"Havard, its Kazi and Hanna, we need shelter!"

The door opened and they ran inside. Quickly it was shut and a large wooden board was placed across it in addition to the normal locks.

"Kazi, see to the Hatchlings. Hanna, join the Younglings." Havard pointed to the centre of the room where the last of the children could be seen descending down a staircase hidden under a opening in the floor. A lady Jivan grabbed Hanna's hand and led her forward. Once they descended, the door was lowered into place. Hanna could hear something heavy being dragged on top of the door. There was a light ahead and the stairs opened to a cramped room filled with benches and pillows. A lantern hung from the centre to light the small space. Hanna wanted to ask what was going on, but she noticed that everyone was holding their breath, listening intently to what was happening above.

After covering the door with a carpet and large chair, Havard continued locking the windows with heavy wooden shutters. Down the hall in the Hatchling room, Kazi and the others did the same. With the windows firmly locked, they proceeded to slide lids onto all the cradles and lock them in place as well. From the cupboard they grabbed knives and swords and stood ready in case anyone should break in.

Then the waiting began. Kazi could hear muffled shouts and screams, banging of doors or perhaps a cart being turned over, and then it was quiet. Time moved slowly. Hanna did not want to be the first to break the silence. Finally, after what felt like an eternity, but was more like thirty minutes, they heard furniture being dragged and a moment later the hatch opened up.

"All clear." Havard said.

Hanna clambered up the steps feeling claustrophobic and desperate to be out of the cramped room.

"What's going on? What was that all about?"

Havard pointed down the hall.

"Please assist Kazi with the Hatchlings. He will explain."

Hanna took off down the hall. Her heart was racing and she still felt panic in her gut. When she got to the end room she found the door was locked shut. She knocked.

"Kazi, its Hanna, Havard sent me to help."

She heard a click and he opened the door. "He gave the all clear?" he asked.

"Yes, but I don't know what's going on. What's happening to the cradles?"

Hanna pushed her way in and went to the nearest cradle. It looked more like a treasure chest. It had a lid and a giant metal lock on it. Kazi went to the fireplace and reached up inside. Hooked on the inside of the chimney was a key.

"I'll unlock them all. You can slip the lids off. They are attached, see?" He unlocked the first one and showed her how the lid swung completely around to hang underneath.

"It's the quickest way to secure the Hatchlings and babies. If anyone breaks in here it would take too long to smash the lock, so they would have to take the whole cradle with them. It's pretty tricky to make a quick get away with a crib under your arm," Kazi said as if it all made perfect sense.

"I still can't imagine why anyone would want to steal Hatchlings."

"It's the crystals they want. Since we keep the crystals with the Hatchlings, this protects them both. Let's finish opening these and then we will go find out what happened."

They unlocked the cradles and the windows then made their way to the fountain in town where most everyone was heading. Kaine stood on a small platform beside the fountain.

"We are safe; no villager was killed in the raid. One Kameil was killed in the attack; one was badly injured and will most likely die as well. I'm afraid the rest got away." The crowd peppered him with questions.

"Did they get into the nursery?"

"Were the Hatchlings safe?"

"What about the crystals?"

"Is Hanna safe?"

Hanna was surprised that someone should ask about her specifically.

"Yes, I'm here." She was puzzled, but counted on Kazi to explain later.

"The Nursery was not breached. In fact, they didn't attempt to break in. That is part of the reason they caught us unaware. They broke into other buildings. We are not sure if they didn't know where the Nursery was or if, perhaps, they were searching for something else. I ask everyone to check their homes and shops. If you had a break in, note everything that was taken and report to the main hall in twenty minutes. Everyone else please return to your duties. Jagare are all on watch right now and the area is secure."

With that Kaine hopped down and headed to the hall to wait for the reports from the villagers.

Kazi pulled Hanna towards the stables. "Let's go check the stables and make sure all the horses are accounted for."

Hanna looked nervous. She couldn't bear the thought of Jade being stolen.

"Kazi, why did someone ask about me? There is a whole village of people to worry about, why me?"

"I told you before, with that gem around your neck, you are at risk. You would make an easy target, you don't have a lid and a lock." He gave her a wry smile.

Turning pale, Hanna said, "Oh. I'm glad you were with me. I would never have thought to go to the Nursery. Now I understand why Havard said it was the safest place for me when we first visited."

They got to the stables and found their horses in the stalls where they had left them. They went out the back door and were about to head to the field when a Jagare stopped them.

"You two should stay back in the main village for now."

Kazi said, "We were just going to check to make sure all the horses are here."

"The Horsemaster is doing that now. Go back. Be safe."

Kazi nodded. They went to Cardea's and wait to hear about the details of the attack.

After a few hours, Leader Chieo arrived at the cottage.

"Ah good, you are both here."

"What happened? What did they take?" Kazi was eager to hear the news.

"You heard they broke into cottages and shops?" They both indicated they had. "They took food and blankets. Some dishes were missing. Also, they broke into the blacksmith shop and took weapons and tools. We need to get this information to Master Juro and the Sanctuary. There may have been similar raids in other villages. Kazi, has your father returned yet?"

Kazi said, "No. I think he will be here tomorrow if he hasn't had any problems along the way." Kazi suddenly looked nervous. It was possible his father would cross paths with the Kameil that had just raided the village.

Sensing his tension Chieo said, "Krigare will be safe. He is used to the dangers of the road and will be on guard." He turned to Hanna. "I'm afraid though this event has forced my hand. Hanna, we are no closer to finding your home today than we were two weeks ago. We need answers and now we have even more questions. Master Juro may be able to help. He is the wisest of us all and the most knowledgeable Juro on Galenia. It is time to get his input."

"Yes I agree." Hanna realized it was time to commit to the task of going home.

"I'm glad to hear that. Master Juro resides at Kokoroe." Chieo paused to see if Hanna would start to understand where he was leading.

"Oh Kazi, isn't that the name of the school you said you were going to?"

"Hanna, I think you should consider going with Kazi to the school. I think there you will find more answers than here. Master Juro will guide you."

"Will it be safe to leave with those Kameil out there?" Kazi asked.

"That's why I'm sending a Jagare with you."

Hanna thought for a moment. "Why doesn't he come here?" she asked.

"Master Juro seldom leaves Kokoroe as he has many responsibilities there. Also it would take more time, for the message would need to travel to him, telling him of our need and then he would need to travel back here."

Hanna could see the truth of it. She was nervous at the thought of going further away from where her home should be, but she conceded that staying put wasn't getting her any closer. Knowing Kazi would be with her was comforting as she trusted him and enjoyed his friendship. She looked around the cottage, sad at the thought of leaving the new home that she so quickly became attached to. She sighed; it was good while it lasted.

"When do we leave?"

"As soon as possible. If Krigare is back tomorrow we will let him rest for the night and you will set out the next day. I don't think we can afford to wait more than two or three days so let us hope for his speedy return."

CHAPTER SEVEN

Friends and Foes

Hanna moaned.

They had been riding all day with a brief stop for lunch and she felt spent. After only two weeks learning to ride she was fairly at ease in the saddle, but six hours in one day was wearing on her. Her travel companions didn't seem to be bothered in the least.

Havard from the nursery ended up being the Jagare to escort them on their journey. He scouted ahead to make sure the path was clear and then joined the party again. He appeared tireless as he rode back and forth covering twice as much ground as the others. Kazi's father was the village messenger as well as a mapmaker. He was on the road a lot so this was an everyday event for him. Kazi often went with his father and so he, too, was used to these long days. Hanna hadn't felt this miserable since she was back home. True, the pink haze helped filter the brightness of the day, but her eyes still ached. Her legs were stiff and she was sure her bruises would prevent her from sitting comfortably for a week. Her stomach rumbled constantly even though they had regular meals. She never ate much at one time and was more used to constantly nibbling throughout the day. This proved somewhat tricky while riding.

"Please someone, tell me we are almost there!"

Krigare chuckled. "I was hoping not to make camp for another two hours. We can stop for a bit for a stretch though, I understand you are not used to this form of travelling. Havard, could you find us a safe spot to rest?"

"Thanks." Hanna said then turned to Kazi who rode next to her. She whispered, "What does he mean 'make camp'?"

"Where we set up to eat and sleep for the night."

"You mean we won't be getting to Kokoroe today?" Hanna asked, more than a little concerned.

Kazi grinned sheepishly. He had some notion that Leader Chieo hadn't informed Hanna of the length of the trip and figured at some point he would have to tell her. He had put it off as long as possible and was not looking forward to this moment. Knowing he could no longer avoid it, he tentatively began to explain. "No Hanna, it will take some time to get there."

"How long?" Hanna asked raising her eyebrows.

"Close to two weeks but..."

"TWO WEEKS!"

The horses started when Hanna shrieked. Krigare turned his horse and looped around to come up beside Hanna. He had also suspected the girl wasn't aware what would truly be involved in the trip, but understood they couldn't risk delay so it was thought the details would sort themselves out when needed.

Krigare said, "Yes, if we travel for most of the day with brief rest periods we can reach Kokoroe within fourteen days. That will include stops in BaDaal and Erdo, but I prefer to stop as little as possible."

"But two weeks!" Hanna exclaimed. "I've already been gone from home for two weeks and then by the time we get back it will be up to a month and a half! My mom will be freaking out!"

Krigare replied. "That may be true, however, you could sit back in Kayu waiting for the chance your home will suddenly appear or you can come with us now with the hope of finding some answers. I thought you'd prefer to take action."

Hanna breathed deeply. She knew Krigare was making a good point. She would absolutely go crazy if she continued the daily trip to the forest to be disappointed time and again; however she couldn't help but voice her fear.

"What if it appears and I'm not there? I could miss my chance to get back."

"That is the chance you are taking," Krigare said, "and if getting home was your only concern, leaving may not be your favoured option, but perhaps you should consider this further. What if you get home and in a day or two you end up back here? We don't know how you got here. How are we to prevent it from occurring again? Or even happening to other people? I think, Hanna, this is bigger than you."

Hanna blinked. She had never thought of the big picture before, so absorbed with her own concerns. Krigare was right. In fact, her mother may have ended up here, too, maybe at a different location. Hanna was somewhat relieved. The guilt she had been carrying about enjoying herself, learning to ride, making new friends, was lifted. With the realization that there were more important issues than her immediate concern, she felt freed. It was like being given a permission slip to skip school.

"Thanks Krigare. You have a good point. I would rather head to Kokoroe and see if we can solve this mystery."

"That's the spirit," Kazi piped up. "We'll have a great time, you'll see."

She sat a little taller in her saddle. This new perspective made her feel like she was a vital part of an important mission. She was grateful, though, when Havard returned ten minutes later with news of a safe place to rest. Regardless of her mind being in a better place her body was still struggling with her cause.

* * *

JOURNEY TO KOKOROE

On the third day, they arrived at BaDaal. They had made fairly good time in spite of the breaks and occasional periods when Hanna chose to walk instead of ride to stretch and work out her aches and pains. She was glad the weather was warm, but not sweltering. The nights cooled down a little yet their bedding kept her warm and Krigare was kind enough to bring a tent along for them to sleep in as she understood he normally went without. She managed to suffer through the less than ideal journey with little complaining, but she was indeed glad to be staying in the village for the night.

BaDaal was very much like Kayu. It had the same layout of the town, same style of cottages and shops. Even the people appeared to be similar. They may have been interested in the guests that stayed overnight at the inn, but were content with the story of leading the children to school to begin their education. It was a reasonable story as many did make the trip but it was a little early to travel as the next semester was still a few weeks away.

They enjoyed the hot meal that was provided and after restocking some supplies for the longer trek to Erdo, they went to bed early that night. The next three days on the road continued uneventfully. They stayed on the main road that led to Kokoroe. The woods flanked the road on either side making a pretty path to follow, but also left them somewhat vulnerable if anyone wished to stage an ambush.

Stopping for lunch at midday, Havard led them to a glade hidden under the canopy of trees just off the road. After securing his horse to a tree and having a quick bite to eat he took off at a jog to scout ahead. He returned within ten minutes.

"Krigare," he said in hushed tones, "there is a band of Kameil not five minutes up ahead. They look settled, for now, so I'd say we are safe here for the moment. When we continue on I suggest we cross the road and make our way through the trees for a time. While you finish up I'm going to go listen in and see if I can find out what they are up to."

Krigare nodded. "Good plan. I will ready the horses for your return."

Havard crept low between the bushes. He could hear them before he could see them, but chose to slip in closer for the better view. Although they were far from any towns their voices were hushed.

"I'm not sure I want to go through with it. How can we trust him after everything?"

The man who spoke resembled a Jivan in his late twenties. His eyes had dark shadows under them and he was gaunt looking. From his raspy breathing, Havard knew he was low on Essence.

"Buroc, we've been over this. What choice do we have? If we don't get some Essence soon most of us will die."

The answer came from a larger Kameil who more closely resembled a Jagare, but was also very lean yet still in better condition than Buroc. The group was made up of five men, all sickly looking.

"I know but what do you suppose these missions will be? The Yaru weren't very forthcoming. I don't want to hurt anyone and raiding villages leaves little to be desired."

The larger man snorted, "They turned us out remember? My village wouldn't even acknowledge they knew me! If you ask me, they get whatever we give them."

A younger Kameil of about seventeen agreed.

"Mine did the same to me. They feared I was diseased."

Buroc sagged, "But you know what it was like. When we were part of the village we would have done the same thing. We didn't know! After those soulless addicts began ripping through the nesting grounds and killing everyone in sight; how could we expect anyone to respond with something other than fear?"

"I'm glad you can still forgive them, but I have a wife and child to think about. If you want to stay here and suffocate to death then go ahead. I'm going to find Mateo. Anyone who wants to join me will be ready to leave in the morning."

Buroc hesitated then sighed, "Yes, all right, I'll go with you, but I'm not going to be his slave." Buroc starred down at his feet, a regretful look on his face.

Havard slowly retreated away from the encampment. Once he reached a safe distance he jogged back to his group and found them saddled and ready to move.

"We should be able to avoid detection. They won't be moving until the morning. They talked of strange things – I will tell you more when we get away from here."

They crossed the road and headed into the brush on the other side. Havard left his horse for Krigare to bring so he could scout up ahead at a run which was much quieter on foot than on his horse. For an hour they travelled this way until Havard led them back to the road. He rode beside Krigare with Kazi and Hanna following closely behind, eager to hear his report.

"There was discontent within the group. From what I heard, they used to be part of one of the main villages. Clearly they are Kameil – they looked very ill and weren't breathing well. Their clothes were thin and worn. They spoke of missions and the Yaru. Have you heard of them?"

Krigare tensed. "Only vaguely. One of the nesting grounds over by Darat was attacked. All of the guards but one had been killed and the place was left in chaos. The survivor mentioned the ambush was unlike any he had heard of. It had started out much the same as others; crazy, barely recognizable men attached attempting to get to the crystals, then others arrived. They were organized and stealthy; most of the guards were dead before they even noticed the new attackers. They came at night and were dressed in black. He referred to them as shadows. The crazed men chanted death cries 'Yaru, Yaru' as the shadows retreated into the night."

Even the stolidly calm disposition of Havard shuddered at Krigare's retelling.

Havard said, "More news to give to Master Juro. One thing was clear," Havard let out a sigh, "they were going to meet Mateo."

With that he kicked his horse ahead to once again take the lead.

Kazi was deep in thought after what Havard said, somewhat shaken by the news. Hanna waited until Krigare had moved further away before she spoke.

"I didn't follow most of that, but I know one thing: everyone seems very skeptical of this Mateo fellow. Care to fill me in?"

Kazi stared off into the distance, looking as if he was trying to remember something from long ago.

"There are few different versions of the story, minor details changed here and there but they all end the same. Around a hundred and eighty years ago there was a Juro who was fascinated with the Hatchlings. His fascination turned more into an obsession and he began asking questions about mixing the races. This was against our ways; there are reasons we don't do this. He moved from village to village trying to convince anyone to take on his vision. In one village he came across a Jagare who listened to his cause. She was fascinated with the arts of the Juro. Together they plotted against the order of things – he began teaching the Jagare the works of the Juro and they planned to have children together. They soon heard about a Jivan who was cast out of his village for constantly interfering with the duties of the Jagare. Because of his meddling, several young ones were killed by the Beasts." Noticing Hanna's blank expression he added, "Beasts are large animals that raid villages and steal livestock or even small children." He acknowledged Hanna's look of horror and continued his story.

"The Juro and Jagare sought out this Jivan and he joined their cause at blending the races – changing the world. They became known as The Three. They wanted to create a 'superior' race;" Kazi explained, rolling his eyes, "one that was capable of controlling the Essence like a Juro, had strength like a Jagare and contained Essence throughout like a Jivan. Once it was known that they were attempting to blend the races, they were cast out of society for their refusal to abandon their cause. It was thought that their new race would be disastrous to the world. The Juro reasoned that it would be unnatural and would therefore destroy nature. Regardless, the Three carried on with their plan and created a new race we now know as the Kameil. As you've heard, they are a weak and sickly race. Eventually, it was rumored they created one Kameil who turned out differently; he was not sickly like the others. He is known as Mateo. He continued their work after they died, but he was more determined than his parents. We are not sure what all he does, but we know the Kameil race has increased unnaturally fast since his known existence and now there are...disappearances. The attacks and raids have been more frequent and much more violent."

"Why did Hamlin say Mateo was just a ghost story then?"

"Our village is the farthest southwest. Mateo is based somewhere in the far eastern quadrant so our village hasn't seen or had much contact with the Kameil or Mateo. It's easy to think he's not real when you are so far removed."

"Why are you so sure he is real?"

"I've traveled with my father. I've seen the raids and heard many stories of what has happened to people. The raid that just happened was Kayu's first. We've been attacked at the nesting grounds before, but never in town. For a village raid to be this far is...unpredictable."

"What do you mean 'this far'?"

"The Kameil are more typically known to stick much further to the east of Kayu. The question is why did they come here?"

Hanna suddenly understood. "Which was why Chieo was anxious for us to be on our way. So, let me see if I understand all that you've told me. The Three, each from a different race, were unhappy with how things were and wanted to change?"

"Right."

"You said they wanted to mix races? So would that mean only Juro can marry Juro and Jivan stick with Jivan...?"

"Yes, and Jagare marry Jagare."

"I can see how that *could* upset someone. I mean, what if you fell in love with someone of a different race?"

"Hanna I love many who are of a different race than me. What difference does that make?" Kazi asked.

"I mean, what if you wanted to marry someone from a different race."

"Who would want to do that?"

"Well obviously that Juro did. He even got kicked out of his home for it."

"But don't you see Hanna? Their Younglings were sick. Most of them died. In fact, it's been wondered for years how the Kameil have even survived."

Hanna wasn't sure what to say. Kazi appeared to be content to follow traditions without question. Hanna always questioned the way things were. She understood what it was like to be different – not to fit in. When hearing about the Kameil, Hanna felt sad for them.

Instead of pity for the Kameil, Kazi seemed to hold them in contempt. She wondered if the Juro and Jivan had been in love, for their story sounded far too scientific, like it was some sort of experiment. The romantic in her saw a Romeo and Juliet love affair and she wondered, if she fell in love with someone she wasn't allowed to be with, would she risk losing her home for them? Knowing her kids would be sick, would she still have them? She hadn't thought of such deep questions before but she knew one thing about herself – she wasn't one to do something just because it was expected of her. The more she learned of the Kameil the more she felt she had in common with them.

* * *

As the days moved on, Hanna became better at travelling. She could ride the horse for longer stretches at a time and even found ways to munch small snacks while she rode. A cloud had hung over the party since encountering the Kameil, and conversation was at a minimum. She had thought long and hard about what she had learned and wondered if her new knowledge was causing her to act differently toward her companions as she felt like there was a wall between them. She decided to lighten the mood and push aside her thoughts about the Kameil for the time being so she didn't damage her friendship with Kazi over something she knew so little about.

"Kazi, what sort of things do they teach at Kokoroe?"

Kazi brightened at the new topic and the wall disintegrated.

"Wonderful things! Everyone learns history and takes a class in Community Living. We learn lots about our world. The Juro spend the longest time at this school since that's where they learn their arts. The Jagare also study some empty-handed fighting. I'm so excited to be going; I've never travelled there before."

"I like history. I've always found the Egyptians and Greeks to be so fascinating. It would be kind of neat to sit in on one of your classes, but it's almost summer, school must not start for a few more months..."

FRIENDS AND FOES

Kazi wasn't sure who Egyptians or Greeks were, but let the comment pass without any inquiry.

"Oh, school goes year round. We have semesters; after you turn thirteen you go to school at the start of the next semester. All the schools are on the same schedule so when you have completed training at one you can use the break to travel to the next. Some students choose to visit home before continuing."

"You will be going to more than one school?" Hanna asked surprised.

"Yep. I'll start with Kokoroe and when my studies are done there I will go to the Citadel. That's where I get to choose my trade and spend most of my time training. I'll stay there until I am skilled in my trade – usually two to four years. The last school is the Percipio where I will spend a year studying math, sciences and perfecting my trade."

"Is it the same for everyone?"

"No, not at all. You can choose to go to Kokoroe or the Citadel first, but the Percipio is always for the older students. Depending on your race and trade, your length at each school varies. Sometimes students will take a break from their studies to be with family. If there is a shortage of tradesman in a certain area you may be fast tracked a little and sent off early, but that doesn't happen too often. Also, some students choose not to go to the Percipio because they feel their knowledge is complete enough for the trade they've chosen."

"It's good there are so many choices. Do you have any idea what trade you will choose?"

"I have given it a lot of thought. I enjoy the horses, but I can't see myself working in the stables forever. My mom, as you know, became a baker and although I do appreciate her talents I'd rather be outside than in the kitchen all day. I love travelling like my dad does, but he is away from home a lot so I'm not sure that is the job for me either. I'm still thinking" He laughed.

"Well, if you weren't worried about doing it forever and just made a decision on what you liked, what would you do?"

"Well, you may laugh, but I'd kind of like to be a Minstrel. I could travel all over the place singing and playing music."

"That sounds great!" Hanna exclaimed. "So the only thing that's stopping you is being on the road all the time?"

Kazi chuckled. "That and I have no idea if I can carry a tune! I'll have to wait until I try a music class to see if I have any skill."

Kazi had a daydreaming look about him. He turned to Hanna and said, "I can't wait until we get there! It's supposed to be an amazing place. Unlike any I've seen."

Hanna hadn't given much thought to what she'd do when she left home. Both her parents were in real estate and often they worked late. That definitely wasn't her dream job, aside from the hours, the whole sales thing did not appeal to her. She too had dreamed of being a singer, but she didn't think it was something she could earn a living at. She wondered, if she lived here, would her career choice be much different than what she would choose back home?

* * *

Their days became habitual. With great pleasure, Hanna and Kazi were responsible for feeding, watering and saddling the horses when they stopped. Hanna found spending time caring for Jade was therapeutic; she often found herself talking to the horse, sharing her concerns. Jade would nuzzle her, comforting her. At least that's what Hanna felt, but she knew it probably had more to do with the oats she carried in her pocket than any intentional consoling the horse was doing.

FRIENDS AND FOES

While they tended the horses, Krigare would set up the camp and cook the food. As for Havard, he scouted ahead and hunted for small game for the evening meal. Hanna liked Havard. He didn't say much and when he did, he was soft spoken, except for the time he talked about the Kameil camp they had found. At that particular moment, he sounded firm and determined. Usually after scouting he would ride alongside Hanna for a while and inquire as to how she was doing. He gave her tips on ways to sit more comfortably in the saddle and seemed to know when the best time was to walk for a bit to stretch her legs before they became cramped.

Her favourite part of the day was after dinner. They would sit around the campfire and listen to stories Krigare told. He seemed to revel in the fact that Hanna was new to this land and would fill her in on all the little details such as what the differences were from village to village or how long it took to get from one place to the next. She was fascinated when he told her of the different cities that he had travelled to and thought how she would like to see them. During these stories Kazi would add in some detail here or there; he seemed to know what extra tidbits Hanna would enjoy. Hanna found it entertaining to listen to Kazi and his dad finish each other's sentences. Not only did they seem to share similar thoughts, but also Hanna could see the Essence flow between the two as if they were connected somehow.

Quietly whittling some random piece of stick, Havard would only join in the conversation when the opportunity presented itself to correct some exaggeration, much to the dismay of Krigare.

Hanna thought it was amusing how different the two were. Where Havard was tall and brunette, Krigare was short with the same acorn coloured hair as Kazi. Havard was stoic and reserved, Krigare was boisterous and talkative. Krigare was full of adventure but Havard hinted at a simple life. Havard had a fatherly demeanour and

90

Hanna felt safe in his presence. Krigare was much like Kazi and she found their friendship a refreshing change from the people back home. They were not concerned with the collection of material things or striving for wealth; such concepts were entirely foreign to them. Although, it appeared that Krigare did seem to enjoy his share of gossip, it seemed to have a harmless quality to it; it was more to enliven his anecdotes for the pleasure of his audience rather than out of any form of malice or personal gain.

It was the first time Hanna could remember feeling like she wasn't being judged. There was still this overwhelming expectation on her; she was to ride and keep up, do her fair share of the work and not complain. It was hard at first but surprisingly she found it getting easier as she went along. She even enjoyed the work. This she attributed to the infectious happy-go-lucky manner of Kazi.

Six days after they left BaDaal they arrived at Erdo. Hanna loved the entrance to this town. The narrowed road was covered by a solid canopy of green as the trees merged together. The town itself had an interesting layout. It was made of three ring roads one inside another. Each road was packed with buildings leaving no space between them so the only way to the centre of town was down the main road that cut straight through each ring. Like a bull's-eye, a three-tiered fountain dominated the main square. Hanna wished she had more time to tour around each ring road, but they arrived late and left early, seeing only the small inn where they slept and the view from her window.

As they rode she scratched Jade behind the ear. In fact, Hanna had become quite attuned to Jade's needs; she understood when the horse was hungry or tired or even just restless. Without much experience with horses she thought this was probably what most equestrians were able to do. Just then though Hanna knew something wasn't right.

"Krigare, I think we need to stop."

Krigare slowed and spun his horse to face her.

"What's the problem?"

Hanna patted Jade's neck. "I think, I think there's something wrong with her front left hoof."

She hopped down. Jade lifted the indicated hoof without any additional coaxing. Krigare joined Hanna as she examined and then removed a sharp stone that was wedged in.

"Good catch Hanna, had she taken a few more steps I'm sure it would have caused a puncture which could have become abscessed. How did you know? Was she favouring that leg?"

Hanna thought for a moment. "No it just seemed to be bothering her."

Kazi joined in, "But how did you know it was bothering her?"

"I just got the feeling that she didn't like walking on that foot. I don't think I can explain it better than that."

Krigare and Kazi exchanged puzzled expressions.

"Is something wrong?" she asked.

Krigare smiled. "Not at all. Let's move before Havard wonders what's keeping us."

Hanna was sure he was holding something back, but just shrugged it off; she figured if it was important she would find out about it eventually.

CHAPTER EIGHT

Sights and Goals

Nandin looked back.

The clearing had been completely emptied. Within the hour of Mateo's announcement the camp was packed and ready for travel. Only two people had chosen to return to their homes as they had wives and children they were not prepared to leave. Two Kameil were left to escort them home while everyone else began their journey further east. Their company consisted of pack mules carrying the remaining food and other supplies as well as fifteen Kameil (some on horses and some on foot), eighteen potentials, the five Yaru and Mateo.

Mateo rode upon a powerful, large, black stallion. The Yaru led the group, two of which scouted ahead and set the trail. There were no roads this far east so they had to struggle through the dense woods of the forest.

Before they had ventured out, Nean and the other Yaru had made their way among the men encouraging them to carry on. They were still dressed in black, but had removed the headpieces so they were less intimidating. Nandin longed to talk to Nean some more, however, their encounter was brief before the camp was disassembled and the journey began. Nean assured Nandin that there would be plenty of time for them to speak more when they reached their destination, but for the time being it was the Yaru's job to lead the men and ensure their safety.

SIGHTS AND GOALS

Nandin was plagued with guilt and full of doubt. Although he had sounded so determined in his decision when he had said it earlier, the responsibility he was shirking sat uneasy on his conscience. Recalling Nean's observation that farmers weren't rare helped to steady his resolve. The assumption he was qualified to be Yaru caused his conviction to waver. He was eager about training and being like the Yaru, but he was worried that they had made a mistake in choosing him. He was just a farm kid after all, nothing special. He wasn't even a Jagare. How could he possibly be capable of what he had seen in the Yaru? And this vision of giving people a choice beyond their race, being able to change one's destiny, all sounded so plausible when he first heard Mateo speak of it, but the more time passed, the more skeptical Nandin became.

Jon was also skeptical but for completely different reasons. He had no desire to change his stripes and thought the whole enterprise seemed scandalous. It was what Mateo hadn't said that concerned him the most. The skills the Yaru showed were impressive, but what did they use those skills for? They would hardly be useful when hunting and even if they did encounter bandits in their travels would they need such elaborate maneuvers? He had an uneasy feeling about the whole thing, but he knew the only way to find out more would be to carry on.

The festive mood of the last few days continued as they travelled, although, the potentials were somewhat taciturn towards the men now revealed as Kameil. Making up camp gave the men time to better understand their hosts as they gathered around the campfire while enjoying their evening meal. Mateo kept to himself. The Yaru joined them briefly before retiring to the command tent early on, leaving the potentials alone with the Kameil. They learned that all the Kameil in the group had been born as Kameil and that their life had been filled with struggle for survival. Some of their villages had found fumaroles,

94

cracks in the ground which spewed Essence in gas form. Inhaling the gas on a daily bases had been the key to their survival, but was also dangerous. The gas was extremely hot and unpredictable. New fumaroles would open up in unexpected places, sometimes right under their camps. The fumaroles could disappear all together in just weeks or months so the community always had to be prepared to move. The Kameil themselves still didn't trust the potentials enough to tell them where they found these fumaroles or how many people lived in their communities, but they wanted them to have an understanding of the hardships they had endured until Mateo found them.

The men were surprised to learn that the Kameil had heard of Mateo's existence and knew the rumour that The Three had created him, but they had never met him before. When Mateo found them he helped their people so they didn't need to live in such dangerous places. He brought them to the valley where they discovered many other Kameil resided. Even though Mateo was unlike them, he treated them with respect, as equals and not as outcasts or lower beings like the other races had.

The potentials were weary of these tales at first, as many had witnessed the raids by the Kameil, some resulting in deaths of Hatchlings. It made it difficult to accept the hardships of their travel companions completely.

One night Jon had expressed his opinion while chatting around the fire.

"You all paint a bleak picture, one that makes our kind sound heartless, but you seem to forget, our attitudes are based on a foundation of terror and murder at the hands of the Kameil."

"Which Kameil are you referring to Jon? Have any of you seen any of us before? I know no one in my community, in my generation, has set foot in one of your villages or cities."

"That's a legitimate point," Jon replied to the Kameil who had spoken. The Kameil tilted his head acknowledging Jon's acceptance.

"I have stood guard," Jon continued, "during multiple raids of the Crystal Pockets and now that you mention it, those Kameil did not look like any of you. They were bald or close to it and their eyes were sunken with dark circles under them. They were ghastly pale, corpse like creatures, hardly recognizable beings and they were viscous."

Jon shuddered as he relayed his account.

He admitted, "We always assumed this is what all Kameil become over time."

"Addicts." The man spat on the ground as if the very word left a bad taste in his mouth. "You describe those we don't even associate with. Greedy, selfish animals! They take and take, caring only for the rush they get from the Essence until it kills them. They will steal from their own families, mothers, even children if it gets them their next high. No, those are not Kameil, they are outcasts, even among my people."

Many of the potentials were shocked when they heard this. It appeared as though some of their beliefs had been misguided.

Another potential leaned forward unshaken by this revelation.

"I have seen these Addicts but that's not all. Different Kameil attacked my village. They appeared somewhat sickly, but not to the extent Jon just described. They came and they stole. What have you to say in their defence?"

"I have heard of some, desperate enough to raid a village, however, these are foreigners to me. I ask you this gentleman: would you really judge an entire race by the actions of a few? If a Jivan in a city far from your own commits a crime should I accuse all Jivan of being criminals?"

"It seems to me that we have been living with blinders on," Nandin observed.

96

JOURNEY TO KOKOROE

Jon was wavering. He knew that there were a few other "potentials" that had joined with Mateo only to discover where the Kameil were and what they were up to. He himself was planning on gaining this knowledge to take back home or to The Sanctuary in order to mount a major campaign to rid Galenia of the Kameil once and for all. Now his resolve was shaken as he realized he had assumed much. Perhaps, when he did venture to The Sanctuary, it would be for a different cause, one for the salvation of a people instead of its destruction. He needed proof and was willing to stick around to get it.

* * *

On day three of their trek the forest gave way to a wide, fast paced river flowing south. The expected splashing and crashing of the waves as they hit rocks and the riverbanks seemed magnified as another river off in the distance added to the sound. The rivers, being of different sizes and shapes, produce their own echoes that overlapped each other creating a symphony of noise. A wooden bridge spanned over the river where it narrowed, ten meters from where they had emerged.

"What is this place?" Nandin asked of no one in particular.

Hodon, who was walking slightly ahead of Nandin, Jon and Kal, slowed his pace to come alongside Nandin.

"We are entering the Valley of a Thousand Rivers," he answered. "Not all the rivers have bridges and the ones that do are not easily found. If you didn't have a guide to lead you through the valley it could take weeks or even months to find your way."

Nandin noticed Jon give Kal a meaningful look and knew they were planning on mapping their route as they went – Jon didn't seem to be the type to leave his fate in someone else's hands. Already the venture they were on was challenging Jon's disposition. The Jagare, being responsible for the protection of the people, had more reason than most to dislike and distrust the Kameil for they had the largest causalities at the Kameil's hands.

They wove their way across the rivers; some heavily treed at their banks, others carving their way through rocky fields of thick grasses. After two days of traversing through the brush, across bridges and wading across knee-deep waterways, the men were grateful when their destination came into view. Mountains lay straight ahead and to their left. As they crested a ridge they stood in awe of the sight before them. The sounds of the rivers they left behind still echoed but another, more intense sound of water thundering as it plummeted from a great height captivated their attention.

"White Wall!" A potential exclaimed.

Murmurings of agreement rippled through the group of men. They had all heard of the giant waterfall that bordered the eastern lands, crashing down a mountain's height into the Sea to Beyond. It had always seemed like a mythic creation added to maps as some sort of grand hoax, but now as they approached the mountains and heard the thundering of the falls they knew it was a reality. The density of the trees and the noise of the rivers had prevented any remarkable distinction before they crested the ridge. Now standing on the hill before the cliffs and mountains, there was no denying what caused the powerful din they heard. Once the initial awe of the waterfall faded they drew their attention to the mountain range in front of them.

Two mountains stood close together creating a valley between them. A massive wall made from dark red bricks had been constructed blocking passage into the valley. As they drew nearer to the complex, they discovered that the wall was, in fact, one side of a tremendous building. The bottom half was solid bricks. The upper portion included windows that were evenly spaced around the entire structure, which was capped with a black slanted roof. A heavy black steel gate wide enough for a wagon was the only interruption in the otherwise continuous structure. The lone sentry stationed on top of the building alerted someone down below of the new arrivals and the gate began to open. They potentials marvelled at the impossible building as they passed through the iron gates, but it was the site beyond left them dumbfounded. The valley was much larger than any of them had imagined; however, it was the city that filled it that left them astonished.

The lower portion of the building on this side of the gate was exclusively dedicated to shops with large windows and doors. There were bakeries and butcher shops, as well as tanners and various clothe makers. On one side of the gate a building was devoted to blacksmithing and contained an armoury full of swords, spears and other weapons.

Children played in front of the marketplace; some drawing in the dirt, others engaged in a game of tag. Everywhere, women and men could be seen doing chores such as scrubbing clothes or cutting wood. Now and then people would poke their heads out of one of the upper windows and holler down to someone below. The noises of an everyday city could be heard, but oddly enough, the sound of the falls completely disappeared once a thick wooden door closed behind the gate, sealing them in.

Beyond the marketplace lay hundreds of brick houses, row upon row of low, one-story buildings. People smiled and some even waved as they made their way deeper into the city. The Kameil that had been with them for the trip separated from the group as each went their own way, saying their farewells as they left until it was only Mateo, the five Yaru, the eighteen potentials and Hodon making their way through the city.

The men silently walked on for another half an hour leaving the sounds of the market behind. Faint, indistinguishable echoes occasionally greeted them, but otherwise the empty streets remained quiet. A stern face in a window or someone bustling past was the only hint of the civilization residing in this part of the city.

Nandin spoke softly, "I wonder where everyone is."

Hodon who always seemed keen to enlighten the new potentials said, "Working at the quarry of course. These houses are closer to the quarry so this is the part of the city where the quarriers mostly live."

Jon leaned closer to Nandin and Kal so as to be unheard by Hodon. "The folk we do see don't seem nearly as welcoming as those closer to the market."

Nandin and Kal nodded as they spied another person peering out their window, glaring at them contemptuously as they passed.

When finally they cleared the last of the houses, the men bringing up the back of the column stumbled into those in front who stood frozen as they stared at the castle ahead. It was a majestic structure standing another ten stories taller than the outer wall that surrounded it. The wall itself was double the height of any forest tree. The red-bricked rectangular castle was impressive in and of itself, but it was the fact that it was floating high above the ground that had the men gawking. The Yaru were already mounting an arched bridge that stretched up to the gate of the castle wall. Hodon beckoned the men forward and they, once again, followed along to the bridge. So intently admiring the castle above, they had neglected to notice at first that the castle was not simply floating above the ground, but was above a massive pit. Once aware of the immense hole, the potentials were reluctant to continue. Hodon attempted to reassure them.

"This is the quarry I mentioned. Nothing to worry about, come on. The castle has been hovering above this pit since before any of you were born – or your parents for that matter."

Finally the men continued on, most choosing to walk in the centre of the bridge with their eyes fixed on their destination, trying to resist the temptation to look down into the pit below. Those brave enough to stray to the edge quickly overcame their curiosity and joined their comrades in the belief that the middle of the bridge was, after all, the safer position.

Gratefully they reached the castle. Even though it was floating it had the pre-tense of normalcy once through the gate. The gate was secured shut with yet another solid wooden door once they were inside. Jon's look of concern was barely concealed as it closed. They stood in a small courtyard with the stables off to the left and the keep, the central tower of the castle, straight ahead.

Mateo turned his horse and spoke to the new arrivals. "Gentlemen, welcome to my home."

A man approached Mateo, bowed and faced the group. He was dressed in a long white robe with large dangling sleeves where his crossed arms were hidden from sight. Around his waist he wore a bright blue sash, the same colour as Mateo's robe. He was short compared to Mateo, but was only slightly shorter than Nandin. His long brown hair had grey streaks and the wrinkles around his eyes revealed he was no longer a young man.

"Let me introduce you to Hatooin, my personal assistant. Any question you have may be directed to him. He will guide you to your new quarters and then retrieve you to join me for dinner."

With that he quickly dismounted as a young boy rushed forward to take the reins of his horse to take away to the stables. They watched as Mateo made his way across the grounds and disappeared into the keep. Hatooin waited until Mateo was gone and slowly all eyes fell on him.

"This way please." Hatooin led the party to a door in the outer wall that revealed a staircase. After climbing two flights, they found themselves in a long hallway that led around the grounds. As they walked they gazed out arched windows that provided them with a view of the castle grounds as they passed by. When the wall reached the keep, the hallway continued into it but now, without the inner windows, sconces were set in the walls to light the passage. The hall ended with another flight of stairs. Going up one more flight they entered a corridor lined with doors. Hatooin stopped at the first one and opened it.

"Please choose a room to stay for tonight. At this time your lodging is simple, a bed, side table and lantern. If your stay continues we shall see about a more personal atmosphere; for now enjoy your view of the gardens. I will leave you to rest and will return to collect you for the evening meal." He bowed, turned and walked back down the stairs.

The weary travellers chose their rooms and quietly entered, each exhausted and lost in his own thoughts.

Nandin was quick to remove his boots and wash his face and hands in a basin sitting next to the lantern. Although dead-tired, he realized he hadn't been this excited since he went to school. Doubt still tugged at him, but he kept pushing it to the back of his mind. When he had seen the community he felt a twinge of guilt. Again reminded of how he had abandoned his village leaving them one farmer short. Bringing in the harvest would be difficult. He rationalized though, that they could just request an extra hand from one of the cities or schools; help would come. They would have had to do this very thing years ago if Nandin had insisted on finishing school, which was completely in his rights. No, he thought, he would not let guilt ruin his adventure. For the first time in his life he was thinking about himself. He collapsed on his bed, allowing sleep to embrace his tired body.

Jon walked to the window of his room. Out the windows he saw a huge garden filled with decorative trees, flowers and a fountain. No one could be seen down in the garden below, but he still had images of children playing in his mind. How could this be? In the care of his people's most feared villain was a community full of families. Most seemed healthy, happy and by no appearance in need of rescuing or having cause for destroying. Was it possible they had been in the wrong? Maybe Nandin was right. How could they be so blind? Mateo's castle was a city unto itself with hundreds of individuals in the compound. He wagered that a few thousand people lived down in the valley. He wasn't sure what to make of it all. He needed more time to decide what to believe.

* * *

Hatooin returned an hour later. He rang a bell, which successfully got everyone's attention as they popped their heads out their doors. By the yawns and stretches the men exhibited it was clear most had taken the opportunity to nap. There hadn't been much else to do in the mostly empty rooms. Hatooin led them back down the stairs and through a door leading into another long, empty corridor. After turning down a few other passages they finally entered a large dining hall. Four large tables connected to make a square leaving an empty space in the middle. The five Yaru sat at the head table, flanking a high-backed chair that still remained empty. The potentials were directed to the other three tables and filled up the remaining seats.

Nandin was situated facing the empty chair; he studied the Yaru who surrounded it, no longer in the black outfits they had been wearing ever since they were introduced in the clearing. They were laughing and chatting amongst themselves. Nandin noticed the different sizes and builds of the Yaru, but in some way they still resembled each other. Before he could contemplate it further, Mateo entered the room. He wore a long, solid black shirt and pants of a similar design that he had worn before, however, the material appeared to be the familiar cotton. He wore a bright blue sash around his waist and simple sandals on his feet. His hair was tied back except for one long, thin braid. Even though Nandin could no longer see Mateo's muscular chest he could still sense the power that resided there. The light, which was provided by sconces along the walls and a magnificent candle-lit chandelier, revealed motion in Mateo's eyes as he gazed at the potentials.

"Honoured guests, I am so glad you choose to join us. I believe you will be pleased you did."

Hatooin pulled out Mateo's chair but remained standing next to Mateo.

"Let me formally introduce you to my Yaru Captains and your new instructors. Mayon, Thanlin, Plyral, Sim, and Nean." As he said their names they stood and bowed in acknowledgment.

Mateo motioned to Hatooin, who rang his ever-present bell, and the room filled with people carrying platters of food and jugs of ale, wine and ice cold water. Nandin felt honoured to be joining Mateo and his Yaru for dinner, but he sensed some of his comrades still were a little uneasy around them. He wasn't sure if it was from the confidence Mateo instilled or the power he exuded but in his presence, Nandin felt euphoric.

Mateo spoke loudly to be overheard above the din of the dishes. "Tonight we feast. Tomorrow your first lesson will begin. Let's become better acquainted."

This was the first time any of them had actually been given the opportunity to speak with Mateo as he never joined them around the fire on the journey and always rode slightly ahead. As the meal began in earnest the men began to chatter. They became more comfortable with their host and began asking questions about what the training involved and what purpose it was for. Mateo and the Yaru listened with interest, but evaded answering questions by adding only minor details to the information that Mateo had already shared with them in his speech at the encampment. Mateo instilled admiration of all those around him. Even Jon, who was determined to despise Mateo, couldn't help but be in awe of him. He was captivated and just wanted to hear him speak more. He asked how Mateo planned on making them Yaru, but before an answer was forthcoming, Hatooin arrived to return them to their rooms.

Some potentials chose to chat with each other awhile, excited about the upcoming training. Nandin felt content to retire to his room and sleep. Jon lay in bed, staring at the ceiling, fretting about Mateo's plans. Mateo had said they contained something at their core that was the key to making them Yaru; what was this key? How was he going to make them Yaru? This question kept him awake most of the night.

* * *

Mateo paced in his study, quietly contemplating his plan. He took a seat, leaned back in his chair and rested his chin in his hand. Hatooin knocked on the door and then entered, carrying a hot mug of tea. He placed it on the desk and turned to go.

"Thank you Hatooin. Please, sit."

Hatooin pulled up a chair.

"I'm so close I can feel it. Do you think our newest subjects will exceed my expectations?"

"Well Master," Hatooin replied tentatively, "they look like a healthy group, but no one in particular stands out to me. I do sense...."

Hatooin hesitated, unsure if his Master was in a mood for him to cast doubt on his latest experiment.

"Go on."

"I get the feeling they may be here under false pretenses. That, perhaps, they are not as eager to share in your plan as they have let on."

Mateo snickered.

"Is that all? That's hardly new. In fact, how many recruits have ever been overly willing at first? Why should that make any difference now?"

Hatooin considered a moment.

"Yes, this is true, but you are training them to be powerful fighters. Isn't that risky? What if they discover what happened to their fellow potentials that chose not to join? Eventually someone will let something slip and they will know those two didn't make it back home."

Mateo thought for a moment.

"Usually if the treatment doesn't work they become Kameil and that doesn't pose much of a risk to me," he mused "but if it does work I need their committed loyalty. I need to know who is trustworthy already and who needs further convincing. What do you propose?"

Hatooin puffed up. Mateo had asked him for his opinion before, on rare occasions, but as the community grew he relied more and more on Hatooin. Hatooin surmised that Mateo's isolation over the years had diminished his people skills and Hatooin's role had become more essential. He reveled in the fact that he was the chief advisor to the most powerful being on Galenia.

"I think we proceed with the plan, giving the treatment to all of them. I suggest we move them to prime quarters – next to the Yaru. We could assign a Yaru to a group of three or four to mentor. Place your most loyal servants to tend to their needs while keeping their ears open for anything suspicious. Once we have determined who is insincere in their commitment, you can try harder to turn them to your cause or...deal with them as you see fit."

"I'd prefer not to dispatch any Yaru, but what you suggest is sound. Thank you for your council. You serve me well. If any of them don't take to the treatment, we may need a contingency plan to avoid it negatively affecting the rest of them. Do you think we should quarantine them to this building?"

Hatooin thought for minute then said, "Maybe for a few days while they gain their strength, but I think seeing and being part of the community will make them more at home. It will be easier to commit them to your cause."

"Is there any resentment towards me with the Kameil? If there is it would hurt our cause more if the new recruits are among them."

Hatooin caught the reference to "our" cause, another sign he was elevated in Mateo's opinion.

"Only among some of the quarry labourers, those that have worked there the longest seem to resent their situation. The Kameil that have most recently arrived think of you with only admiration. You chose wisely bringing them here."

Mateo said, "Yes, a choice based on your suggestion. Hatooin you've proven to be of great value to me. How can I further reward your loyalty?"

Hatooin had already been provided with prime living quarters with his own bath and servants to meet his needs. He was among the first to receive the treatment to restore the Essence that had been robbed from him during one of Mateo's experiments. His word was second only to Mateo within the castle grounds; outside the castle the five Yaru were given higher command. Hatooin had worked closely with Mateo for years in the lab and enjoyed the work they performed there.

"Master, you have done right by me. What more could I ask for?"

"I've noticed you have yet to take a wife."

Hatooin chuckled. "One day perhaps. I have my eye on a few candidates."

"Well, let me know when you've chosen one. I'm sure she would have a few ideas of a reward. Thank you for your thoughts. We will proceed after the morning meal."

Mateo indicated that Hatooin was dismissed. Hatooin rose and gave a quick bow. Mateo watched him as he left the room. Hatooin's pride was not lost on Mateo. He sensed it when he first met the man and had been playing to it ever since. He needed talented people he could trust. Hatooin was no Yaru, but he had his uses. He understood group mentality and had personal insight to the Kameil. Mateo knew they had lost faith in him when he didn't help them after his failed experimentations; he had been busy with his own concerns. Unfortunately, the damage was done and now he needed their help to achieve his latest plans. Hatooin had helped to begin to repair that damage. In a few more years, he would have the manpower necessary to successfully accomplish his goal.

CHAPTER NINE

Encounters and Intrigue

Their destination was within reach.

Five more days of travelling and the heavily worn dirt trail they had been on became a cobbled road, which marked the final part of their journey to Kokoroe. The clickity-clack sound of the horses' hooves echoed off the stones adding a new dimension to the last few miles of their trek. The road widened as it intersected with roads from Situ and Korode.

In addition to the change in road, they had also experienced a change in scenery. The trees thinned out until there were just a few clumped here and there. The road led up and over rolling hills and they could see mountains off in the distance. Both Kazi and Hanna stared with excitement when the first glimpse of Kokoroe came into view.

With mountains as a backdrop, the school dominated the top of a hill allowing them to see the great gates long before they arrived. As they drew closer, the large mass took shape. The structure was a pillared archway that had three large openings, the one in the middle being taller and wider. They were rectangular in shape, but what made them eye-catching was how they were topped. The multi-tiered roof had ends that flared out and up giving an appearance of wings. The whole thing was coloured deep red and the tiled roof had a reflective quality that made it sparkle in the sun. More and more details revealed themselves as they approached: trellises stood between pillars in the two flanking openings and vines climbed up them, making solid walls of greenery with a hint of colour from pink and blue flowers. A large black iron gate stood under the main arch. Tall trees followed an attached iron and wood fence that faded off into the distance around the school grounds.

Hanna marveled at the enormous structure. When finally they were on top of the hill they dismounted their horses and led them up to the gate. Hanna reached out to touch the designs and upon closer inspection discovered they had texture. Looking up she realized there were carvings all the way to the top of each pillar that were accented with black paint, giving them dimension.

Havard walked up to the side of the gate where a golden rope hung. When he pulled it a loud gong sounded, echoing like waves rolling upon a shore. A tall brunette woman, obviously a Jagare, opened the gates and welcomed in the travellers. She was dressed in deep burgundy pants and shirt and wore a golden rope for a belt with keys securely attached.

"Greetings Krigare. It has been some time; I am pleased to see you again" she said closing the gate behind them.

There was a break in her composure when she first noticed Havard.

"Havard...what a pleasant surprise." Her tone was even, but they locked eyes and some unspoken communication seemed to occur.

Havard bowed. "Hello Jaylin."

Hanna noticed that as they spoke the Essence between them seemed to intertwine as if it was trying to pull them together. Kazi exchanged glances with Hanna; he might not be able to see the Essence, but he was still able to sense that there was something between the two of them.

Krigare bowed. "Greetings Jaylin. This is my son Kazi and you've met Havard, our village guardian."

In acknowledgment to Havard's charge of the Hatchlings she bowed, "Your noble work is a compliment to all Jagare."

As she took Kazi's hand she said, "I have heard many tales of you, brave Kazi. I wonder if you will prove to be an adventurer like your father?"

Kazi looked pleased that his father had spoken of him and with such high regard. Jaylin turned to Hanna.

Krigare said, "This is Hanna. She has been a guest at our village."

Jaylin bowed to Hanna. "Welcome friend. I am Jaylin the Gatekeeper."

They walked farther into the compound as they spoke.

"Krigare, do you bring messages for Master Juro?"

Krigare nodded while patting a bag he had slung over his shoulder.

"Very good. Someone will see to your horses. I will lead you to the guest quarters to freshen up and rest while I arrange a meeting in two hours' time."

They tied their horses to a nearby hitching post and followed Jaylin. Hanna was surprised at the appearance of the school grounds. Large grey stones were nestled into a field of white gravel and created a pathway that they now followed. Also in the gravel were stone sculptures of different sizes; some looked like oddly shaped towers while others were carved in the shape of little houses with windows. Decorative bushes and rounded trees were scattered amongst the statues. Ahead were several square buildings with flat black roofs. Before Hanna got a chance to see much more Jaylin led them to the first building. Instead of the stone or wood buildings she had seen in the villages, this structure had sand-coloured walls that looked like hardened paper. There were black supports that made a large grid pattern across the whole wall. The black doorframe protruded out and was topped with what looked like a flattened top hat with the ends sticking out past the door's casing. It was a smaller version of the roof that covered the whole building. The double doors were also black, but had no door handles. Hanna was wondering how they opened when Jaylin slid one to the side.

As they walked over the threshold they entered a small foyer with smooth stones making up the flooring, the same beige walls and another sliding door facing them. Two long wooden benches were placed against both walls and several baskets of towels were tucked underneath. Jaylin slid open the next door to reveal a square, open roofed garden. The same oddly shaped trees and bushes were situated in more gravel that surrounded a small pool in the centre. A few stone benches circled the pond and interestingly-shaped boulders seemed to be placed randomly throughout the space. A wooden walkway bordered the garden, which allowed one to walk to any of the sliding doors that lined the remaining three walls.

Jaylin motioned to the doors with her hands.

"Any of the rooms on the left or across the garden are currently unoccupied; feel free to choose the one you wish. The corner door on the left is where you will find the toilet. If any of you are interested in washing up, you are welcome to go to the bathhouse. It is usually empty at this time of day as most students are in lessons. I will return for you when Master Juro is ready."

She went back through the sliding doors they had entered from. Kazi flashed Hanna an excited look and bound down the wooden path to the first door. He slid it open to reveal a small room with a bed, low to the floor, a small area rug and some open shelves against the wall. There were no windows, but the walls were translucent enough to let light through. Kazi shrugged, went in and was about to collapse on his bed when Hanna grabbed him.

"Wait...you're a little dirty. Maybe you should visit the bathhouse first?"

Kazi looked down at his arms and legs.

112

With a chuckle he said, "You're right, but in case you haven't noticed, you're not that clean either."

Hanna laughed. "I guess two weeks riding horses and camping will do that to a person. Let's go see what this bathhouse looks like...where do you suppose it is?"

"Havard and father will know; they've been here before."

They followed Krigare and Havard as they, too, needed to clean up.

They led them to the building next door. It was of similar design, but included images on the doors. Hanna hesitated until Kazi explained that the symbols meant male and female. When they slid open the two doors there was a wall dividing the entrance. Kazi, Havard and Krigare entered one side of the divider so Hanna took the other. The entrance had an L-shaped wall so even with the door open no one could see inside. Closing the door behind her, she walked around the wall. Instantly she felt the moisture in the air, which was infused with the smell of lavender. In the middle of the room was a large, steaming pool. Wooden walls with matching door jutted out of the far corner; she thought it most likely a sauna. There were several cubicles along one wall that she discovered were showers when she peeked into them. She was delighted; she hadn't had a shower in such a long time. Back at the village she had used a washbasin and cloth to clean herself and on the road they sometimes found small streams they could rinse off in. She didn't realize how much she missed showering until this moment. She sat on a bench, facing a wall of cubbies; some held towels and some were empty. Seeing no one else in the room she quickly undressed, stuffed her clothes into an empty cubby, grabbed a towel and headed for the closest shower stall.

She draped her towel over a line that hung across the stall. She didn't see any handle to turn the water on, but she did notice the showerhead had a cover on it. When she slid the cover off, warm water splashed down on her. She closed her eyes and enjoyed the refreshing sensation. After she was thoroughly soaked, she looked around and found some glass bottles filled with what she figured must be shampoo. When she finished washing she slid the cap back over the showerhead and grabbed her towel. She looked around the stall to discover she was still alone, so made her way to the hot pool, placed her towel on the side and slid in. All of her tired aching muscles just let go. She leaned her head back and breathed in deeply. She had been concerned at first when she smelled the lavender, worried it may be too strong and cause her a headache, but it proved to be mild enough that she was able to enjoy it. She felt herself starting to doze off and thought better of it. She swam around a little to stretch out. Climbing out of the pool she grabbed the towel and headed to the sauna. She opened the door enough to glance in to ensure it was also empty and make sure it was actually a sauna, and then went in. There were two levels of benches against the wall and a metal bin filled with hot rocks. She filled a ladle from a bucket of water on the floor and poured it over the rocks. The rocks sizzled as steam rose into the air. Hanna lay down on the top bench and smiled. She felt so warm and at ease. She knew she couldn't stay too much longer because all this relaxation would cause her to fall asleep and she certainly didn't want to wake up and find the room full of people. As if to confirm her fears, she heard a door open. She lay still and listened. She could hear footsteps. There was the rustling noise of fabric being moved. Hanna wasn't sure what to do. She thought she would wait until she heard the shower turn on or perhaps movement in the pool and then try to sneak out. Instead, she heard the door slide open and shut again. She waited. When no further sounds could be heard she opened the sauna room door slowly. There was no one in the room. She quickly walked back to her locker to discover her clothes missing. In their place was a long white robe hanging on a hook beside the locker. Hanna guessed that someone must have taken her dirty clothes to be washed. Gratified, she thought it was turning out to be a great day. She finished drying off and put on the clean robe. She also found slippers on the floor under the robe and she slid those on as well. She walked out the door and made her way back to the guest quarters. She passed the room Kazi had entered earlier. Hearing deep breathing, she knew he was sound asleep already. She went into the room next to his, slipped under the covers of the bed and quickly drifted off to sleep.

* * *

Two hours later Kazi was waking Hanna from the best sleep she'd had in weeks. Wiping the drool off her cheek she stretched and sat up. Kazi laughed as he gave Hanna a hand standing up.

"It's time for dinner." Noticing she still wore her robe he added, "I think you should get dressed first though."

He winked and walked out of the room, closing the door behind him. Hanna hesitated for a minute remembering she had left all her extra clothes with the horses. A quick glance around the room revealed a folded pile of clothes on one of the wooden shelves. She held up a pair of tan pants and a long, light blue top. She slipped into the clothes. It felt like she was wearing pajamas as the pants were very baggy and the top hung almost to her knees. She was just puzzling out how she was going to keep the pants from falling down when she noticed a white sash that had fallen on the floor. It was almost a foot wide and longer than she was tall. She wrapped it over her top several times around her waist. She tied it in a knot leaving some of the sash hanging down. When she opened the door she saw Kazi waiting in the garden. He came over and adjusted her sash so the extra hung down her side instead of her front. She was surprised when she noticed he was dressed exactly the same way.

"There are some sandals on the floor under the shelves" Kazi said.

Hanna found them and put them on and they walked out of the guesthouse. Havard was standing just outside the door. He was beaming.

"Now you two look like true students of Kokoroe. Krigare is meeting with Master Juro. We shall join the others for dinner and meet up with him later."

"Havard, how do you know Jaylin?" Hanna hoped she wasn't too out of line asking, but she couldn't help being curious.

Havard stared ahead with a far off look in his eyes.

"We went to school together. We have been friends for some time but have little opportunity to see each other."

Kazi grinned, "It kind of seemed like there may be more to it than that."

Havard gave Kazi a friendly slap to the head. "There may have been, but our lives took different paths."

It was clear he wasn't going to say more. Havard began walking; Hanna and Kazi fell instep beside him. They passed a few more buildings that looked similar to the guesthouse but varied in size; some were two or three stories tall. The winding path led to a stone bridge that stretched over a wide creek with large trees on either side, blocking out much of the view ahead of them. The bridge connected to a hexagonal gazebo with two more bridges leading off in different directions. They took the passage to the left through the trees and under an archway, smaller but similar to the one at the entrance to the grounds except it had only one arch instead of three. They stepped out onto a brick patio that was surrounded by three buildings, each facing in towards the centre of the patio. The buildings resembled the ones they had seen already, the main differences being that the wood supports and the roof were a darker shade of red instead of black. Another difference was that there were giant red pillars in front of each and the roofs extended out, creating a covered walkway joining all three buildings. In the gaps between each building there were archways, leading to more unseen places. Two of the structures were similar in size as the guest quarters, but the third was the largest building they had come across. Havard led them to the third building and went in. The ceiling was high with exposed black beams. Wood posts stood vertically supporting the beams and the wooden floor was covered with several rows of long, wide mats that ran the width of the room. On top of each mat sat four low, square tables. Eight individuals of varying ages sat on cushions at each table. Hanna noticed that most of them were dressed identically to Kazi and herself with a few exceptions; some had tan tops instead of blue and there were different coloured sashes among them.

A stack of shelves held shoes near the door they had just entered. As they removed their shoes and placed them on the shelves a Juro approached them. She was younger than any Juro Hanna had met so far, but considering she had only met four it didn't count for much. It seemed only one Juro lived in each village unless they were married, like the couple she had met while staying in Erdo.

"Welcome friends, my name is Yoshi. If you will follow me I will take you to your dining table."

Havard motioned for the kids to go first. Hanna was grateful that the table they were taken to was in a corner, as she was in no mood to stand out today. She noticed some people glance her way as she went across the room. She responded with a nervous smile, but tried to be as invisible as possible. As she walked past the tables, she noticed that amongst the Jivan and Jagare there were more Juro than she had ever seen in one place. She made a mental note to ask Kazi about this when they were alone again. Yoshi took a seat at table occupied only by Jaylin the Gatekeeper.

Once they were seated Jaylin spoke. "I trust you have found your accommodations adequate?"

Kazi and Hanna exchanged grins. Hanna replied, "More than just adequate. I had the best nap ever. The bathhouse was amazing! I haven't felt this clean in...I don't know how long."

Jaylin laughed. "I'm glad you are enjoying yourself so far Hanna. Now that you are clean and rested I imagine you are hungry?"

They both nodded their heads earnestly hoping that food was soon to follow that question.

Havard spoke, "It seems to me these two are always hungry." He gave them a wry grin with a nod of his head. "Will Krigare be joining us?"

Jaylin shook her head.

"No, I believe he will be dining with Master Juro as they seem to have much to discuss. Kazi, I know you will be starting school with us in a few weeks, Hanna do you know how long you will be with us?"

"Not really. I was hoping Master Juro would be able to answer that question."

If Jaylin thought that Hanna's situation was odd, she never let on, seeming content to leave the mystery for someone else. Catching movement out of the corner of her eye, Hanna turned and saw the set of double doors, across from where they had entered, open. Several people pulling carts hustled through. The carts looked like tables with two large wheels and two legs and were topped with platters of food and dishes. The first cart went down the centre row then to the far aisle where the guests sat. The boy, no more than thirteen, that pulled the cart, set it down on its legs and then handed out wooden bowls and ceramic cups to everyone at Hanna's table. He placed several dishes of food in the centre of the table along with two large jugs. When he was done, he gave a quick bow and headed to the next table to repeat the same procedure. The other people pulling carts had gone down the other aisles also setting out the meal and dishes. Everyone patiently waited. Once finished, they lined the carts up against one wall, then they each made their way to different tables and sat down. When they had all been seated a chime sounded and eating commenced. There were large wooden spoons or tongs used for dishing up the food that consisted of chicken pieces, rice and a variety of vegetables. Hanna noticed there was no other cutlery and waited to see what the others did. She was surprised to see that, once they filled their plates with serving utensils, they used their fingers to scoop the food and eat it. Although this was typical of how they had eaten most of their meals on the road, during her stay at the village they often used spoons, knives and forks (which had only two or three prongs). She surmised that since they were eating with their hands that maybe this explained why she was given an extra bowl: one must be to use as a finger bowl. As if reading her mind, Jaylin poured water into the extra bowl and passed the jug along. She dipped her fingers into it, shook them out and reached for the other jug. She poured herself some water in her mug and passed this jug as well. After Hanna filled her own cup she took a long drink of the water and found it was refreshingly cold, unlike most of the water she had had so far.

"Jaylin," Hanna asked, "how come this water is so cold? It seems most of the water in the villages is only slightly cool."

Jaylin nodded.

"Yes, that is typical. We are close enough to the Spire Mountain range that it is practical to get blocks of ice to cool food allowing us to store it for a greater length of time. As the ice melts we collect it and have chilled water to drink. It is a refreshing treat."

Hanna nodded, attempting to appear amazed at this innovation, but silently chuckled to herself. What would they think if she told them about the freezers and refrigerators she had back home? When she had first come to Galenia she told Kazi about all sorts of details of her home, but after a while she started holding back a little as he rarely understood what she was saying and often was so in awe she thought perhaps it was better if she kept some of the more advanced innovations to herself. She didn't know if he would think she was magical or just making it all up. It often felt like she had gone back in time thousands of years and the idea of phones, computers or even electricity were just a bit too far outside of their realm of reality. At that thought, she looked around and admired all the sconces on the walls and the lanterns that hung overhead. She loved the glow they gave off, so much better than the bright fluorescents from school and the halogens at home, although it was much more convenient to flick on a switch instead of lighting the wicks one lamp at a time. She thought it kind of funny how she had taken so much for granted: two weeks to get to a place that would have taken her just hours by car, the amount of effort involved in washing clothes by hand, bathing in creeks or with buckets. The everyday requirements of life here took up so much time, it was amazing that there was ever time left in the day to do other things. She understood why the villages had become so interdependent; it would be much more difficult to achieve anything if they worked alone. For the first time she wondered if that innovation back home was really for the best if it cut people off from each other so completely?

When it seemed most people had finished eating, different students rose and again moved the carts down the aisle to collect empty plates and food platters. As Hanna watched them move efficiently from table to table, Yoshi rose.

"If the three of you would follow me, Master Juro will see you now."

Havard, Kazi and Hanna rose and followed her through the room and out the main door. She led them down the covered archway to the next building over. As

120

they went, Kazi explained that Master Juro was the most advanced Juro in the world and therefore the most respected. He reminded her to bow and thank Master Juro for his time.

The building they were led to was two stories high. Once inside they saw several couches and chairs in a circle in front of a large fireplace with a low table in the centre. A raised area had a variety of tables, tiered stands of votive candles in the shape of pyramids and large brass pots which shone in the glow of several lanterns. Yards of gauze fabric hung from the ceiling, thick enough to prevent anyone from seeing in, but they were slightly opened so large cushions could be seen in addition to a low table topped with more candles and rolls of parchment. Sitting at one of the tables was Krigare. He looked up as they entered and hurried over to greet them.

"Ah Kazi, seeing you in the students' attire brings back memories. It's like I was just walking these grounds myself for the first time." He smiled as he patted his son on the back. "Kazi, Havard, we are to wait here. Hanna, Master Juro is in the meditation gardens out back; Yoshi, would you show Hanna the way?"

Krigare bowed to her. Yoshi nodded and motioned for Hanna to continue following her. They went down a hallway that led away from the main chamber passing a few doorways and walked outside. The gardens were breathtaking. Trees, mosses and plants of varying shades of green were surrounded by brightly coloured flowers of reds, blues, yellows and pinks. Hanna could see a waterfall spilling into a creek that meandered down a hill, at the bottom of which a wooden bridge led over the creek. There were stones everywhere, some in the water, others following a pathway in among the bushes. Some were big enough to sit or climb on. Stone statues were strategically placed; however, they looked like they had always been there. Yoshi led Hanna down the path, over the bridge and around a hill. There she saw sand that had been raked into a pattern that looked like waves of water and a few boulders of irregular shapes sat in a seemingly haphazard fashion in the sand. The creek continued through the greenery and a second bridge crossed to another section of the garden. Hanna noticed someone was on this bridge.

Hanna blinked and blinked again not sure if what she was seeing was real. The person she saw was obviously a Juro given his size. He had long grey hair and a beard tied every three inches or so making it look thin. He wore a robe of a pearly sheen that picked up other colours as it moved. His arms came together in front and his hands were hidden in his sleeves. His legs were crossed in a sitting position, but what was amazing was that he was floating four feet off the ground. He had a brighter pink glow than anyone she had seen and it encompassed him. His bright blue eyes seem to pierce her soul as they approached.

Yoshi bowed low.

"Master Juro, may I present Hanna?"

Master Juro nodded and looked at Hanna with a penetrating stare. Hanna tucked her hair behind her ears as she so often did when she was nervous.

"Hanna I see that I've made you uneasy. Would you prefer if I were to walk?"

Hanna shook her head. "Oh no sir, but I would like to know – how do you do that?"

He smiled slightly and said, "Yoshi would you be so kind?"

Yoshi bowed, passed Master Juro and began walking at a steady pace. As she did, Master Juro began following her, still floating in the air. Hanna came out of her stunned state and quickly caught up to walk beside him.

"The simplest explanation would be to say that I create a magnetic pole." When Hanna looked confused he added, "Imagine two magnets. If you put like poles together they resist each other; the stronger the magnet, the stronger the resistance. So my magnetic pole is the same as the grounds and therefore I float above it. I use this magnetic property to move as well. Yoshi has an opposite pole from the one I've created therefore I'm attracted to her," Hanna suppressed a giggle as she apparently was the only one who found humour in that comment. "As she walks I am pulled along. Make sense?"

Hanna looked concerned, "So you can't move unless there is someone around to, um, pull you?"

Master Juro tilted his head. "No, I have other means of movement; I just prefer to float when I'm with someone as tall as you. I prefer to look into your eyes."

Hanna chuckled. "That's the first time anyone has referred to me as tall."

Master Juro nodded his understanding.

"I realize you must have many questions as all this is new to you. Would you be so kind as to answer a few of mine first?"

"Sure thing," Hanna quickly added, "Master Juro." Remembering Kazi's advice, it seemed the respectful thing to do.

"Krigare told me many things and I have read Leader Chieo's report. Now I would like your version. Would you please tell me how you came to Galenia?"

Hanna told her story right from when she was following Cardea to the time when Leader Chieo suggested she make the two-week journey to Kokoroe. He asked a few questions about her home, questions she thought were odd such as what her parents did and what her town looked like. Before she got too carried away he held up his hand.

"You have convinced me that you are, indeed, not from this world. How you got here is still a mystery to me...but we will solve it. How are you feeling? You are able to breathe easily?"

"I'm fine. With the crystal I've been able to breathe without any problems. Can I ask you a question now? It's something that's been on my mind for some time now..."

He nodded.

"It's just, if I am from a different world how is it we just happen to speak the same language?"

"That is a most astute question. Do you remember a time when you were low on Essence?"

Hanna thought back. When she first awoke she had been without Essence for a long time, but they had given her the gas, and she was able to recover. She also remembered coming back from the woods and how tired and weak she was.

"Yes, I was starting to run out after the first time we searched the woods for my home."

"What do you remember about how you felt and how others sounded to you?"

Hanna thought for a minute. She recalled her breathing becoming difficult and feeling dizzy. She was so weak when they got back to the cottage she almost collapsed on the bed. Then they suggested something about resting...

"Oh yeah, I remember that it sounded weird like...like I was under water."

"I thought as much," he said. "If you were without Essence, and able to remain conscious, you would not be able to understand a word that was said. You see, the Essence is in every living being in our world. It connects us. I can empathize with the animals and even the trees. From what Krigare told me I believe you experienced this with your horse. This is a rare ability, I might add; it takes many years for a Juro to be able to establish this connection. You, however, seem to do it by instinct." He tilted his head, "You are a unique case. As far as I know, you are the only one of your kind on our world. Perhaps we will have a chance to further investigate this conundrum. Of course, discovering how you got here needs be our first concern," noticing her anxiety, he quickly added, "followed by how to get you home. I am afraid Hanna, this may not be a problem with a quick solution."

Hanna was getting use to this sort of news and acknowledged that there was no point in getting upset about it. She realized there wasn't anything she could really do anyway.

"Until we have this matter resolved, how would you feel about staying with us at Kokoroe and learning about our ways until we can find some answers?"

Hanna smiled. "That sounds great. It really is beautiful here."

He added, "I would like to ask you to refrain from sharing your story with the others; I think it would be easier that way. Kazi knows the truth, but he can be trusted to keep it to himself. How much about your homeland have you told him?"

"Well, I started telling him about all sorts of things like my school, what my parents did and the things I did for fun, but I found that most of it just sort of confused him so I held back."

Hanna blushed at this as she felt like holding back was close to lying.

Master Juro said, "This is good. From what you have told me, your world is very different from ours and although Kazi accepts the truth, it may be too much for him to take. I am glad you have realized this as well. Can you handle the burden of keeping this other worldly knowledge to yourself?"

Hanna thought for a moment.

"Yes, I think so. There has been so much to see and do, I haven't run out of things to talk about yet." She smiled to herself.

"Excellent. For now, we will claim you are the adopted daughter of Cardea and Hamlin as, from what I hear, that is not far from the truth. Your injury stands and how you came into the village can be told if needs be. We will tell them you came from beyond the mountains. Many will think you are Kameil as you will only be able to keep that crystal around your neck secret for so long. It will benefit you and gain trust if we mention that you have The Sight. That may bring about more questions, however, you will be fully accepted here."

As they continued to wander the gardens, Master Juro pointed out interesting details along the way such as how certain plants grew or the relevance of particular rock carvings. When they returned to the bridge, he bid her farewell.

"Thank you Hanna, it has been a pleasure to meet you. We will spend much more time together I'm sure. Since the school semester does not start for another two weeks I will ensure that you and Kazi are kept busy."

Yoshi nodded at Hanna, who began following her. She stopped, remembering Kazi's words, and ran back to Master Juro.

"Thank you." She said and gave a deep bow.

He nodded in response. Hanna joined Yoshi again who led her back through the gardens and into the house to her friends.

* * *

Master Juro sat beside the fire. He had spent the last hour in quiet contemplation. Hanna's arrival had caused him greater concern than he had let on to the girl. He sensed some dark aspect to the event that brought her here and was fearful for his world. Now he gathered with the other four leaders of Kokoroe to inform them of Hanna and her situation. They met in the main chamber of his home and were sitting on chairs and sofas surrounding the fireplace. He trusted each of them as they had all been at Kokoroe for many years. Etai, who sat beside him, was his oldest friend; although she was over five hundred years of age, she was still younger than him. Her long grey hair

126

was left hanging down her back and was bejeweled with minuscule sparkling stones.

Master Juro had been her teacher when she first began her lessons, but over the many years her admiration of him became more that of a colleague than an adoring student. She sat silently as she thought about what he had just told them.

Biatach, a Jagare, laced his fingers as he listened to Master Juro explain how Hanna had entered the world. In addition to being in charge of the physical training of the students, he was also head of security. His hair and neatly trimmed beard were dark, his face darkened from spending most of his time outdoors. He had an intimidating demeanor, but those who knew him understood his purpose was to bring out the best in each of his students.

He said, "Mahou," using Master Juro's first name instead of his title, "this is troubling news. How do you propose we proceed?"

Mahou explained the cover story he wished Hanna to use and why he thought her true origin needed to be kept secret.

Biatach replied, "How are we going to convince anyone of this story? They will think she is Kameil and when have we ever brought a Kameil into our home? Now we are going to teach her our ways? They will think she is a spy."

Jillian, another teacher, but of the Jivan race, leaned forward. Out of all the leaders she knew the most of the Kameil as she had studied and taught history. Her auburn hair had gems similar to Etai's. Unlike Etai, her hair was pulled back and up onto her head. As fascinated as she was by the Kameil race she didn't forget for one minute what they were capable of. "Yes, Biatach is right. How do we know she is not a spy?"

Mahou gave a slight nod. "She is a spy, or she will be."

The others looked on with confusion.

ENCOUNTERS AND INTRIGUE

"I think others will trust her once they learn that she has The Sight."

Everyone froze at this and listened with rapt attention. They all knew that someone with The Sight would gain as much respect as any Juro as it was typically the first skill a Juro acquired.

"This makes her somewhat of an anomaly. I think we can claim she is from beyond the mountains and has been outside of our struggle. She will need to prove her alliance to us. Training her in our ways and sharing our history with her should easily bring her to our cause. At that point, I think we will be able to convince her to spy for us. The fact that she can pass for a Kameil works in our favour. She will be able to penetrate their camps and bring us intelligence which no one else is able to do. Of course, this plan will take much time before it can be successfully executed."

"Does she not wish to return home?" Etai asked.

"Yes she is keen to return; she has yet to except the truth." Mahou said.

Etai replied, "What truth is that?"

Mahou sighed. "There is no going back. I don't fully understand how she got here yet. There may have been some sort of temporary tear between our worlds. It's not natural whatever it is and it is extremely dangerous. There have been signs of deterioration of Essence in the area. I suspect Mateo is behind it, but I'm not sure how. It is imperative that we find out before something disastrous occurs. From what Chieo said in his message, they have been searching the area daily, trying to find a way back into Hanna's land. I'm going to insist for this to stop. It is too big of a risk. If they stumble upon her world there is no way of knowing if they will make it back and if they do, we don't want anyone else following them. We need to contain the situation."

Sohil, another Juro teacher who had been silent so far, turned his head, "Yes and alert the other Juro in case there is another tear, as you call it."

"Good idea Sohil," Etai said. "I agree the girl could prove to be a valuable ally, but do we really want to put her at risk?"

"I think before too long we will all be at risk. We will prepare her the best we can. we need to find out more about Mateo's plan and what he is doing. Sohil is correct; we need to discover if there have been other tears." Mahou paused. "If there have been, perhaps we can figure out how they were caused."

Jillian frowned. "She is still young. Do you really think she will be much help to us?"

Mahou nodded. "I have every confidence she will be instrumental. There is something about her...we must train her. She has the best Tahtay's any student could hope for. Between you four and those at the Citadel, I think she will do just fine." Mahou sat back with a cup of tea in his hands and said softly, "Yes, she will do fine indeed.

CHAPTER TEN

Practice and Patients

The morning meal was pleasant.

Once again they dined with the Yaru but Mateo was absent. The Yaru explained that they were going to break into smaller groups with one Yaru to lead them. Hatooin arrived and requested the first volunteer to meet with Mateo for their Yaru treatment. Nandin stepped forward.

"Excellent. Master Mateo will be pleased at your eagerness. Follow me."

Hatooin led Nandin up a few flights of stairs to a heavyset door. Hatooin produced a key and unlocked it. Nandin was mystified, never before had he seen a room like this. There were shelves full of bottles and jars of various sizes and shapes, some thin and tube like while others had bulb bottoms. There were books and scrolls on the shelves and some parchment posted on the walls. Long, high tables were full of glass jars and strange looking contraptions and tools. Plants and herbs were everywhere. In the corner was a desk full of papers and writing instruments. In another corner two chairs were positioned in front of a fireplace. Several doors were lined down one wall and large map with pins all over it dominated another wall. It was unlike any room he'd seen before.

Mateo entered through the door farthest away from Nandin. He was dressed in simple cotton trousers and a shirt with the sleeves tied tightly to his arms. Enthusiastically he crossed the room to greet them.

"Master Mateo, this is Nandin. He volunteered to go first."

Mateo inclined his head.

"Nandin, thank you for your trust. Remember this day, for we are about to change your life. The procedure is to increase your Essence evenly throughout your body. At first it will make you a little dizzy and you will feel as fatigued as if you have just finished running for a very long time. You may experience some tenderness. All this will pass in a few days while the Essence binds to you. After that you will feel better than you can possibly imagine."

Nandin cast his eyes down feeling a little uneasy, but unwilling to turn back.

"What must I do?" he asked.

Mateo led him to a wall with numbers written vertically on it. He made a mark at Nandin's height; then Mateo walked over to the wall of doors and opened one to reveal a small, cramped room filled with one high table, several wall sconces and a smaller table full of various metal instruments. Nandin suddenly felt extremely nervous. He wondered what he had gotten himself into.

"You will need to remove your clothing and lie on this table, I will do the rest."

Nandin did as he was instructed. He closed his eyes and tried, without much success, to imagine he was dreaming. Hatooin placed straps around Nandin's chest, legs and head.

He said, "We need you to lie perfectly still. These will keep you in place while you receive the treatment."

Nandin breathed deeply, trying to stay calm. Hatooin used a moistened cloth to wipe at Nandin's arms and legs speaking quietly as he prepared him, "There are three treatments; one for your blood, one for your bones and one for your air. We will do one at a time to make sure it takes. The air is the easiest, we shall start there."

PRACTICE AND PATIENTS

He placed a mask over Nandin's nose and mouth. The mask was attached to a bag made from an animal's bladder that Mateo held. Slowly he released the Essence contained in the bag as Nandin breathed in. The room started spinning and everything was blurry. The harder Nandin tried to focus the fuzzier things became.

Mateo put the bag down and held his hands an inch over Nandin's chest. He began moving his hands as though he was pushing or pulling water, with each pass moving further down Nandin's body. When he finally reached Nandin's feet he motioned to Hatooin who had picked up the bag. He pressed on the bag causing Nandin to breathe in deeply once more. Mateo repeated his movements, this time progressing towards Nandin's head. Nandin closed his eyes, hoping that it would prevent his nausea from taking over; it didn't help. Mateo placed his hand on Nandin's forehead.

"Rest Nandin. I will return shortly."

Hatooin covered Nandin with a blanket and extinguished the lights as he and Mateo left the room. Nandin fell asleep.

When Nandin awoke he was surprised to see that the lights were back on and Mateo and Hatooin were standing over him speaking. He had no idea how long he'd been asleep.

Noticing Nandin stir, Mateo said, "Great news. The first treatment went exactly as planned. You are doing well. Now we will treat your blood. You will feel a sharp pinch but it won't last."

Hatooin hung a bag, of pink liquid on a pole that hovered above the bed.

"What you see here is Essence in liquid form. It took me years to discover how to achieve it. Try to relax."

Nandin felt the promised sharp pinch on the inside of his elbow. He gasped then slowly exhaled. A warm sensation began to travel up his arm. He could feel it spreading throughout his body. There was a metallic taste in the back of his throat, but no matter how many times he swallowed, it would not go away. His lips started twitching and every now and then his arm would jolt. Mateo once again placed his hands over Nandin. This time he squeezed his fists and made a movement like he was milking a cow. Nandin thought this was all very interesting but his focus was still blurry and he was having a hard time keeping his eyes open – and then, he passed out.

Nandin awoke; again unsure of how much time had passed. Hatooin stood by him, watching, as if waiting for him to open his eyes.

"Welcome back Nandin. Phase two has been successful. I will alert Master Mateo that you are ready to begin the last treatment. First have a sip of water."

Nandin didn't know how he was going to drink when he was still strapped down to the table. Hatooin placed a tube into Nandin's mouth and squeezed a water skin. The cool liquid trickling onto Nandin's tongue was the most refreshing water he could ever remember having.

"That is all for now. We do not want you to get sick."

He left the room briefly and returned with Mateo.

"Nandin you are almost there. You will be a splendid Yaru, you will see. This small discomfort will be worth it." Mateo paused, "I have saved this next treatment for the end as it can be a bit more...uncomfortable. We need to roll you onto your side. Then Hatooin is going to place a stick in your mouth so you don't accidentally bite your tongue."

Hatooin loosened the straps and gently rolled Nandin over. He opened Nandin's mouth, placed in the stick and strapped Nandin down again in this new position. Mateo held a long pointy piece of metal.

"Brace yourself."

Slowly he slid the metal into Nandin's spine. Nandin bit down hard on the stick. Pain erupted down his back and he had to fight back tears. There was a slight popping sound and then a burning sensation began to course in both directions along his spine. Hatooin held the metal object as Mateo placed his hands on Nandin's back. Nandin could feel Mateo's fingers on his skin as he began massaging down Nandin's spine. Methodically, Mateo continued massaging along each of Nandin's bones; right down to his toes and up to the top of his skull. At some point the pain melted away and Nandin was left feeling numb. Once more he dozed off.

* * *

The potentials followed the Yaru to one of the upper levels of the castle. The whole floor was open, being one enormous room with large pillars throughout. The pillars had thick bundles of fabric wrapped around them at different heights and various weapons lined the walls such as staffs and swords. Large leather sacks filled with sand hung down from the ceiling as well as a few balls the size of oranges. Several crates filled with rice, sand, dirt and gravel sat on the floor. Boards of different thicknesses sat on open shelving and a few wooden stands with dowels protruding out of them were placed haphazardly at one end of the room.

Before separating their groups, Mayon spoke.

"Each of us Yaru Captains has a specialized skill in which will be training you in. Mine is with the sword, which is why I'm often referred to as Blades."

He stepped back and Thanlin stepped forward.

"My skill is in hand-to-hand fighting."

"I am known for my skill with the bow and arrow," Plyral said and stepped back.

With pride, Sim said, "My endurance allows me to run long and far."

"And I," said a voice from above, "am particularly good at climbing."

Everyone looked up. Nean was hanging from the beams overhead. He swung to a pole and shimmied down.

The potentials had listened with mounting excitement; it was going to be an interesting day. The Yaru led each of their groups to a different area of the room. Nean's team sat on the floor and began doing stretches while Thanlin's learned breathing exercises and arm movements. Plyral gave his men ropes to jump and Mayon, or as the men quickly preferred to call him, Blades, took his group over to the crates. Jon, who was part of Sim's group, started running laps. While jogging, Jon looked out the windows and was surprised how far he could see. Details of the city beyond the castle went by in a blur, but he looked out past the valley wall to the field and trees beyond. They were truly high up.

After a while they rotated exercises. Occasionally, Hatooin would reappear and take another volunteer away. The men became more and more eager to volunteer as they became fatigued from their workouts.

By lunchtime, a third of the potentials had been taken away. The others were exhausted and grateful to break for lunch. They had been promised a demonstration after their break; they all looked forward to it.

After their meal they returned to the training room with the Yaru.

"Gentlemen, if you could stand to the side here, we will begin with our demonstration." Mayon said.

Nean ran forward, flipped in the air landing on his feet and continued running to the wall. He leaped up onto the wall and grabbed invisible handholds. When he reached the top he grabbed a beam and swung hand-over-hand pushing down ropes that had been hidden. As each rope dangled, another Yaru grabbed it and quickly pulled himself up using only his arms. Once they were all at the top they sat on the beam. Mayon swung his legs to be on the same side of the beam and then leaned backwards until he was hanging upside down. Thanlin climbed over top of him until Mayon held him by his ankles. One by one they made a human chain until Nean scrambled down and flipped onto the floor. One at a time they swung to the ground, flipping as they went. The potentials applauded with enthusiasm.

Next they got out small, sharp metal objects and began throwing them in what appeared to be some random way at the wall. When they were done, they climbed again using the metal objects for hand and foot holds. At the top of the wall they pushed off again, rolling as they hit the ground. Two of the Yaru grabbed a large rope and strung it from one post to another at a height three feet off the ground. Once it was secure they took turns running across it and flipping off the end. They jumped over the rope two or three at a time in different directions; sometimes landing on two feet, sometimes flipping as they went. They continued climbing and tumbling a few more times while Plyral undid the rope and set up a wooden dummy with a sack for a head. When he was ready, they grabbed hollow reeds and placed small darts inside. With deadly accuracy, they blew the darts hitting the dummy in the neck or heart. Grains of sand spilled from the sack onto the floor.

The potentials watched and cheered with each new display of their talents. The Yaru were amazingly fast and smooth. They moved with stealth, hardly making any noise. Every man in the room was impressed; moreover, they were eager to possess the skills they had seen. As Hatooin continued to request volunteers more and more men willingly stepped up.

When suppertime came only six potentials remained untreated. Their hunger outweighed their concern as to where their companions had gone and how they were doing. After their meal they were taken to a common room where they played cards. Hatooin entered the dimly lit room.

"Master Mateo is done for today. He apologizes that you six will have to wait one more day but the treatments are quiet taxing. Twelve in one day is impressive. Please, continue enjoying your games. When you are ready to retire, any of the Yaru can show you to your new quarters."

Hatooin had thought it wise to allow the remaining potentials the privilege of staying in their new rooms. He knew the last ones were most likely the ones with the least desire to be there. Keeping them one more night without the treatment was a risk so providing them the better suites would help appease them a little longer.

Now that Jon was rested and well fed he once again became anxious. He didn't think there would be much chance of escape, but just sitting around waiting to be whisked away for some mysterious treatment wasn't in his nature.

"What exactly are the others doing and why haven't they returned all day?" he asked to no one in particular.

The Yaru looked up from their cards and glanced at each other. Some silent communication occurred as Mayon stood up and said, "Come. Let us sit by the fire and discuss this further."

They laid down their cards and made their way over to the hearth where large chairs with cushions faced each other. Nean and Sim grabbed a few more chairs so there would be enough seats for the eleven of them.

"It has been a long day and I think I speak for all of us Yaru when I say it has been a pleasure training you. We look forward to all of you joining our ranks." Mayon glanced at his fellow Yaru.

The other Yaru nodded their heads in return.

Plyral added, "Everything we have demonstrated to you today is in your grasp to learn and master. You will find your patience will be well rewarded."

Mayon continued, "Four of you being Jagare are already strong and capable of much, I see your doubt at the need for any improvements."

Jon inclined his head, skeptical as to where it was leading.

"Do any of you claim to have the abilities we displayed to you today?" Mayon waited in silence.

Seeing no response was forthcoming he said, "I thought not. With these new skills, imagine the protection you could offer your people." He paused to let that thought sink in.

"All five of us have undergone Mateo's unique treatment. Not only have we endured; we have improved every aspect of our beings. I will not lie to you: the process is strenuous. Your companions are in recovery; it will take a few days. But when they have recuperated they will be stronger and healthier than ever before, as will you be."

Jon sat back. Strenuous? That could be a discreet way of saying painful. His options were limited. Although promised that he would be free to leave if he chose, Jon doubted the sincerity of the offer. He had seen too much. Upon returning home his local Juro would want to know everything he had discovered. After the precautions Mateo had taken to keep this information hidden, like the giant wall, Jon doubted he could just stroll out the front gate. If he tried to run, surely he would be caught, what chance would he have against any Yaru? If he went along with the treatment it would even the odds somewhat; at least he would possess the same skills and it would allow him to continue to play the part of a willing participant and learn about Mateo's real plan. It would also give him time to speak with those below in the compound and find out their real story, that is, if it wasn't what he had been told. If everything was on the up and up then perhaps he could do some good here. Maybe he could stop the attacks on the villages. He sighed. It was obvious; his best course of action was to see it through. With that decision made, he realized how tired he was.

"Okay, what's this about new quarters?"

CHAPTER ELEVEN

Recovery and Discovery

Nandin sat up with a start.

He dreamt he was strapped to a table, unable to move while someone tortured him with sharp objects. His head spun from the quick movement and as he put his hand against the wall to steady himself he realized it was not a nightmare. He gazed around the room and discovered he hadn't been here before. The room was much larger than the previous one he had stayed in; in fact, it was the largest bedroom he'd ever seen. The bed he lay on, was twice the size of his usual single cot and topped with a big fluffy comforter. A compact table with a lamp sat close by with soft shoes placed in front. Nandin slipped these on as he continued to admire his current space. The door was on the same wall as the head of the bed and across from the door were two giant windows that went almost from floor to ceiling. Large fabric curtains blocked the view as well as most of the light, leaving the room in a grey haze; albeit just bright enough for Nandin to perceive his surroundings. A huge fireplace with an elegant mantle holding more lanterns dominated the wall parallel to the bed. In front of the hearth lay a sheepskin rug surrounded by deep cushioned chairs with small tables to accommodate drinks while relaxing by the fire. In the middle of the room a round table with four chairs held a pitcher of water and a couple of mugs.

Nandin rose and found his legs wobbly. He slowly shuffled to the table to find water for his dry and scratchy throat. When he made the four steps to the table he

140

dragged out a chair and fell onto it, surprised by how exhausted he felt. He reached for the water, but could barely will his arm to lift the jug; it felt as if heavy weights were dangling from his elbow. At that moment his door quietly opened. A woman of middle years peeked around the door.

"Oh sir, you are awake! Let me help you with that!" She rushed over and took the jug out of Nandin's hand.

"Sir you shouldn't be out of bed. Have some water then let me help you back." She held a filled mug to his lips and helped him drink. He felt so weak he didn't even bother protesting at the assistance she offered. After a few mouthfuls she helped him stand and hobble back to bed.

"Don't worry," she reassured him "you will have your strength back in a few days. I attended the first Yaru after his treatment you know, so you are in good hands."

She tucked him back under the sheets and he fell back to sleep before his head hit the pillow.

Again time eluded him when next he awoke. The lady who had assisted him before was still in the room – or in the room again, he wasn't sure which. She sat on the bed next to him. When she noticed his eyes open she leaned forward. She raised his head a little then spoon-fed him some soup. He finished the soup and then pushed himself up into a sitting position.

"I don't mean to be rude, but who are you?"

She let out a chuckle. "Sir, I am your attendant for now. Any needs you have you just let me know and I will do my best to meet them."

She patted Nandin on his leg and gave him a warm smile. Nandin was taken aback. He had never heard of anyone having a servant before. Even at the schools there were no attendants as such. There were individuals who chose to stay and take care of the compounds, but even the Masters didn't have personal servants. Nandin's cheeks burned red, as he didn't know what to make of this latest development.

"Ah, okay, thanks. What should I call you? I mean, what is your name?"

"Oh, call me Hattie."

"Okay, Hattie. So how long have I been here and where exactly is here?" Nandin regarded the room he was in.

Hattie said, "You were brought to your new quarters right after your treatment two days ago. You woke this morning for that little excursion across the room and that was enough to tucker you out until now. It is suppertime and I just thought I'd pop in to see if I could get a little more food into you. I've only managed to get you to take drops of broth or water since you haven't really been very lucid. Perhaps now you could manage a little bread?"

Nandin indicated he could and she got up and went to the table where she retrieved a plate of bread. Nandin reached out, grabbed a slice and unceremoniously stuffed it into his mouth.

"How are you feeling?" she asked.

"Weak. Stiff. Sore. Not very Yaru like."

She laughed. "All in good time. You have had a pretty intense procedure; it takes time to recuperate. Would you like to try a warm bath?"

Nandin agreed that soaking in a hot tub sounded wonderful, although he was unsure if he could make his way to a bathhouse any time soon. He was about to say this when she stood up.

"I will turn on your bath water. You will love the water closet you have."

Nandin gawked. "You mean I have my own bath? We have plumbing in our own rooms?"

Hattie gave him a crooked grin.

"All the Yaru do."

She left the room via a door he hadn't noticed on the other side of the fireplace. As he waited for her return, Nandin swung his legs over the side of the bed and slipped his feet back into the comfortable shoes he had used earlier. He put weight on his legs to test his strength and found he was still a bit too weak yet to venture on his own. Hattie returned to the room and rushed to his side.

"I hope you're not planning on walking on your own again, I don't think you're ready for that just yet."

Hattie proved to be quite capable as she aided Nandin across the room and into the next. Nandin sighed when he saw the tub full of steaming water. At home he usually washed up with a bucket of cold water or down in the streams. The last warm bath he had enjoyed was at school and those were in large public baths. A private bath in his own room was a definite perk of his new situation. Hattie helped him get undressed and then he sank into the tub.

"I will give you your privacy. I will return before the water cools."

She closed the door as she left the room. He breathed deeply and relaxed his aching body. He glanced around the room and noticed a floor length mirror in one corner and a chair in front of a sink with brushes and shaving supplies laid out. A wardrobe sat against another wall. He wondered what clothes might be behind the doors. After twenty minutes of soaking, Hattie returned. She helped Nandin get out of the tub and into fresh clothing. He pondered if she was the one who had dressed him after the surgery; last time he could recall, he was naked on a table.

As they returned to the main room and over to the bed, Nandin noticed that the bed had been outfitted with clean sheets.

"Thank you for your help and your kindness Hattie."

Hattie smiled. "You are most welcome sir. I am glad to be put to good use."

"Please, call me Nandin."

"As you wish Nandin sir."

Nandin chuckled but could tell Hattie was unlikely to drop the formality anytime soon.

"How are the others?" he asked. "Are you helping them as well?"

"They are all on the mend you will be glad to hear and no, I am your attendant; they have their own."

Nandin settled back under the blankets and was surprised he was ready for sleep again. He wondered how long this recovery would take.

The next morning Nandin woke as Hattie entered the room. She carried a full tray of food. As the smell of the porridge reached him, Nandin's mouth began to water and he realized he was famished. He sat up and slipped on his shoes feeling stronger than he had on the previous day. A little too confidently he popped out of bed and almost fell back down.

"Easy Nandin sir, you may be feeling a little better, but before you can be jumping around you need to eat and regain your strength."

"Point taken," he said as he steadied himself, using the wall for support. Slowly he made his way to the table and sat down in the chair Hattie had pulled out for him. The heat that came off the porridge warmed his face as he leaned over the bowl. His hands were shaking, but he managed to scoop some up and get it to his mouth. After a few more spoonfuls he felt fatigue in his arm and let it plop to the table. Without hesitation, she took up the spoon and fed him the rest of the bowl. She helped him with the juice and offered to help with the toast, but by that time he had resumed enough strength to hold it himself.

"Excellent sir, I think after another rest we can start with your exercises."

"Exercises?" he chuckled. "Hattie I can barely eat, how could I possible do any exercises?"

"Don't you worry, we will go slowly but we need to get you moving a little and get your blood pumping. Trust me, it will help."

Nandin raised his hands in submission. "I am at your tender mercies. I will bow to your better judgment."

She laughed as once again she helped him return to his bed. Silently Nandin watched as she gathered the dishes and left the room. Although his body was tired once more, his mind remained alert. He looked around the room again enjoying the relaxing pace of things. He couldn't remember a time where he just lay in bed doing nothing. He felt sick a few times over the years, but nothing that had kept him bed ridden. At the very least, he had stayed indoors and helped his mother with the household chores. Never once in his memory did he have nothing to do. He wondered if he would be able to tolerate it for long.

Soon he began to appreciate the details of the mundane, from the brick patterns in the walls to the grain of wood in the chairs, the smooth design of the mantle and the way the fabric in the curtains folded. Then something caught his eye. The curtains didn't go all the way to the ground, as neither did the windows, except for one. What he could see of the casing was not quite right; he thought perhaps it was a door. When Hattie came in next, he would ask her to open up the curtains so he could confirm his guess and besides, he thought, he really would like to see the view. Shortly after that decision he dozed again.

Hattie returned and gently shook Nandin awake. It didn't take much. He was glad to see her again.

"Okay sir, if you are ready we will begin. The first few exercises require you to lie on your back so just stay as you are."

She pulled back his sheets and kneeled on the side of the bed. She lifted his leg and bent it towards his chest as far as it would go and then straightened it again. She did this several times, and then repeated with the other leg. She rolled his ankles in circles and rubbed his feet. Next she sat him up and they did several arm stretches. Nandin had to admit the exercise helped. He could feel the strength returning with each new stretch.

"Nandin sir," she said, "these are the basic ones I want you to start with. As soon as you feel you are capable, do these on your own several times a day. Now with my help we will see if we can take a walk around the room. Please make sure I'm here before you attempt this on your own; it would be much more difficult to pick you up off the floor than to give you support to walk."

Nandin accepted her advice and they began slowly moving across the room.

"Hattie, would you be so kind as to open the curtains? I would sure like to look outside."

Hattie said, "Oh sir, my apologies. I've been keeping them shut so as not to disturb you as you slept, but of course you must be tiring of staring at the walls! Besides, we could do with a little more light in here. Here, hold onto this chair for support, while I pull them open. You have one of the best views this palace has to offer."

She pulled back the fabric to reveal a bright blue sky and a brick balcony. Nandin expected more. Seeing his expression she chuckled.

"You need to get a little closer." She returned to his side to help him to the window. He noticed the long window was indeed a door. When he was close enough to place his hands on the glass he gasped at the sight. He had never seen the view the others had in the training room, so he was surprised that he could see beyond the castle wall, past the outer building and into the forest, but he could also see much further than that. He could clearly see the mountains to the north and what he thought must be buildings to west. Hattie opened up the glass door.

"Care to venture outside?" She held out her hand to help him over the casing and onto the balcony.

He made his way to the railing and gripping it tightly as he gazed down at the establishment below. He could see people scurrying about but it was difficult to make out what they were doing; Nandin felt as if he were among the clouds.

* * *

Three days after awakening Nandin had regained much of his former strength. The exercises increased to include sit ups, push-ups and jumping jacks and he was able to do them by himself. He had fallen into a routine of eating, stretching, gazing off his balcony or sitting in one of his large armchairs to read a book he had found on the side table, a rare but much appreciated item. Once a day, Hattie would give him a massage to ease his aching muscles and he would end the day with a hot bath. He was, however, starting to get a little restless. Until this moment, walking across his room took a great deal of effort so he hadn't thought much about leaving his space, but now he began to feel somewhat like a prisoner; albeit one living in luxury. He would ask Hattie if he could wander the place when she next came in.

There was a knock at the door. Nandin was sitting in his preferred chair by the cold fireplace that hadn't been lit, as the early summer was warm enough.

"Come in," he said. Expecting Hattie he continued the page of the book he was on.

"Are you enjoying it?"

Nandin was shocked when he looked up to see that it was Mateo who had entered. So far, his only visitor had been Hattie. He quickly stood but Mateo waved him back down.

"Please, sit. I would like to speak with you if you are up to it?" he said in a questioning tone.

"Yes, I'm fine thank you. Actually, I feel great today."

"I heard you were recovering very well. I apologize for not checking in on you sooner, however, since you've experienced no complications I thought I'd wait until you had some strength back. So, all things considered, have you been enjoying your apartment?" Mateo gestured around the room.

Nandin chuckled, "All things considered, yes. I would say it is the best place I've ever stayed but..." he paused considering if he should speak his mind. Mateo indicated that he should continue. "I could use a change of scenery."

"I understand. I can do something about that. I find the gardens can be very therapeutic. Come, we shall walk and talk."

Nandin followed Mateo out of the room. He wasn't sure if he could handle the trek all the way down to the gardens and back again, but he wasn't about to complain now that he was venturing out of his room.

As they walked down the hallway in silence, Nandin thought about the comment Mateo had made about him not having *complications*.

He looked up and saw Mateo was studying him.

"What's on your mind Nandin?"

Mateo was an intimidating individual both in height and presence, but Nandin got the feeling he preferred directness.

"I was just wondering if any of the others had experienced complications."

Mateo was intrigued. "I'm glad you caught that and even more pleased you brought it up. As a Yaru I need you to be aware of the implications of what you hear. You're off to a good start. To answer your question, yes, there were some. A few patients required more applications of the Essence as it didn't bind at first." Noting the concerned look on Nandin's face he added, "but they are all recovering just fine now. You, however, have recovered the fastest."

Nandin thought for a moment then said, "That's probably because I went first."

"That may be, but I think there is more to it than that. In my experience, the most willing patients seem to take to the treatment the quickest. Sometimes, it seems, that if the mind resists, so too will the body."

They came to the end of the hallway and Mateo opened a large door perpendicular to the rest. They entered a small box like room - the floor was a wooden platform

148

with ropes strung all around. Mateo reached over to a sizeable brass bell that hung on the wall and rang it. The noise echoed off the walls and faded as it spread down a shaft below them. Nandin felt a breeze coming from below. Suddenly the floor began to move. He grabbed at a handrail secured to the floor to steady himself as they were lowered into the building. Before he could ask what was happening Mateo explained.

"This is a lift and lower platform. With the building being so tall it would take much time to climb all those stairs, so I had this made. At the lowest level there is a man leading a mule who is connected to rope pulleys; as he walks he can *lower* or *lift* the *platform*."

Nandin asked, "So does it only stop on the top and bottom levels?"

"No. As you will see there are several doors we will pass that we could exit through."

"So how does he know when to stop?"

Mateo pointed to a box in the corner of the platform. Nandin looked inside and saw another bell.

"Just ring that bell and it will stop at the next door."

Nandin was relieved and grateful for the platform. He knew now he would be able to get back to his room without collapsing from exhaustion. They emerged on the main floor. To get to the gardens they only had to go down a short corridor.

"Nandin, you may visit these gardens any time. I recommend, while going through your final stages of resurgence, you take your attendant with you. As for the rest of the place, once you have been given a proper tour you will learn where you can and cannot roam. Some areas, like the treatment facility, are strictly off limits as it would be dangerous to interrupt a procedure." He paused then added, "Besides, I'd hate for you to get lost."

He gestured toward the building they just left. Nandin looked behind and gazed at the top of the structure.

He laughed. "I would also hate for me to get lost."

Mateo let out a chuckle. "Yes, in fact, some of those floors we don't even use so if you ended up on one of them it could be years before you were found."

Nandin definitely did not like the sound of that. The gardens would keep him content for now. As they walked, Nandin had a sudden realization; instead of feeling weaker as they went, he felt quite the opposite. He wasn't sure if it was due to the fresh air, the gardens truly being therapeutic or if it had something to do with Mateo, however, Nandin felt like he had been drinking wine every time he was around Mateo and this time was no exception. Mateo stopped at a bench, motioned for Nandin to sit and then leaned against a large boulder facing him.

"Why do you want to be a Yaru?"

Nandin was a little surprised at the question but answered it without hesitation.

"When I heard you speak in the woods, you made me believe I could be something more than I am, that I could make a difference in a way that mattered."

"I am pleased to hear that. Did you not have any reservations about leaving your family and home behind?"

Nandin lowered his eyes.

"I spent my life in the village. Only for a brief time did I get to attend school because I was called back early to help. I never thought about how my life could be different until you spoke and the truth is, this life sounded more compelling."

Mateo laughed. "I'm sure it will be that. Tell me, what was your trade?"

"I was a farmer."

"A worthy profession, you fed your village, but I can understand how that would be...lacking in adventure."

"So what will you have me do?"

"Train. Be the best you can be Nandin, and when you are done, we will find the most suitable assignments for you. Tell me, how are you feeling now?"

Nandin flexed his hands and stretched his legs. He felt a tingling sensation throughout his body.

"You know, I feel good. I feel really, really good."

Mateo stood. "Excellent. You are ready."

They made their way back to Nandin's room. Mateo asked him to enjoy his next meal, rest a little and then he would send someone to give him a tour.

Nandin realized that wearing his bed clothes around the castle would not be appropriate so he looked in the wardrobe to see if there may be something more suitable in there. He chuckled to himself to think that three days stuck in the room and he had yet to open the doors. When he saw the black clothing that the Yaru had dressed in hanging there he was giddy. As tempted as he was to try them on, he thought it a little too presumptuous to wear just yet. Instead, he chose a pair of grey pants and top since they looked like they would be the most comfortable; they were similar to the ones he had worn at school. He noticed there were a variety of outfits that would be worn by any number of individuals in his village and he made a mental note to ask someone about this.

Shortly after he changed there was a knock at the door. He opened the door and Nean entered. He bowed to Nandin. Nean was taller than most Jivan yet did not exceed the height of a Jagare. He wore his hair tide back today and he was wearing similar clothes to Nandin, except they were black. Nandin thought his expression was mischievous.

"Well Nandin, are you ready for your tour?"

"Yes that would be great. I was beginning to wonder if I'd ever get to talk to you again. You've been rather busy since we've met."

"Too true. Not to worry though, we will be seeing plenty of each other from now on."

Nandin led him to the table that held a platter still containing some fruit along with the ever-present water jug.

"Care for something to eat or would you like some water?"

Nean replied, "No thank you, I'm fine. How are you enjoying your adventure so far? I bet you're not bored."

Nandin laughed. "Hardly. Although this isn't exactly the adventure I had imagined."

"Oh and what did you imagine?"

Nandin smiled. "I thought there would be more girls."

"Ha! All in good time my friend, all in good time. I kept a spot open on my team for you, I think you'll enjoy my specialty."

"What might that be? "

Nean's grin broadened. "I'm exceptionally good at climbing. I'll demonstrate when we get to the training room since you missed out during the first training session."

Nandin tried not to look disappointed. "You've already had a training session?"

Nean whispered in a conspiring tone. "Not really. It was just something to keep the men busy while they waited. You are the first of the new Yaru to leave his quarters."

Nean understood Nandin's puzzled expression.

"Yes, you are Yaru now. I'll show you."

He led Nandin back to the lift-and-lower platform. "Normally we'd take the stairs, but I want you to save your strength."

They rode the platform down passing several doors until Nean rang the bell to signal the stop. They entered the training room and Nandin was amazed at its size and deduced that it took up most of this level of the building.

Nean said, "Let me show you what we have here."

He led Nandin to the wall of weapons and pulled down a sword that was in its scabbard. He handed it to Nandin. It was surprisingly light. As Nandin pulled it from its scabbard he discovered it was shorter than he expected.

The blade was straight and the grip was square. It was simple yet elegant in its design.

"This certainly doesn't look like a hunting weapon. What do you use these for?" Nandin asked.

"Protection. It can be useful against those who wish to attack first and ask questions later. Mostly it's just a security measure. If you do your job right you won't need protection," he said giving Nandin a wink. Nandin replaced the sword. Nean made his way across the room jumping up and hitting the sand filled leather sacks that hung from the ceiling as he passed by. He stopped in front of several crates filled with a variety of substances.

Nean said, "Come over here. Make a fist and punch into the bin of rice."

Nandin did so and his fist was buried up to his forearm.

"Okay, now the sand."

Again Nandin punched but this time his hand didn't go in so far.

"Again with the dirt and then the gravel."

With each punch his hand penetrated less and less. When he hit the gravel he swore and pulled his hand out which now had a few minor cuts on the knuckles.

"The purpose of this exercise is to toughen your hands. Now you know what to expect, you would be wise to stick with hitting the rice until you've hardened your hand a little."

"You couldn't have told me that to start with?" Nandin scowled as he shook his hand.

"Can you always learn from what you are told?" Nean asked sarcastically. "I find some lessons are more effective if the student has first-hand experience." Nean grinned. "If your hands are toughened they won't bleed so easily, which is advantageous since there will be plenty of opportunities for your hands to be cut." Motioning to Nandin's bloodied hand he added, "Now you don't need to take my word for it, you have learned on your own."

Nean could tell Nandin was not pleased with his first lesson and knew it was time to improve his mood.

"Okay, let me show you what I can do."

He ran to the far wall and scampered up. Grabbing onto the beam he shimmied across, hand over hand, knocking ropes as he went like he had done during the group session. He climbed down one rope and when he hit the ground, he ran, grabbed a rope and swung from one rope to the next going up to the top as he went, like a monkey swinging through vines in a jungle. He flipped himself up to the top of the beam and ran along it and then when he reached a pillar, he climbed down using his hands and feet like an animal descending a tree.

"Impressive Nean. That was well done." Nandin applauded enthusiastically.

Nean bowed. "Thank you. Now, I'm sure you are anxious as to how I'm going to demonstrate that you are Yaru."

Nandin said, "After the last lesson I don't know if I'm as anxious as I was."

"Yes, I suppose that may not have been the best way to earn your trust. Let me have another go, this one will be more fun." He rubbed his hands together gleefully.

Nandin laughed. "Okay, okay, what do you want me to do?"

"Have you any skill with the bow and arrow?"

"I wouldn't say skill. I learned how to use them at school, but it wasn't one of my better abilities."

"Good. Then this will be the perfect test for you."

He handed Nandin a bow and arrow. "You see that wooden dummy with the target painted on it? Aim and hit the centre."

Nandin laughed. "That's clear across the room! I'd be lucky to even hit it."

"Excellent. Aim and hit the centre."

Nandin notched his arrow, lifted the bow, pulled back the string, released and watch the arrow soar through the

154

air and hit the ground, covering only two thirds of the way to the target. He looked at Nean expecting him to show signs of disappointment but saw instead he had a steady grin on his face.

"Now try again. This time close your eyes."

Nandin complied.

"Plant your feet firmly on the ground. Breathe deep. Now as you pull back the bowstring feel the Essence moving through your arms. Open your eyes, aim and hit the centre of the target."

Nandin notched another arrow and followed Nean's instructions exactly and released. The arrow shot through the air, straight and true then hit the target six inches from the centre. He blinked in amazement.

Nean clapped him on the back. "Now all we need to do is work on your aim. Welcome to the club my friend."

Nandin looked pleased with himself. Things were about to get very interesting.

CHAPTER TWELVE

Recognition and Revelation

Hanna was excited.

It was her first day of school at Kokoroe and she couldn't wait to get started. For the last two weeks Hanna and Kazi had been assigned odd chores, like helping in the kitchen or doing laundry, to keep them busy. They spent two or three days working in one area and then moved on to the next. Hanna had a new appreciation for modern conveniences. She spent three days washing laundry by hand and hanging it to dry; by the third day she could barely lift her arms. They were so heavy and sore after constantly holding them above her head while attaching clothes to a line. Scrubbing the floors on her hands and knees didn't prove to be any easier of a task. So exhausted and sore at the end of each day, she quickly got over being shy in the girls' bathhouse. Most of the students had their showers, saunas and hot tubs at the end of the day and no one showed concern about being naked around each other. At first Hanna had tried to be private about having a shower, but there was no way to get in the hot tub alone or unseen; bathing suits were not used. The hot tub was the best way to relax stiff, sore muscles so whatever discomfort she originally felt at being nude, faded away out of a stronger need to ease her pain.

Of all the chores she had been assigned her favourite was tending the gardens. Although pulling weeds proved to be about as much fun as scrubbing floors and equally hard on her knees, the atmosphere was much more enjoyable. Often she was given an area to herself to work and she would sing and daydream as she crawled along. Another part of garden duty was cleaning the ponds and feeding the fish. She enjoyed listening to the trickle of the fountains and waterfalls leading from one pool to another. Hanna relished the moments she could steal some time to just sit and enjoy the scenery.

It was during one of these quiet escapes that she realized how good she felt. All the time she had spent working out in the bright sunlight and not one migraine. As she pondered this, she realized she hadn't had one headache since she came to Galenia. No ringing in her ears or nausea to prevent her from being productive. No strange auras in front of her eyes or throbbing pain in her temple to cause her to go into hiding. This realization brought her some peace of mind; it was hard to want to go back home when she was finally free of such debilitating pain.

Now with school about to start she realized something else about herself. She liked to learn. In fact, she had so many questions about this world around her she could hardly wait to begin. This was so uncharacteristic of her since back home she dreaded school. What she began to recognize, though, was that it wasn't school, *per se*, that she disliked but more the atmosphere. Large noisy classrooms, bright fluorescent lights, chaos in the hallways between classes and crowded, sweaty lunchrooms. Just thinking about it made her feel stressed. But here it was different. She had learned that the classes consisted of no more than ten students with the exception of what she thought of as gym class. Many sessions took place outside in the courtyard or even in the gardens. She also found that the students here were very friendly. So far she had felt accepted and respected even before Master Juro mentioned to everyone that she had The Sight. She wasn't sure if there were other status symbols that set people apart, but so far she had not sensed there were such things as popular kids or nerds. Knowing she was already accepted, she approached the first day of school with great anticipation and a little relief from the labour she had endured. She knew she was not completely free of the chores because every person at Kokoroe, with the exception of the teachers, were expected to take turns assisting with each job, however, the amount of time would be greatly reduced, she hoped.

Kazi and Hanna had been kept so busy they didn't have many opportunities to make new friends. Krigare and Havard left a couple days after they got there so Jaylin and Yoshi were the only people they knew and consistently saw. Not only did Yoshi give them their tour, but also she was the one who led them from chore to chore and showed them what to do. She was kind, but not talkative. She hinted at things that they may learn, but was never forthcoming with details. They did manage to discover that their first class of the day was History.

Hanna quickly dressed and descended the stairs to the courtyard of her apartment building. She and Kazi had been given new rooms once it was established that they were both to be attending school.

The building she was in was on the other side of the bathhouse from the guest quarters. It was two stories high with the same design as the guesthouse except that there were rooms on two levels and it was for the female students only. Another difference was that the courtyard was cement with only a few potted plants. It was the hub of the dormitory as many of the students hung out there, visiting, playing games or doing various chores. The housing for the boys was on the opposite side of the pathway so Kazi didn't have far to go to meet Hanna. Hanna was beginning to recognize faces, but knew none of those girls were in her class since the newest students would be beginning today and therefore had only just arrived.

Kazi was already in the courtyard when she appeared; he always was a step ahead of her.

"Good morning Hanna. Ready to learn?"

In addition to his school clothes, he wore a big goofy grin that showed that he, too, was excited about their first day.

"You bet, but I think I'd like to get some food first; I won't last long without it."

Kazi laughed. "Ah Hanna, you're always thinking with your stomach. Come on, let's go eat."

They quickly made their way through the grounds greeting familiar faces as they went. At the long hall, as it was known, they ate quickly, then made their way to the school hall where their first classes would begin.

After climbing the steep staircase, they entered the building and made their way up to the second floor. When Yoshi had given them a tour of the grounds she had made sure to show them where the school hall was and where their first classes would be held. At this moment Hanna was grateful she had, for it gave her a certain level of comfort knowing where to go. Instead of large tables or metal desks with hard plastic chairs, this room was filled with floor cushions and wooden trays that were low to the ground, just high enough to get your legs under Hanna presumed. There were a few potted plants in the room, a large cushioned chair (which she assumed was the teacher's) and a low table tucked into one of the corners. When last she had seen it, it had been empty but today there were a few students already sitting on the cushions. Kazi and Hanna found a couple empty places near the front and sat down. Sure enough the tray tables fit nicely over her crossed legs. A few more students entered into the room and took the remaining seats. Before Hanna could turn to introduce herself, a middle-aged Jivan lady came into the room. She wore a long navy robe with a pearl white sash, which hinted at pinks and blues as she moved. Her auburn hair was pulled back, which could have given her a stern look except that her face was round and her cheeks were rosy. She wore a smile that looked as if it were always present.

A hush fell over the room as those who had been whispering noticed the teacher taking her seat in the large cushioned chair.

"Good morning. I am Tahtay Jillian. I will be your guide through history over the next few months. You may be familiar with many of the tales you will hear, but it is my endeavour to sort truth from myths, delve deeper than you've been and bring these stories to life. It is essential you understand how our past has determined who we are today. How we live. How we think. And how we grow. Without this understanding you may fall from the path we have chosen as some before you have. We will discuss this and venture as to why. When we talk about our past it is helpful to also talk about not just what happened but when. So there you have it. Our goal is to deal with the what, the who, the why, the how and the when. Any questions?" Greeted by no response, she added with a smile, "Then let us begin."

Hanna was enthralled as she listened to Tahtay Jillian speak about the beginning of the known history of Galenia. Prior to 1100 years ago, during what was referred to as the Time of Endurance, their culture was in survival mode. They lived day-to-day trying not to be killed from too much Essence or lack thereof or by wild animals, some known as Wolcotts which, from what Hanna saw from drawings, looked like a cross between a wild boar and a wolf. The people lived mostly like nomads roaming from place to place following food and searching for Essence; however, back then, it was only known as the life source. The historians surmised, some tribes knew where to find Essence and others just chanced upon places where they felt healthier. One of the main reasons for this was that the tribes consisted of only one race. The Juro were able to find and safely manage the Essence, yet were vulnerable to the Wolcott and the Mystic Flyers. At first when Hanna discovered that the Mystic Flyers were dragon like creatures she was rather excited, but when she learned they were the size of elephants with a wing span of what she estimated was fifty feet and they could carry children or even small adults she thought perhaps fear may be a better, safer approach. The Wolcotts were equally impressive and fearsome having the girth and rage of a large bull with razor sharp tusks the span of her arm and the cunning of a wolf. The Jagare, being strong and skillful hunters were capable of dealing with the Beasts, but struggled when it came to securing their life source. The Jivan, not being particularly good hunters, had to devise a reliable food source and began learning the ways of farming, but were still vulnerable to attacks and issues concerning the Essence. So, for all these reasons, a coming together of the different peoples occurred. Details of the initial event were vague, as this part of history had been written many years after it occurred and was based on oral stories and cave paintings. Whatever the case may be, the time was known as The Alliance and was marked as year one. After fifty years, the Sanctuary was built as a place for the leaders of all tribes to convene and deliberate. By year eighty, the schools came into existence; each school was run by a different race to teach their skills and share the knowledge they possessed.

The end of the first lesson left Hanna filled with mixed feelings. The history of these people was fascinating and she had thoroughly enjoyed the lesson, but she found that being an outsider had never been as abundantly clear to her. Sure there were bits of Galenia's past that she could relate to, but this world's history consisted of enough differences that she could not delude herself into it calling her own. The Essence was something she struggled to fathom. Although she had experienced first-hand the effects of being without it, she could hardly imagine an entire population driven by it and deprived of it. As she thought this over it dawned on her that the Kameil were experiencing just that. She wondered, given their history, why wouldn't they help the Kameil? She would ask when she felt the time was right.

Tahtay Jillian dismissed the class. "After lunch you will make your way to the exercise grounds where Tahtay Biatach will begin your physical instruction."

Hanna turned to Kazi and said, "I thought her name was Tahtay?"

Kazi explained, "No that's more of a title, her name is Jillian. All the teachers here are Tahtay."

"Why only here? I didn't hear anyone call the teachers back in the village Tahtay."

"No, of course not. Let's see, how do I explain...it refers to the phase they're at. The village teachers would be the first phase of teaching and many stay there, but some move on to the next phase. They teach at the schools and are honoured as Tahtay. If they continue with their training they can eventually become Leaders and then Masters."

Hanna said, "Oh, I think I get it. So all the Masters were once Tahtay?"

"Yep, you got it." Kazi replied.

They continued to chat as they made their way back to the Long Hall for lunch. A girl who sat beside Kazi in class joined them.

"You're The Seer right?" she inquired. She had shoulder length black hair and was about four inches taller than Hanna. She smiled revealing sparkling white teeth that were perfectly straight.

Hanna looked puzzled. "The seer?"

Kazi answered, "That's what people have been calling you since they found out you have The Sight."

He turned to the girl and said, "This is Hanna. I'm Kazi."

Hanna blushed. She had talked to a few of the students on occasion, but no one had called her The Seer before. No one bowed to her or treated her differently, like they had back at the village, even though they knew she had The Sight. She didn't consider it strange since no one treated the Juro students like that either. She had learned from Kazi that this school had the largest population of Juro anywhere in the world. They stayed here and trained for most of their lives until a village or city needed them. Most of them had brief visits at the other schools, but usually not until they were much older. Apparently it took a long time to learn their art and even though they were long lived, they didn't have Hatchlings very often so there wasn't a huge Juro population. Kokoroe provided the best opportunity to find a spouse and several even had Hatchlings while at school. Since they dominated the school it would be strange if everyone held them in reverence, especially before they were even capable of using their gifts. The fact that anyone would single her out in this community of potential wizards was unexpected.

Realizing she had made Hanna uncomfortable the girl nervously apologized.

"Hanna, I didn't mean any offence. I was just curious. I mean, I think it would be really cool to see the Essence. As you can most likely tell, I'm Jagare so that's not something I could ever do. Oh where are my manners, I'm just prattling on! My name is Celine. I just got here yesterday. I'm from Situ. Have you been there before? Oh, of course you haven't, I'm sure I would have heard if you had since it's such a small town. Where are you two from?"

Hanna and Kazi laughed. "We're from Kayu."

They continued their conversation until they reached the long hall where they met a few more of their classmates, though none quiet as chatty as Celine. After lunch they all made their way back to the training grounds in front of the school.

A male Jagare stood in front of the school on the stone patio that was considered the training grounds. He wore navy pants and top with a pearl white sash like Tahtay Jillian's. Hanna thought he looked like a martial arts instructor from back home. His hair was short and he was so tanned Hanna couldn't tell what shade his skin may have been had he spent a life out of the sun.

"Please spread out." He said to the ten students as they arrived.

"I am Tahtay Biatach and will be your physical instructor. For this week I will be teaching you some stretching and breathing exercises. Starting next week you will be joining the other students at the start of each day doing these exercises."

He demonstrated the first few movements: breathing deeply with legs apart and raised his arms and moved them left to right while breathing out.

They joined in and mimicked his slow even movements stretching arms and legs. Hanna felt like she was doing ballet but on the spot and without the turns.

After half an hour, Tahtay Biatach bowed and said, "Follow me to the training field."

He led them to a field of grass with a large sand pit that had a variety of equipment spread across an area the size of a football field. He turned to face his students with his back to the field.

"You have been told that Kokoroe was founded by the Juro and therefore we concentrate on the abilities they have, correct?" Tahtay Biatach asked.

Once everyone acknowledged they knew what he was referring to he continued.

"What this course behind me was developed for was to train them to escape. Remember, they were an entire community of individuals no higher than my waist and even though they were able to hunt and track they were in constant danger from the wildlife. If ever caught unawares they were no match for the mighty Wolcott or Mystic Flyers. Historically, the best chance for survival was to run and hide. They needed to be able to climb trees or scale cliff faces to get to the safety of higher ground or caves. As you advance in your abilities you will be doing just that. For now we will build your strength, speed and agility."

He motioned over his shoulder. "For the first part of this course you will need to leap from stone to stone without falling into the sand. The sand represents water in this task, at some point you will be jumping stones in a stream. Falling off the stones is dangerous. Why?"

A Jagare named raised his hand. "If the water is deep you could drown or it could slow you down. If you were being chased, you'd get caught."

"Exactly. Also you could twist an ankle or bang your head; you get the picture. Past the stones you will see a wooden wall with a hanging rope. Use the rope to scale the wall. The wall is our rock face."

Another boy raised his hand, "What does the rope represent?"

Tahtay Biatach replied in a serious tone, "A rope."

Everyone chuckled as he continued explaining. "Sometimes they would live in caves in the rock face. A rope could be lowered to get to the cave."

He gestured to the right and said, "Next, after you scale the wall you will then crawl under a net that is low enough to the ground that you will need to be on your bellies. This may not be particularly difficult but remember this is a test of speed. The net is the brush in the woods; keep your head down, you wouldn't want branches poking out your eyes or scratching your face. Once you are free of the net, run to the large log that acts as a bridge; currently it is only waist height off the ground. In reality these logs may have spanned over ravines large enough to hold a small village. Don't fall." Pointing to the farthest point across the field he said, "Lastly there are hanging ropes – swing from one to the next and land on the other side of the finish line. These ropes symbolize ropes or vines that hung from trees, which they used to safely traverse high above the forest floor."

"Okay, we will go one at a time. Run your fastest; do your best. Let's see how you do."

Hanna was worried. The rocks seemed okay, the net and the log may be slow going, but she dreaded that wall. She didn't know if she would even get a foot off the ground and it was at least ten feet up. She was never a good climber nor did she have much upper body strength. The last time she tried to pull herself up anything it was on a playground and that was when she was ten.

One by one people volunteered to go next. She hoped, if she put it off long enough, class would end and she could skip it all together. She watched as Kazi slipped off a rock into the sand. He looked sheepish, but got back on and kept going. He got to the wall and struggled as he slowly went up. She couldn't see him land on the other side. He must have done all right as she could see the net shaking in the distance as he wormed his way through. He managed over the log, not too quickly, but he didn't fall. As he swung to the finish line his classmates applauded him as they had every other student who had made it so far.

A Jagare student went next and he traversed the course fairly quickly without too much effort. A Juro student went after him and did much better at the stone jumping than Kazi but really struggled getting up the wall.

Finally there was no one left but her. The Tahtay regarded her as she stepped up to the start line.

"It's Hanna isn't it?" he asked.

"Yes," she said softly.

"What seems to be the trouble, you look concerned?"

"I'm afraid I won't be able to make it over the wall," she admitted.

"Don't be," he said. "Be afraid of the Wolcott that is chasing you, for when he catches you, he will bite off your head. Now RUN!"

She didn't hesitate. She leaped from stone to stone like a ballet dancer leaping across a stage. She easily raced across the field to the wall, leaped up, unaware that she was already halfway to the top with the jump, pulled herself up the last few feet, and jumped to the mat below, landing with a roll. She dove under the net, scuttled through and ran across the log like she had done it a million times, then swung on the ropes to the finish line. Her fellow students applauded with enthusiasm although their expressions were one of shock.

Kazi went to her. "How'd you do that?"

"I don't know," she said "I just – ran."

Noticing his expression she added "The guy before me did it like that too."

"Yeah, but you're not Jagare. " He leaned in to whisper, "You're not even Jivan. You're more like a Kameil, but they wouldn't even make it across the course, they would collapse first."

He paused. Hanna wasn't sure if he was upset or what. He clapped her on the back and said loudly, "That was FANTASTIC!"

They all laughed at Kazi's remark. Tahtay Biatach reached the group and congratulated everyone on their first efforts of the course.

He turned to Hanna and said, "I guess that Wolcott will be going hungry. Well done."

Hanna smiled. She didn't know how she managed to breeze through the course, but it had been easy. She wondered what other surprises lay in store for her. So far, she liked what she had discovered.

* * *

Time passed quickly. Throughout the week Hanna did little more than learn history and do physical training. Her class became very good at following Tahtay Biatach's

167

lead during the breathing and stretching exercises and they would be ready to join the others at the start of the next week. The obstacle course changed only a little over the week as Biatach wanted them to improve their timing as well as finish the course without falling or tripping. Each time Hanna did the course, not only did her speed increase, but her agility was such that it felt as though she was flying.

As for history class, Hanna continued to be captivated. Tahtay Jillian spoke of the joining of the three races and how they combined their skills to create a symbiotic society. A place where each member contributed to the well-being and success of the community. The Juros provided the knowledge on how to manage the life source, now known as Essence, while the Jagare used their skills to hunt for and protect each community they were in. The Jivan were then able to farm without fear of attack or complications from Essence as well as spend their time raising the young. Many other trades began to emerge. Instead of relying on crude handmade weapons, they learned to temper steel. Animal skins for clothing were replaced with woven cloth. Without the need to move in search for Essence or food, towns arose. The first town to grow into a city was Senda as it was located by the Sanctuary; the political hub. Every village leader would venture there and delegates from each village stayed and sent messages back to villages. The more people stayed at Senda the more they needed farmers, cooks and many other trades so it grew quickly. Towns, however, still remained spread out since only so many Hatchlings could use the same nesting grounds; therefore, the towns emerged depending on where the Crystal Pockets were found. Others cities were located next to the three schools: Kokoroe, The Citadel and The Percipio. As the number of students that attended increased, so did their needs for food, clothing and other necessities. The schools were purposely built close to some of the largest and most plentiful Crystal pockets so they could handle the rise in population.

For nearly 900 years the people prospered. Without the constant struggle for survival, there was time for other pursuits. Education expanded, as did the arts. People came to the Sanctuary, not only to make decisions, but to debate questions on life and the world around them. Tahtay Jillian told the story of the Juro who began contemplating the mixing of the races. Jillian's version was very similar to the one that Kazi had told Hanna, but even Hanna couldn't turn Tahtay Jillian's version into some tragic love story. When she told the story she was full of emotion as if she were still mourning the banishment of the Three. She actually shed tears when she spoke of the Hatchlings that died from their union. By the time they were banished they had a strong following; many people left with them. Also, she added a detail to the story that Hanna hadn't heard and from the reaction of most of the other students, it was clear they were also unfamiliar with this detail.

When The Three discovered that their children were sickly or couldn't survive, they stole other Hatchlings. They began doing experiments with the Essence to see if they could change the amount a child would be born with. Once again deaths occurred. The ones that survived were void of Essence and became the beginning of the Kameil race. The offspring of the Kameil were also born without Essence. Tahtay Jillian ended the week's lessons saying she did not understand how any of the Kameil could have survived over the last one hundred and eighty years, but somehow their numbers continued to grow.

Hanna couldn't contain herself any longer; she had to ask.

"Why isn't anyone trying to help the Kameil? It seems to me they were just victims; they didn't choose to be like that."

Tahtay Jillian gave Hanna a knowing smile.

"If only it were that easy. You see we didn't know at first what The Three were up to; truth to tell, once they were banished they were all but forgotten, that is, until the Hatchlings were stolen. After that we were able to only get a glimpse at what they were doing as they had built a fortress and we would not be able to get to them without great casualties. We discovered their failed attempts at breeding when we found the graves of their children that they marked with stones detailing their deaths."

"The kidnappings of the Hatchlings occurred only once, but then other people began to go missing. For generations the Kameil hid away and kept mostly to themselves until a little less than one hundred years ago. As we understand it, Mateo emerged as a powerful being, but we are not sure exactly what he is or how he came into existence. Some believe he is the offspring of The Three, others consider the possibility he was experimented on as an adult. Most of what we know of him came from rumors, which consist of sightings of the largest being ever scene capable of manipulating Essence and faster than any beast. We have no way to separate the facts from the myths. What we do know is that under his influence the Kameil race came out of hiding and have become more aggressive and distorted. Invasions of the nesting pockets began and many Hatchlings have been killed. We were forced to keep the Hatchlings in the villages to better protect them. Communities reported that the disappearances began to increase. Raids have continued, stealing, killing, but during all this, not once has any Kameil asked for help."

"I'm sorry to say Hanna, but even though the Kameil may have started out as victims, they have become villains."

Hanna was dumbfounded. Up until that point she had felt a sort of kinship to the Kameil; they shared a common concern. Now she understood that even with their shared struggle, she was not one of them; their cause was not her cause. The wistful thinking of a naive girl to save a wronged people was now replaced with a new determined resolve – if it were ever within her power, she would help stop the Kameil from bringing anymore harm to these peaceful people.

CHAPTER THIRTEEN

Doubt and Conviction

Nandin was motivated.

Every day he made his way to the training room. Slowly but surely each of the Junior Yaru, as they became known, showed up to join him. Every now and then Mateo would drop in to watch their progress. On the fifth day Mateo pulled Nandin aside.

"I have a favour to ask of you. As you can see, most of the Junior Yaru have fully recovered, but there are a few who are still on the mend. Some of them are being rather difficult and are refusing aide from their attendants. Would you be willing to visit them? I'm sure they would benefit from some company. Perhaps they will be more inclined to take advice from you."

Nandin agreed. "Absolutely. Shall I go now?"

"Yes, thank you. Return to your floor. You can start with Jon. He is at the opposite end of the hall from the lift, last door on the right. Then there are two more in rooms also on the right. You will notice tags on all their doors; they will be easy enough to spot."

Nandin bowed and left the training room. Over the last five days his energy tripled. He opted to take the stairs instead of the lift as he enjoyed the extra work out. He knocked on Jon's door and when no sound was heard and no one opened the door, Nandin cracked it open and glanced into the room. He saw Jon lying on his bed. At first he thought he might be sleeping, but then he noticed

Jon's eyes were open. He went into the room and closed the door behind him.

"Did I wake you?" he asked.

"No." Jon replied, still staring at the ceiling.

"Mind if I sit?"

"Whatever, it's not like I could stop you."

Nandin grabbed a chair and pulled it up to the bed. The room was almost identical to his with a few subtle differences such as the colour of the fabrics.

"Are you all right Jon?"

For the first time Jon glanced over at Nandin. His face showed fatigue and his expression was one of disdain. He propped himself up on one elbow and in even tones said, "Do I look all right Nandin? I've been confined to this room for over a week, barely able to feed myself and weaker than a two year old. How could I be all right?"

It was if the floodgates holding back all the frustration and doubt that Jon had been accumulating finally gave way. He raised his voice as he vented.

"What was I thinking? I let them take me! I let them experiment on me! Now here I am, not even half the man I was! I thought it would make me stronger, give me a better chance to fight them but they've taken everything! My home is lost to me, my strength gone. Why didn't they just kill me? What's the point of breaking me?"

Nandin could see the desperation in his eyes.

"Jon, you're not broken. Look at me, I was where you are and now I am better than I ever was. They didn't lie to you Jon. I think you need to follow Nean's advice. He's always saying 'Get out of your head and into your body'. Come on, let's walk."

He pulled back the bed covers and swung Jon's legs around. Before he could argue, Nandin had Jon standing. Jon yielded a little as Nandin helped him stagger to the window.

"Have you checked out your view yet?" Nandin asked.

Jon gave his head a slight shake to indicate he hadn't. Nandin pulled open the drapes and opened the patio door.

"Come on, let's get you some fresh air."

Nandin helped him out and Jon grabbed onto the rail. As Jon gazed out he seemed to gain strength.

"Breathe deep, it helps."

Jon leaned on his elbows as he watched the people below.

"Nandin, what are we doing here?"

Nandin replied, "I think we all have our own reasons...what was yours?"

Jon grunted, "I thought maybe I could stop them. You know? Stop the attacks and the kidnappings but when I got here, well it's different than I imagined."

He motioned to the community below.

"Yes. We've been assuming all these years that the Kameil were all the same and every wrong done to us could be blamed on any of them and Mateo. We were wrong."

"So what is he doing? Why all the training? Why bring us here at all? Just because he has a dream doesn't mean I want to be a part of it."

"But you chose to come and now you are part of it. I don't think you can turn back. As soon as a Juro got one look at you, you would be a dead man. Don't you see Jon? We have to change the way society sees the Kameil, it can't go on like this. Those children desire better."

Nandin pointed toward the city.

"But I have this nagging feeling that he hasn't told us everything...it seems like he's building an army; I don't want to start a war."

"We are already at war, we just didn't see it. What Nean has taught me is that if we do things right we can stop the killing. We need to open their eyes, not by force, but by using stealth. I'm not sure how, but I know murder isn't a part of his plan. I'm sure it will all make sense soon. For now we need to get your strength back. Come on, let's get you out of this room and go to the gardens. I find them...therapeutic."

Nandin chuckled to himself. He didn't think Jon would go if he heard that it was Mateo who first told Nandin about the healing properties of the garden.

* * *

Mateo listened as Hatooin reported Jon and Nandin's conversation. Mateo had requested that Hatooin listen in personally and not use any of the other servants. From everything he had witnessed of Jon, he knew he was the least willing person there. He was concerned that Jon had the power to cause disdain in the Junior Yaru and at this point that was something he wanted to avoid. Jon had required multiple doses of Essence. Nandin was the opposite. He took to the treatment and recovered quickly. His attitude and commitment was infectious and those around him seemed to benefit greatly from it.

Mateo risked a one-on-one between Nandin and Jon to see if they could bring Jon to their cause. If not, they would have to dispose of him. He couldn't take the chance that his newfound Yaru might rebel; he already had enough powerful enemies, what he needed was strong allies.

When Hatooin had finished his report, Mateo said, "It seems our young friend Nandin is a man of many talents. He couldn't have done better if we had coached him."

He thought for a moment. "His conviction sounds like mine. I think I should like to test him."

Hatooin asked, "Shall I arrange for a meeting?"

"Give him another week. I think the Yaru need his presence at the moment. When everyone has settled into routine, including those who have yet to begin, then I will meet with him. And I think it is time to have the group gather for meals again."

"I will see that it is done Master." Hatooin bowed and left the room.

Mateo felt a sense of achievement as he thought about his latest prodigy. He pulled out his journal and made some notes. He knew it would take a long time training the Junior Yaru before they could match their teachers' abilities, but he thought with a few more men like Nandin he may be able to obtain their absolute loyalty quicker than the last time.

His plans were achievable, but they weren't easy. He knew he walked a fine line, too far one way or the other and the results would be disastrous. He needed Yaru who could walk that line without wavering. It would take time. This dream had started with the Three one hundred and eighty years ago, what was a few more months?

* * *

It had taken a few more visits to get Jon, and the few others who were struggling, to recoup and embrace their new roles as Yaru, but finally Nandin managed to get each of them to the training room to join the rest. Jon had been reluctant, but was beginning to appreciate his newfound skills. Being Jagare, he had been strong and able in many areas and seeing the Yaru perform, although impressive, hadn't convinced him that they were extraordinary; only that they had been trained and practiced in a different way than he was familiar with. Now he understood that he had underestimated their skill. As he executed each task they set before him, he could tell that he was much more than he'd been; he was stronger, faster and had more endurance than before. He was anxious to test his new skills outside the training room. Currently he was practising running dive rolls over barrels.

Nandin felt pride that he had managed to get all the men on board. Some, like Jon, had felt betrayed by Mateo.

They thought he had stolen the power they possessed; instead of healing and getting stronger their depression robbed their minds and made them physically weak. Once he managed to get them out of their doldrums, their strength returned and then improved quickly. As he watched them carry out the challenges their Yaru trainers gave them, he knew with satisfaction that his influence had an impact on their current success.

Nandin was still a student himself and was also participating in the drills, but as the men obviously looked up to him, he had become the spiritual leader of the group. The men were eager to share their successes with him as, not only was he confident and full of conviction, but he was also the most talented of all the Junior Yaru. When he was shown a new exercise, everyone would stop and watch to see how he did. Sometimes he would even add a little something additional like an extra flip or double arrows to his shot.

Mateo entered the room and motioned for Nandin to join him.

"Master Mateo, it is good to see you."

"I'm hearing good things about you Nandin," Mateo said proudly. "How are the men doing?"

Nandin knew Mateo would be aware of how the men were doing in training as the Yaru trainers would have undoubtedly filled him in so he deduced that Mateo was asking more about their state of mind.

"Much better. I think even Jon is beginning to enjoy himself."

"I'm glad to hear that. Do you think they are up for a tour of the quarry? It will give me a chance to explain what it is we do here."

"That would be great; we still have a lot of questions."

Mateo nodded thoughtfully. "I imagine you do. Get them together and have them each choose a horse from the stables. Be prepared to leave in an hour's time."

Nandin bowed. "I will make sure we are ready."

An hour later, eighteen junior Yaru were sitting astride their horses. Mateo emerged and retrieved his horse from a stable boy who had it saddled and ready. Mateo was an impressive figure on his stallion, which was at least seventeen hands high; he towered over the men who were on smaller breeds meant for speed and agility verses power. Sentries opened the gates and they followed Mateo onto the bridge. Part way down the bridge he stopped to face the men.

Gesturing over the edge to the pit below he said, "Here is a great view of the Kameil hard at work."

Jon had wanted to know for some time and finally saw his opportunity to ask.

"Where did all these people come from anyway?"

Mateo replied, "I'm sure you are all familiar with my parents? I believe you refer to them as 'The Three'?"

"They were your parents?" Nandin asked.

Mateo tilted his head side to side.

"More or less. That's how I've come to think of them. Anyway, these are their descendants as well as their followers."

Jon muttered something under his breath.

"What was that Jon? I didn't quite catch that." Mateo asked.

Jon turned his horse so he could look Mateo right in the eye. "I said, or the descendants of those who were kidnapped."

"Kidnapped? Is that what people are saying? No, no one here has been kidnapped. Everyone here came willingly. They left the accepted society for their own reasons; mostly because they wanted to make choices not available to them. Here a person can choose to do what he wants to do and be with whom he wants to be. We have no use for the rules of so-called civilized society..."

Witnessing Jon's bravery at questioning Mateo and then Mateo responding with no hostility, another Junior Yaru asked a question that had been on all their minds.

"What about the Hatchlings? They were stolen..."

"Hatchlings?" Mateo paused and looked up at the sky as if trying to remember. "Oh yes, the Hatchlings. Actually, that's how all this," he motioned to the city and complex around them, "began."

He turned his horse around and continued down the bridge. Even though he spoke loudly the men rode closely so as not to miss a word he said.

"When The Three first arrived in the valley, their dream was to create a combined race. Unfortunately, all the babies they had together hatched without any Essence. Kenzo, the Juro, was able to keep the babies alive, but without crystals they wouldn't survive long. New to the area they were unaware of any crystal pockets so out of desperation Dedri, the Jagare, and her Jagare comrades went back across the rivers to the closest Crystal Pocket they knew of. Naturally, it was being used as nesting grounds so there were several Jagare guarding it. Dedri pleaded with them to spare a few crystals so that her children may live, but they refused. They spat insults at her, said her children deserved to die since she chose to live without morals..."

Nandin, who rode next to Mateo, noticed he had a wistful look in his eye. As he told the story it was more like he was recalling a memory, not just retelling a tale.

"So when they refused to give them the crystals the 'outcasts' tried to take them. It turned into a bloody fight. Jagare on both sides died. Dedri was fighting for the lives of her children and was driven by desperation; she was victorious. They took only a handful of crystals, as they were not greedy. When they were leaving, they took stock of the massacre around them; regretful it had to come to that. And then, they noticed the Hatchlings. They were torn about what to do. If they left them there they would surely be eaten by any number of wild animals. If they returned them to the town, they would be arrested or hanged. In addition, Dedri's children would die. So they took the Hatchlings with them."

"When they returned to the valley, and the others heard about the tragedy that had occurred, they realized they would not be safe. So they built the wall. And that's when the quarry began. They built the walls thick enough to also become their homes. The upper levels are still apartments today, but we use the lower ones as shops as you noticed when you arrived."

When they finished crossing the bridge Mateo led them to the edge of the pit.

"A remarkable thing was discovered as they began to quarry these rocks. You see, these stones have an increased amount of Essence in them; more than any other stone. So, The Three no longer required crystals in order to heal their young. You asked where these people came from? Some come from the direct line of The Three, but most are children of their followers. The followers agreed to treatments from The Three, hoping to increase their Essence, but ironically losing it completely. Hence the Kameil race grew at an alarming rate. Keep in mind even after they came to this valley nearly two hundred years ago, others still sought them out. As it happens, The Three were not the only ones discontent with the rules that had been set up by those in charge. The freedom I speak of is not for my sake alone."

He looked each of his men in the eye and they nodded to him, acknowledging his statement. Even Jon felt his resistance wavering.

Another Yaru asked, "I was just wondering about the castle...why was it built here and floating as it is?"

"Ah yes, the marvel of the floating castle. The rocks in this valley have a strong magnetic force. As you may have noticed there are other rocks that are hovering here and there, but none as mighty as that which the castle was built on. As for why it was built, well there is a practical reason. The Three needed a lab to do their research and study these stones; it made sense to keep it close to the quarry. It started out as a much simpler structure and was added onto as the need arose..." he paused to see if anyone caught his pun. It seemed the men were too involved in his explanation to catch the wit. He sighed as he continued. "Also, adding floors was a good use of the extra rocks that had been cut. Speaking of which let me show you how this whole mining operation works."

Mateo continued to explain as they rode around the gaping hole.

"At the bottom of the pit they chisel out new rock chunks and place them into a wagon containing large buckets. They carve the road as they go so the wagon can be right close to where they are working. Once they've filled the wagon it returns up here..."

They had reached the far side of the pit where the base of the two mountains merged into a valley. Mateo dismounted and tied his horse to a hitching post; he waited while the others did likewise. Once everyone was ready he led them to the closest contraption. Two men stood on top of a tower holding a bucket that was attached to a rope; the other end of the rope was attached to a mule. As Mateo approached, they released the bucket and it was lowered to the ground as the mule walked closer to the tower. When it reached the ground Mateo unhooked it and walked to an unhitched wagon that was nearby. Inside the wagon were several more large buckets that were filled with chunks of rock.

"We start by hooking up these buckets," he signaled to the man holding the harness of the mule and he began walking the mule away from the tower.

"The rope is on a pulley system so when the mule walks away it pulls the end of the rope tied to the bucket up to the top of the tower like the lift-lower platform in the castle."

He waited while the bucket was hoisted all the way to the top.

"Now the men up there will tilt it until all the rock chunks fall down the ramp breaking up as they go."

They heard the loud clunk clunk as the rocks tumbled down a steep ramp then crashed into a large bin at the bottom that was elevated a few feet off the ground.

"This here is kind of a neat contraption." he tapped the side of the bin. "This side slides up so the rocks can slowly be released into these buckets below it."

The man who lifted the side of the bin waited while the rocks tumbled into one of the buckets. If the rocks got stuck he took a rod with a large hook on the end and pushed or pulled the rocks down using the hook. Once the bucket was full he slid it down the rollers it sat on, then placed an empty bucket under the bin. He slid the side of the large bin a bit further up to allow more rocks to tumble and repeated the same push pull with his hook.

Mateo grabbed the full bucket, which was obviously very heavy but he made it look as if it were empty.

"After they fill a bucket they move it onto one of those wheeled carts and bring it to the next tower...unless I'm here of course, then I can just pick it up myself."

He winked to the man by the bin who nodded his appreciation as Mateo led the Junior Yaru to the next tower.

"As you can see, this tower is much like the last one, however, the ramp is a bit steeper."

He hooked his bucket up to the pulley, nodded to the man leading the mule and the bucket was lifted to the top.

"These rocks will get tumbled down this ramp for a few passes until the stones finally break into something you can hold in your hand."

He picked another bucket of the smaller stones and again the men followed him as he weaved between the towers, buckets, men and mules. They came to a circular stone basin with a hole in the centre. A wooden axle rose from the hole and was attached to a heavy oak plank that rested on its side on the outer rim of the basin. The plank was longer than the width of the basin and two mules were harnessed to the plank, one at each end. In the basin sat a massive boulder that fit snugly against the edge of the outer and inner rim.

"This is the final step; we dump these rocks into the basin."

He shook the bucket, spreading the rocks out evenly throughout the basin. After filling one side, he walked around the plank and mule to dump the rest of his rocks into the other side. When he finished, he smacked one of the mules on its hindquarters causing it to walk forward. As the mules walked, the plank pushed the heavy boulder forward causing it to roll. It crunched the smaller stones as it went.

"The boulder will continue moving round and round crushing the rocks until nothing is left but a fine powder."

Mateo wiped his hands together brushing off the dust that had settled there.

"Once it is powder, it is brought to my lab where I refine it. That's the tricky bit. Now come and take a look at this."

The men were somewhat surprised how excited Mateo was about the whole process. He had seemed very passionate when he first spoke to them out at the clearing, but since then he had remained fairly subdued. Now he was like a child showing off his favourite toys. He showed them to a large rain barrel. He took the lid off and let them each take a look.

"Give it a smell," he said. "Anyone care to venture what this is?"

"Liquid Essence?" one of the men asked somewhat astonished. Even though they had all been treated with it, the concept still amazed them.

"Ha!" Mateo said. "That is what it looks like but no, not exactly. This liquid is what makes liquid Essence possible. After I refine the powdered rocks, I mix it with this liquid and voila! I have the ideal substance. It is what allows the extra Essence to bind to you."

Nandin looked around the quarry. "Where does it come from?"

Mateo smiled slyly.

"Good question. As we cut away the rocks this stuff began to seep into the pit. It was rather slow at first; it drizzled out of cracks. Right away I knew it was something important. It runs clear and has no smell, yet it has a distinct taste and a different consistency than water. For years I worked with it until I successfully created liquid Essence. Now you may have noticed we don't have much need for the stones themselves now that our buildings have been completed."

He pointed to another area where a simple structure was built. It had no walls just a frame and a roof, presumably to provide shade. Several people chiseled rocks on tables or on the ground depending on the size of the stone.

"We still have some people carving the stones for replacement bricks or to add extra levels on the homes, although, for the most part, what we want is this liquid. Some month's back, we came upon a pocket and we were able to get a whole barrel of the stuff – that's the most we've ever had in one go! Normally we are lucky to get a few litres in a year. So, we keep digging and we keep collecting it."

Nandin asked, "What do you use all the powder for? Seems to me there would be enough made from one bucket of rocks to go with that liquid you've collected."

Mateo made a fist and lightly tapped Nandin on the shoulder.

"Right you are! Much more than needed for the liquid but you see, we are still in need of Essence. As the rocks are chiseled and then tumbled and crushed, Essence is spread into the air; enough so that all the Kameil within this valley can survive without any additional doses. But that's only when they are in the valley. When they leave, their Essence is quickly used up. So here I was, with all this fine powder that contained Essence. It gave me an idea and after much trial and error I was able to create Essence capsules! Little pills with a high concentration of powdered Essence. Of course, it's not like the Kameil could just swallow a handful of this dust. I had to refine it: remove all the other stuff from it."

Jon asked, "What other stuff?"

Mateo puckered his lips for a minute then responded. "The names of the 'stuff' I created myself, so that won't help you much. Let's just say I removed everything that wasn't Essence. It's what it *means* that's important. Now the Kameil can be away from the valley for an extended period of time – anytime they begin to feel a little low on Essence, they can just take one of the pills."

"You mean the Kameil were trapped here before you made the pills?" Jon asked.

Mateo sighed. "The valley isn't a prison Jon. The wall was built to keep people out, not hold anyone in. There were those who decided they didn't want to stay, for whatever reason, and they left. Of course they are always welcome to come back, however, many haven't returned. Hopefully they have found safe sources of Essence. I was out hunting when I came across a community of Kameil who had been surviving off of fumaroles – definitely not a safe source of Essence. You met some of those Kameil on your way here. They left the valley many generations ago and were unaware of its healing qualities."

He looked around as if enjoying the view.

"Well, I think that's enough of a tour for today. If there aren't any more questions I think we can return to the castle."

Nandin scanned the area trying to see if there was anything he had missed. Content that Mateo had been thorough with his explanations, he joined the others as they made their way back to where the horses were tethered.

They rode back to the castle in silence, contemplating everything Mateo had told them – it was a lot to take in. Jon was still surprised at the number of people that lived there, especially now that he knew many of them had ventured here on their own. Nandin liked Mateo and the more he found out about the history of the place and Mateo's motives, the more committed he was. Jon, on the other hand, was still concerned. One thing Mateo had said didn't quite sit right with him: his followers agreed to a treatment and it resulted in them losing their Essence. He wondered if the treatment was similar to the one he had received and if so, did it mean his condition was temporary or did Mateo perfect it? Jon reasoned that it was Mateo who invented liquid Essence and he claimed he had perfected the process. But did that mean that there were hundreds of failures before him? He could understand the benefits of creating a people with the abilities and qualities of all three races, but at what cost? Hundreds of people who thought they would be part of a new "superior race" instead becoming less than they were; lacking Essence altogether, forming a sickly race now known as Kameil? Jon shivered at the thought.

CHAPTER FOURTEEN

Diversions and Game

Nandin surveyed the room.

It had been a week after the tour of the quarry when Mateo approached Nandin again. Together they stood watching the men practice the skills they had been taught over the last few weeks. Mateo turned to Nandin.

"Do you think they could use a little change of pace?" he asked.

Nandin tilted his head while attempting to ascertain Mateo's meaning.

"What kind of change?"

"It's about time we added some game to our diet. Do you think anyone would be up for a hunt?"

"Absolutely! I think Jon would be the first to volunteer."

"What about yourself?" Mateo asked.

Nandin shrugged his shoulders.

"I'm sure it would be great fun but I've never hunted before. I don't know the first thing about it."

Mateo placed his large hand on the young mans' shoulder.

"I think it is time to learn. Pick four men to join you, some with hunting skill and those who you think would benefit the most from the experience, regardless of their abilities. I will assign two senior Yaru to lead you."

Nandin nodded and headed back to the men as Mateo motioned for his Yaru trainers to join him.

"Sim and Plyral take Nandin and the four men he chooses with you on a hunt. Nean, Thanlin – you two remain here and keep training the others. Mayon, it's time to make contact again with the Kameil in the field. Meet me in my office when you are done here and we'll go over the plan."

The Yaru bowed to Mateo who gave a slight nod then turned and left the room. Sim joined Nandin who had just finished recruiting the four would-be hunters.

"Return to your rooms and change into the appropriate clothing. Plyral and I will meet you in the main hall," Sim said to the gathered men.

The Junior Yaru quickly left the training room to carry out the request. Nandin watched Jon as they made their way back to the rooms. He could tell that Jon was excited about leaving, but was not sure if he was looking forward to the hunt or if he had other plans. After what Jon had confided in him, he was concerned for Jon's well-being. Although his mood had improved Nandin wasn't sure if he would stick around if presented with an opportunity to flee. When they reached the level their rooms were on Nandin grabbed Jon by the shoulder before he disappeared into his quarters.

"Jon, a word if I may?"

Jon nodded. "Sure Nandin, what's on your mind?"

Nandin gave a sheepish grin. "Well, I've never hunted before. I'm afraid I'm a little out of my element. Heck, I'm not even sure if I'd know the right way to put on the gear."

Jon clapped him on the back.

"Ha! Nandin you'll do fine. Go get changed, I will check you over and give you any tips you need. You may have been born Jivan, but if you looked in the mirror you'd see you look more Jagare – add that to what I've seen in the training room and I think you will make a fine hunter. Come, let's not keep the group waiting."

Nandin quickly changed into a pair of light beige pants and a long shirt of the same colour. He added a leather vest and headed to the lift with the rest of the Junior Yaru. Of the men he had chosen, two were previously Jagare and had hunting experience and the other two had been Jivan. Jon and Lazar were excited about trying out their new skills on the hunt while Kal and Purvis reflected Nandin's anxiety. He chose Kal not only because Nandin felt they had become friends since they played dice the first day he arrived at the camp, but he had proved to be rather capable with the bow and arrow; not quite as talented as Nandin, yet skilled none the less. He invited another Junior Yaru slow to mend and had succumbed to depression and thought this expedition would be therapeutic. Although Jon regained much of his former self, Nandin thought this would help with his restlessness. His last choice was one of the most able Junior Yaru, he shared Nandin's confidence in their current roles and he had hunted before.

As the five of them made their way to the main hall, Jon and Lazar gave the others some idea of what to expect on their outing. Sim and Plyral were already dressed and waiting when they arrived. After saddling and mounting their horses, they were led out of the keep, down to and through the city back to the main square where the blacksmith's shop was located. They were all astonished at the amount of weapons and gear that stocked the shelves and walls of the shop. Jon walked confidently around the room choosing the items he preferred to use when hunting. Sim grabbed three short bows and handed them and the quivers to the others. Plyral showed them some knives and explained how to wear them so as not to cut themselves as they rode. In addition, they were given slingshots and rocks; apparently more for practice than hunting. Nandin was glad that there were four experienced hunters able to help the three novices.

Once they were geared up, they stopped in the market to stock up on food for the trip. Nandin was surprised to learn they might be gone a few days, as they would need to get as much game as possible. When Jon learned they were not only hunting for themselves, but all the residents of the castle he became much more devoted to the task for now he was also feeding women, children and those who could not fend for themselves. It gave him purpose. Nandin could sense this shift in him as he took to the task with an enthusiasm he had never seen. Jon also made suggestions to Plyral and Sim as they began discussing the details of their excursion.

As the extent of the excursion began the sink in, Nandin felt even more nervous. Even on the long road to school he had not ridden on horseback, but rode in a wagon instead. The little tour around the quarry was one thing; he just had to follow the horse in front of him. Taking a horse out into the open, where they were likely to pick up the pace, seemed a little daunting. Not surprisingly, Kal and Purvis were also new to riding. It was quickly decided that each of them would be teamed up with three of the more experienced hunters leaving Sim who would act as the lead tracker for the party. Two pack mules were brought to help carry the gear and game they would be bringing back with them. When the gates were opened, Sim led the team north of the castle and into the Thickwood Forest. It didn't take long for the three inexperienced riders to adapt to riding; however, Nandin felt it they had to go any faster than a trot he was sure to be on the ground. Once deep into the woods, they found a clearing where they could tie the horses and set up camp. Sim went off on foot to find some game trails to follow and as they waited Jon, and Plyral went over the hand signals they would use and then taught them to the others.

After forty minutes, Sim returned to collect the men. As they came across the trail Sim had found, Jon pointed out the tracks to Nandin. He showed him how to walk without making noise. They were far from any villages and the only sounds they heard were the birds above, unseen critters leaping from tree to tree and the leaves as they gently blew in the light breeze. Every time Nandin stepped on a leaf a bit too loudly or snapped a twig he'd cringe, but Jon only gave him the sign for quiet without showing any real frustration.

Finally, they came across a stag drinking from a pool of water. Jon signalled Nandin to stop so he didn't alert their prey. He motioned that Nandin was to watch as he carefully moved closer and got into position. The others had circled around the animal on either side as a precautionary measure – it had been agreed that this would be Jon's kill. He notched his arrow and just as the creature raised his head, perhaps sensing danger, Jon's arrow took it down.

Nandin was impressed how quickly everyone caught and killed the animal before it could suffer. The novices were shown where the best places to hit the animal with the arrow were, as Jon had done, and kill it. Then they showed them how to gut it, get it back to the site, and hang it until they returned to the village.

After three days, they had enough game to last the castle occupants for a month. Sim explained how the Kameil did the farming, but there were few among them who made decent hunters and those that did were tasked with keeping the farmlands free of predators; therefore hunting had fallen to the Yaru. With only five of them, they were only able to provide enough for the castle residence on a regular basis, but sometimes they would bring a stag to the valley to give some of the Kameil there a change from their standard fare.

Nandin had managed to catch a few rabbits, but mostly spent the time learning how to hunt. While Jon was in his glory, Nandin wouldn't have minded if he never had to hunt again. There was so much waiting quietly and being still involved; he'd much rather be doing something active. Sim tried to convince him that hunting was good practice for learning stealth techniques as most animals can sense danger more readily than people. Usually people are so busy going about their daily routines they are completely oblivious, but after a sharp look from Jon, Sim amended his statement adding most Jagare were, of course, the exception since they spent their lives being alert for danger. Nandin hoped that the next stealth lesson didn't involve all the blood and guts; it was definitely his least favourite part of the experience.

CHAPTER FIFTEEN

Pathways and Passages

The sun shone brightly.

Hanna was glad that they would be spending their lessons outside. Today, instead of doing their exercise in the afternoon, they joined the other students in the morning to do the warm-up routine. As they stretched Hanna thought it made an interesting display having so many people synchronizing their movements. As everyone exhaled with an audible "whoa" she got goose bumps. It was like they were doing a strange slow motion dance with their voices setting the beat.

After the routine, Hanna's class followed Tahtay Biatach out the back gate for a field trip. They were heading outside the school grounds to attempt some real world applications of the skills they had been practicing. Hanna felt exhilarated. For the first time ever, she was good at a gym class. Back home she had never been very athletic. She took part in a few dance classes and had played soccer for a couple of years, but nothing really clicked. Always being the shortest and the smallest didn't lend her much in the way of an edge for sports, which suited her fine. She was content to just hang out with her friends, when she felt good enough, and cheer on the sidelines. But here she was equal to the best Jagare in the class;

running faster than she ever had and agile enough to complete tasks she never thought possible. She didn't know how she was doing these things; perhaps, she reasoned, it had something to do with the crystal she wore.

Her new skills gave her confidence and she was excited to find out what the next challenges would be. As they made their way behind the school toward the mountains, Hanna noticed that the woods were denser than they were at the front of the school. The terrain inclined, gradually at first, and then more dramatically the further they walked. They followed a narrow dirt path that had obviously been walked on many times leaving a groove with little vegetation to get in the way. When they came to a larger opening where the path split into three directions Tahtay Biatach stopped and turned to face his students.

"There are two paths that lead down and around this mountain range. One will take you across a stream, the other across a chasm. I have sent guides ahead so they can assist you should you encounter problems. At this point, please keep in mind there is nothing chasing you," he winked at Hanna, "so go slow and be safe. Our goal this week is to introduce you to these real world environments. You will find it more challenging than the training grounds."

"Once you have made the crossing you, will come to another junction in the path. The one you are to take has been marked with a white strip tied to a tree. The paths will eventually merge in front of a rock face; wait for me there. I will split you into two groups; one group per path; however, we will proceed one person at a time. Try to make it down the path at a quick, but safe pace and I repeat, slow down at the crossing. This is not a competition and I'm not looking for heroics right now."

He divided the group and sent off the first students. After a few minutes passed and the person ahead could no longer be seen or heard he sent the next pair. He pulled Hanna and another student aside.

"You two have been my fastest and most able students so far. I would like you to go last, but the same rules apply, no crazy stuff out there. Of course, if you hear that someone ahead of you has gotten into trouble, then hurry along in case they could use your help. I'm going ahead now, but I will be in-between the paths; it will be slower going, however, it will enable me to get to either path if something should occur. Count to one hundred and then send the next pair and repeat until it's your turn."

"I have a question," Hanna said, "how do you know that nothing is chasing us? Those Wolcotts still exist don't they?"

Tahtay Biatach replied, "Yes, they still exist, but we hunt these woods often and keep it free of the larger predators. It would be very unusual for there to be anything out here that could harm you. You should be safe."

"Should?"

Biatach smirked. "Well, we are out in the wilderness," he shrugged, "can't predict everything." He turned and took off into the brush.

Hanna and the Jagare student diligently sent off two students until it was their turn. When they finished counting, they glanced at each other, and then took off down their own paths. As Hanna ran she became mindful of the occasional roots across the path or depressions that could cause her to trip. She thought it strange that once she became aware of these things they began to give off a pink hue slightly brighter than everything surrounding the path. If a branch hung low across the path or if a rock jutted out she found she could easily navigate past it without slowing since she had ample warning. When she arrived at the crossing, she could see she had almost caught up with a fellow student who had just made it to the other side. Her path had led to the stream, which could be crossed using a combination of large boulders and a fallen log. The stream was about twenty feet across and was fast-flowing. As tempted as Hanna was to try to run across, she had no desire to go for a swim should she prove less adept than on the training course. She gazed down into the water and immediately regretted it as it made her dizzy and a lot less confident.

"You will do fine." A deep voice said.

"Man! I almost jumped out of my skin!" Hanna exclaimed.

Sitting on a large rock beside the creek, slightly obscured from view by an overhanging tree, was a Jagare whom Hanna hadn't met before, but had seen around the campus. Currently he was laughing.

"Now that would have been a sight! Come on, off you go, since you're the last one I will be following you over."

Hanna grumbled, "It's amazing no one's fallen in if you've taken to scaring everyone as they cross."

He just smiled and waved her on. Hanna stepped out on the first rock and then tested the next rock to make sure it was stable. She increased her pace a little as she continued to test each stone to ensure it wasn't going to move. Halfway across she came to the fallen tree. Its base rested on other boulders causing the end to be raised above the creek by a few feet. Hanna grabbed a branch for leverage and swung her leg up and over. She now straddled it but was facing the wrong way. She saw the Jagare laughing at her partway across the stream. She rolled her eyes at him and dropped one of her legs, holding herself on the log by keeping her arms straight, then swung both legs back over landing with her legs outstretched. She smiled to herself as she imagined she was a professional gymnast on the pommel horse. Continuing with that image in mind she pushed herself to standing ran down the rest of the tree and flipped off the end onto the ground. She turned around to see if her spectator was still laughing, but felt rather sheepish when she saw the scowl on his face.

"What were you doing? I thought you were told to take it easy this round?" he admonished.

Hanna stared down at her feet. "I just got caught up in the moment, sorry."

Realizing he sounded a bit too much like Tahtay Biatach he said, "Well, you're all right so I guess no harm was done. I'm Karn by the way."

He leaped off the tree and gave her a quick bow after he landed. Hanna bowed back.

"I'm Hanna."

"Okay Hanna, what's say we race to the rock face?"

Hanna smiled then took off without waiting for him to say go. She heard him laugh as he ran to catch up to her. She caught up with the student ahead of her who was leaning against a tree trying to catch his breath. He stepped back and waved them past. When she reached the divided pathway she took the one marked with the white strip. Karn was hard on her heels just waiting for an opportunity to get by her, but the path proved to be too narrow.

After another ten minutes of dogging roots and bramble they emerged into a clearing at the same time where the rest of the group assembled.

Hanna bent over with her hands on her knees breathing heavily. She smiled when she saw Karn doing the same thing. Before too long they heard movement behind them and Tahtay Biatach came out from the trees followed shortly by the student they had passed.

"It looks like we are all here. Any troubles?" Biatach asked.

He surveyed the group then made eye contact with Karn and the other Jagare who stood watch over the other path. No one spoke up, however, Karn must have revealed something in his expression to give Biatach pause. Hanna waited for Karn to tell him about her reckless stunt on the log but he remained silent.

Biatach continued, "Very well then, to our next exercise."

Biatach moved into a horseshoe-shaped clearing large enough for all the students and the two guides to stand around while leaving the centre unoccupied. He stood facing the group with his back to the rock face.

"As I'm sure you have guessed, we will be scaling this rock" he said slapping his hand against it.

"Today you have the privilege of this rope that has been securely attached to the top," he gave the rope a tug, "but it will prove more challenging than the wall you have been practising on. Notice that the last few feet jut out slightly. I will have one of the guides climb first. Watch closely. He will be waiting for you at the top so if you are having any trouble he can assist you the rest of the way. Also, we have this additional rope for you to tie around yourselves so if you slip you won't come crashing down. It's not that high, but you could still twist your ankle or even break something if you land badly. Okay, one at a time – we'll go in the same order to give the latter runners a chance to catch their breath."

The guide from the group who took the path over the chasm climbed up the rope. He made it look easy and could have obviously gone faster, but had kept it slow so everyone could clearly make out where he placed his feet. When he made it to the top he peeked over the edge and hollered below that they could begin as he tossed down one end of the safety rope. One by one they each slowly made their way up the rope. When it was Hanna's turn she stood at the base of the rock and gazed up. She thought it looked much higher than the twelve feet it probably was. As she ran her fingers across the dark grey rock she found it cool to the touch and knew that if she wasn't careful she would easily scrape herself on its jagged surface.

She waited for the safety rope to be tossed down again and then Karn helped her secure it under her arms. She felt intimidated by the enormous structure, but took a deep breath and began climbing. Once she got into it, she found it wasn't as tricky as she thought it would be; the practice over the last week had really helped to prepare her. When she got to the part of rock that jutted out she heard the guide above her.

"You're doing great Hanna, you're almost there."

He gave her some useful advice about where to put her feet which was enough for her to swiftly finish ascending.

At the top he grabbed onto her arm in case she needed help pulling herself over the ledge.

She smiled, rubbing her arms that were still trembling from the exertion and excitement.

"Thank you. That was a bit of a rush."

He chuckled as she took a look back down the cliff she had just climbed. She stood and observed her surroundings. The overhang that they had reached was only ten feet across. She noticed there was a cave opening where most of the students had disappeared. Kazi bounded over to her.

"Great job! Now you've got to come see this."

He half dragged her into the cave. The opening was deceivingly small, roughly the size of a door; inside, though, it was rather spacious. The top of the cavern was still too low for most adult Jagare so any that came here would have to hunch over, but there was plenty of room to sit or lay and stretch out. There was no way to tell from where they were how deep into the mountain the cave went as the light from the one lit torch revealed only the immediate area. Shadows danced along the walls and the ceiling giving the cave an ominous feeling. Pictures covered the walls in bright oranges, reds and even purple. Hanna couldn't make out any details from where she stood at the entrance of the cave.

Her fellow students were seated in a semi-circle in the middle of the floor. When Kazi noticed she had stopped following him he grabbed her arm again and dragged her to the circle to sit. The remaining students made their way into the cave and joined the others along with Karn, the other guide and Tahtay Biatach.

"Okay," Biatach said in a slightly raised voice that echoed around the cavern, "they're all yours." Everyone grew quiet allowing them to hear footsteps approaching from further within the cave. The shadows shuddered in an unnerving way as a figure approached. The students held their breath. The shadow that had appeared large at first became smaller as it came closer and closer. Everyone laughed and breathed easily when finally Tahtay Jillian came into view.

"I'm glad you could all join me and it appears everyone is unscathed. Thank you Tahtay Biatach, I think we will be ready to prepare lunch in about an hour."

"I will return then."

He bowed and then led their two guides out of the cave.

Turning back to her students Jillian said, "We've talked about our history, now it is time to see it. In her hand she held a lantern. She un-shuttered it and walked closer to one of the walls. As her light illuminated the wall the images came to life. She explained how the pictures told the stories of how their ancestors lived during the Time of Endurance.

"This cave was home to a group of Juro for many generations as is shown by this mural here which acts like a family's timeline. Come and take a closer look."

As they crowded around she pointed to simple pictures on the wall of a man and woman standing beside each other with a circle joining their hands. Their hair differentiated the figures; men had straight hair and the females curled up. Smaller child-like images were standing beside them, but stacked on top of each other. The children had lines pointing to the right at another pair of adults with hands also linked and more children stacked on top of each other. Every now and then an X would be in the place of where an adult picture should be. Jillian pointed to the first image of the adults, which was very faded, most of the original colour lost.

"We know the circle represents the marriage of two people."

She then pointed at the smaller images.

"These would represent their children and this line is their growth line at the end of which is the child become adult and once again shows another married couple. The lines that end with an X represent a death. The length of the line gives us an idea of how long the child lived before death. Once married, if they died before having kids you will see an X in lieu of children. If the surviving spouse remarried they have a new picture beside the first. Questions?"

Celine said, "Why do some kids have a line that ends in a circle?"

"Yes I was getting there. The lines that end in a circle imply that he was married. You will notice that these family lines show the progression of the females. The men are added into the family line of their spouse. If you look closely you can see that each individual has an identifying mark. Here is a challenge for you: pick a boy on the family line that has been married; note his identifying mark and then find the family line he has been added to. You will find the family lines on every wall. There is no particular place to find them; it is assumed they just fit them in wherever they found room. I have more lanterns here. Light them and follow the passage to find the line you wish to work on. Pick the family line within this area or just a short way down the passage but don't wander too far – we will venture further in a bit."

Hanna joined Kazi, who had picked up a lantern and was standing by the torch, waiting to light the candle. Once lit, they went to the opposite wall to find a different family line. They inched their way down the passage admiring the faded pictures. The walls were covered from floor to ceiling which lent an impressive quality to the artwork, but on closer inspection the pictures were quite simple. Even though the designs were simplistic, Hanna felt a little overwhelmed since there was much detail in every image. There were images of animals stocking prey or being hunted. Other pictures contained images of various types of vegetation along with smaller animals: some familiar to Hanna, others foreign. They found another family line close to the floor so they crouched down to study it.

After a moment of observing the family Hanna pointed to a few pictures.

"Look Kazi, doesn't it seem odd that some of the pictures near the beginning of the line look newer than ones further down."

"That's because they are."

They turned around as Tahtay Jillian crouched down behind them.

"These families are all Juro. Each couple has only one Hatchling every fifty to eighty years so their first child may already have a Hatchling of their own before they have siblings. Good observation Hanna."

She got up and went to see what the other students were finding. Hanna and Kazi returned to observing the wall. Each individual had a symbol on his or her chest; there were squiggly lines, odd shapes, dots and dashes. Hanna traced the line with her finger, pausing at each individual then following the line. They often had to return to previous generations due to a death ending the entire branch. Finally they managed to find a male who married and hadn't been crossed off. Using his finger, Kazi drew on the dirt floor the image on the boy's chest. The real scavenger hunt now began. They continued searching the wall they were on until they felt they were too far removed from where they had started and returned back to the boy they found. Then they searched the same wall but toward the cave opening. After no success they switched walls. After half an hour they finally came across the family the boy had married into.

Hanna let out an exasperated "Eureka!"

Tahtay Jillian came over to confirm they correctly found a match.

"Well done. It would have been much easier to find this back before the walls were so completely covered. What you are looking at are hundreds of years' worth of images."

To the whole group she said, "A few more minutes and then we will move on."

Some of their fellow students had already found their matches and some were still struggling. Hanna and Kazi joined the students who already finished the task and were sitting back in the semi circle. Tahtay Jillian joined them.

"Can anyone tell me what other things are painted on the walls aside from the family lines?"

"Animals."

"Plants."

"Numbers."

Jillian said, "Yes to all of those. What were the animals doing?"

"Hunting or being chased."

"Right. Many of these pictures are telling stories. They depict an animal they caught and killed perhaps or even how the animal may have attacked them. What do you think the plants tell us?"

No one answered this time.

"Okay, let me ask this, did anyone recognize any of the plants?"

A Jivan girl answered, "Yes, I noticed there was a Red Bean Plant."

Jillian smiled.

"How come you were able to recognize that plant?"

"My Ma showed it to me when I was little and told me it was one of the most poisonous plants on the planet. It's easy to spot. It has red beans with black tops and they are nestled in brown leaves. We sometimes take the beans and make them into necklaces. Ma said that was to help remind us not to ever eat them because if we did we would be dead within hours."

"Thank you, that's exactly what I was looking for. So why do you think they would paint this type of plant on the wall?"

Celine spoke up. "As a warning?"

"Absolutely. They didn't have books or scrolls, so the walls were the only way to record their knowledge. They may have told stories, but living for hundreds of years it would be hard to keep track of all the things they learned."

She paused and looked around, "I see a few more students have found their family line connection; I will be right back."

When she returned she brought the remaining students with her.

"We've talked about the stories on the walls as well as the knowledge stored there. I would like to note that we have recorded the wisdom that these walls have given us, mostly when the schools first came into existence. Has anyone else guessed another way these pictures are still connected to us today?"

Kazi raised his hand. "Go ahead Kazi." Jillian said.

"Is this how our writing began?" he asked timidly.

"Excellent! Please tell us how you came to that conclusion since these pictures are different enough from our own writing for this truth to be overlooked."

"Well, it was by chance actually. One of the pictures I saw was partly erased and it looked like the word tree."

Jillian pulled some paper out of a bag she had slung over her shoulder and handed each person a single sheet.

"Go back to the walls and pick any picture. Place your paper so it cuts the picture in half. Then tell me what words you see."

Everyone eagerly followed Tahtay Jillian's advice and dashed to the walls. Voices called out various things such as "Wolcott" or "Man". Hanna felt completely lost. She covered up part of a picture of a jar, but to her it still looked like a half a jar, no words popped out like she expected they magically would. Jillian came over to her and whispered in her ear.

"I don't suppose the writing where you come from looks similar to this?"

Hanna shook her head. Jillian took out a pencil and drew on Hanna's page. She drew the upper half of the jar, a tree and an animal.

"This is how we write jar, tree and wolf."

She drew a few more images.

"Oh I've seen that one before!" Hanna exclaimed. "It's on the girl's bathhouse."

"Right. That's the sign for girl or woman. Do you know any of these signs?"

Hanna looked at the lines and the dots then admitted she didn't.

"This is how we write numbers. The dot is one, two is two, and so on until you get to five which is just a thin line."

Hanna felt a little overwhelmed. Since she'd been on Galenia she hadn't taken notice of any writing; in fact the thought didn't even crossed her mind. It would have been baffling if their written words were like hers. It was unfortunate the Essence didn't translate the written language as well as the spoken word – the idea of having to learn to write a whole new language was daunting. Sensing Hanna's distress, Jillian place a hand on her shoulder.

"Don't worry Hanna, I will help you. Keep in mind though that most of your fellow students only

know a few words, that's why they come to school –
to learn."

Hanna relaxed upon hearing this.

"Thank you Tahtay Jillian."

They walked back into the centre of the room.
Jillian raised her voice to be heard over the chatter
that had broken out.

"Gather round again."

When they were all sitting she continued.

"When our ancestors left their caves to join with
the other races, they needed to bring their knowledge
with them. At first they would just visit sites such as
this, but after a while they devised a better way – this
mainly came about when they started the schools.
Having this knowledge in hand was much more
convenient and they needed to blend the artwork from
one tribe to the next as well as from race to race.
Some of our first books contain these images in their
entirety, but as the blending occurred and multiple
works were needed it became much more efficient to
only copy part of the picture. Over hundreds of years
these have been altered here and there to what was
most functional. The written language has also
expanded beyond the original markings to include
new ideas and concepts that didn't exist during the
Time of Endurance. Let me show you something
really amazing."

She led the group deeper into the cave. They
came to an opening with several tunnels leading
deeper into the mountain. Jillian turned right and they
found themselves in a room half the size as the
original cave. She suspended her lantern on a hook
that was attached to the ceiling. Her class looked
around in awe. Like the first cave, this room was

covered from floor to ceiling in artwork, but unlike those walls, these ones shimmered and sparkled. The entire surface looked as if it had been dusted in gold and tiny pink gems sparkled as they reflected the light from the lantern.

"Essence!" someone whispered.

Hanna understood as she too felt the need to be hushed in this dazzling room.

"Welcome to the map room. This is a map of the inside of this mountain. The small Essence gems you see on the map represent areas where there were larger Essence deposits. We will venture down to one or two of them today after lunch, but most of these deposits have long been empty. The longer they lived here, the deeper they needed to go to set up a nesting ground. Most of these areas are quiet small so could only house a couple hatchlings. Barely any Essence resides in them today leaving the rooms as nothing more than attractions since they are of little use for us now. Follow me to another map room."

She removed her lantern and followed a different tunnel to another chamber. This one was only slightly larger than the last. Once again she hung her light to illuminate the majority of the room.

"As you can see, this map shows the area outside the mountain. On it you will find the locations of streams, ravines, valleys as well as fruit baring trees and bushes. There are also a few Wolcott dens and a nest of Draka, which are one of the species of Mystic Flyers for those of you who haven't heard of them. As large as this map may seem, keep in mind that it only covers this mountain range and the forest up to where Kokoroe is built. It may be that the Juro from these caves never ventured any further than what's drawn here, that is, not until their last generation joined with the other races."

"Take a quick look and then head back to the front cave to meet Tahtay Biatach for lunch."

* * *

Hanna's stomach growled. They made a fire just outside the cave and prepared lunch from the food Tahtay Jillian had brought and the animals Tahtay Biatach and his two guides had hunted while the rest of them were exploring the cave. Time dragged before they finally got to sit down and eat.

Once lunch was finished, they made their way back to the Essence map chamber. After choosing two of the closest crystal caves to go and investigate, they began down one of the unexplored tunnels. Following Tahtay Jillian around several twists and turns Hanna felt positively lost. She was glad that Tahtay Jillian was confident as to where she was going. The tunnels were so dark that the light from Jillian's lantern was swallowed mere feet in front of them. They had brought a few extras, but were saving the candles for when the first one burned down low. They stayed close together as no one was eager to venture far from the only light source. Hanna rubbed her arms to try to keep them warm; the air in the mountain was consistent, but it did feel quite a bit cooler than outside. After thirty minutes of touring through the gloom they arrived at the first nesting grounds. Hanna had expected another chamber like either of the map rooms, but instead the passage just widened. Four small oval holes had been carved into

210

the wall. Brushing away dust that had accumulated over time, Hanna ran her hand across one of the pockets. It was worn smooth by the Hatchlings that had occupied the space in ages past. Clear minuscule crystals could barely be seen embedded in the top of the pockets.

Tahtay Jillian said, "As you can see, this is a fairly small nesting area. With only four pockets for the Hatchlings, the Essence must have been depleted very quickly. The next nesting grounds will prove to be a little more compelling. This way."

Off they went again until the narrow tunnel opened to a huge cavern. They stood on a ledge that went around the perimeter of a pit that went beyond their ability to see. Similarly, Hanna couldn't tell how tall the cavern was since the light was taken over by the darkness before a ceiling could be seen. She felt a cool mist on her face and saw the thin sheet of water falling from an opening high up in the mountain. It moved like a sheer curtain in a breeze and the light added a ghostly glow to it. They followed the ledge to another opening beside the waterfall. They continued down another darkened passage when light burst forth everywhere. Thousands of crystals lined the walls and sparkled as the light from the lantern reflected off their surface causing the room to feel like it was moving. Blues and purples were the dominant colour of the crystals with a few deep reds and lighter pink ones higher up. Clear gems were intermixed with the coloured ones and reflected the most light. The room put Hanna in mind of a giant coloured disco ball turned inside out.

Kazi leaned over to Hanna and whispered, "What I'd give to see what you see."

Hanna was puzzled.

"What do you mean? Don't you see sparkling coloured crystals?"

"Of course I do but you can see the Essence," Kazi replied.

Hanna paused then turned away from Kazi to once again admire the crystals. Her eyes darted around, but the crystals looked the same and then........there! She could see it! The stones were giving off a pink glow! She came closer to the walls and soon she noticed a pattern. The darker the crystal the less of a glow it gave off; the exception being that the clear crystals had no glow at all. There were black crystals imbedded among the others that she hadn't noticed at first because of the little reflection they had; they only gave off the slightest glow – the pink crystals glowed the brightest. The various intensities made it look like the stones just popped out from the wall. It was strange how she couldn't see it at first and then when she peered at it just the right way the Essence revealed itself. It reminded her of one of those Magic Eye pictures which had a three dimensional picture hidden within an obscure pattern. She couldn't help but reach out and touch the jewels. As she ran her hand along the jagged wall she could feel some sort of energy; the more Essence the gem had the more energy it emitted.

Tahtay Jillian was observing Hanna. By Hanna's reaction she knew she was able to see the Essence around the room. When she saw the girl touch the stones she wondered if she could also feel it. She knew Master Juro would want to know Hanna's reactions.

She asked Hanna, "What do you make of it?"

212

"Oh it's marvelous!" she replied. "I've never seen anything like it!"

"Explain what you see." Jillian said.

"Well I see all the coloured gems, obviously, but then I can see them glowing too. The darker the gem, like the black ones, only have a hint of a pink glow and the rose coloured ones are so bright. It's strange how those ones are mostly up high. I'm wondering why don't the clear ones have a glow?"

Jillian reached out and touched a clear stone gem. "These have been drained of their Essence. The gems start out black with just a touch of Essence. As the gems ripen, if you will, they change colour as they take in more Essence. Once they reach the shade of pink they are infused with as much Essence as they can be; these are the only ones that we can draw any Essence out of; they are the ones we use for the Hatchlings. Once the Hatchlings drain the pink crystals of the Essence they become clear. This Demi Geode, that is what we call these caves," she motioned around the room, "would have been one of the preferred nesting grounds. As you can see there are hardly any of the pink crystals here."

"I'm not sure I understand. Didn't you say that the Juro lived here over a thousand years ago?"

"Yes, that's right." Jillian said.

"Well then how come more gems haven't turned pink yet?"

"It can take hundreds to thousands of years for the gems to change which is why they are so valuable to us."

Hanna recalled that Kazi called the crystal she wore a "valuable treasure" when he first gave it to her. Now she fostered a newfound appreciation for it.

213

She joined the others as they continued walking around the "Demi Geode" as Tahtay Jillian called it. When she could finally tear her eyes from the walls she noticed a stone dais in the middle of the room. It was a wide cylinder shape like a pillar but only came up to her chest. Eight smooth oval pockets were evenly spaced around the top of the circle like spokes on a wheel. It reminded Hanna of a giant egg pan her mother used to make poached eggs.

Tahtay Jillian came over to the raised platform.

"This is called a Hatchling table. These divots are where they laid the Hatchlings. They may have placed the newborns in baskets in the middle of the table or in cradles close by. Imagine it. What a wondrous place to be born!"

Hanna could appreciate her enthusiasm. This place was astounding compared to the plain dirt and rock walls of most of the interior of the mountain.

"Okay class," Tahtay Jillian said, "let us make our way back. It will be dinner by the time we return to Kokoroe."

As they retraced their steps, Hanna walked beside Tahtay Jillian with Kazi close on her heels.

"I was wondering, why is it called a Demi Geode?"

Jillian said, "Because it contains only part of the Geode."

Hanna wrinkled her brow. "Okay, I think I'm still missing something. A geode is a rock with tiny crystals or something in them, right?"

"Yes, we call those rock geodes but I'm referring to The Geode. It is the source of the Essence. It is where all Essence begins and ends. Master Juro will give you more instruction on it."

214

It was clear she was not going to elaborate so Hanna refrained from asking any more questions. Instead, she listened to Kazi talk excitedly about seeing a real Demi Geode. He apparently had never seen one before; he had only heard of them.

They made it back to the cave entrance and carefully took turns down the rope to the clearing below. Hanna was surprised to see that even Tahtay Jillian used the rope like the rest of them, but then Hanna realized it was probably the only way up or down from the cave.

As they made the hike back to Kokoroe they took a different path than either the ones they had taken earlier. This path had a bridge that crossed the creek making the journey back much more leisurely. The path was also wider so the group went together, walking in twos or threes.

Hanna was looking forward to a hot bath after dinner. She was tired but so full of new ideas to contemplate. A bath seemed like it would be the perfect end to such an adventurous day.

CHAPTER SIXTEEN

Sustenance and Substance

Hanna was famished.

As the class made their way to the long hall they reminisced about the adventures of the day. Karn saw them enter the building and followed them to a table.

"Mind if I join in?" Karn asked.

"Sure Karn." Hanna replied and introduced him to all of her friends.

Karn exchanged greetings. "How did you find the crossing? I can remember the first time I had to go across the ravine; definitely one to get your blood pumping."

Kazi agreed. "Yep, I refused to look down until I was all the way across. I preferred not to see how deep it was. I'm not sure if I could have done it if I'd known; it was quite the drop."

Hanna was surprised. "If I had fallen I'd just have gotten wet. It seems rather risky to let students cross something that dangerous. Could you have seriously gotten hurt?"

"Oh, absolutely." Kazi said. "But that's why we used a safety rope."

Kazi went on to explain how there was a rope, about six feet above the log they had to cross, which was strung across the ravine and attached to large trees at either end. They connected a shorter rope to Kazi's belt and a metal hook clipped to the overhead rope allowing it to slide along as he walked across.

"You'd still get a bit of a beating if you fell off the log," Karn added, "You could swing into the log or the cliff face if you were close enough. One of my friends slipped his first time and scraped his side. Bruised it pretty good, even tore some ligaments. He was sore for weeks."

He grinned as he recalled his friend's pain.

"Gee," Hanna said, "you seem really choked up about it."

Karn laughed. "He deserved it. He was trying to show off by running across the log. Kind of reminds me of someone."

He looked meaningfully at Hanna.

Kazi grinned, "Okay, out with it! What did Hanna do?"

Karn looked at Hanna who melted into her chair. With pleasure he revealed what had happened during Hanna's crossing. Kazi laughed when Karn mentioned her being backwards on the log and was hysterical with tears in his eyes when Karn got to the point where she did a flip off the end. Hanna blushed. Not fond of being the centre of attention at the best of times she felt embarrassed about the inappropriate, prideful moment she had on the log. Karn put a friendly hand on her shoulder as he went on to tell of a time where he too had acted brashly, but he did it in front of Tahtay Biatach, who didn't let him off with a warning. They were on a hunting expedition and were supposed to wait for everyone to get into position before springing a trap on a Wolcott. Karn had seen an opening and charged the Wolcott with a spear. Fortunately, Biatach had seen Karn act ahead of the plan and sprung the net to hold the Beast in place so it couldn't gut Karn before they had a chance to kill it. He explained how he spent the next week scrubbing dishes while he "contemplated" the reason for following instructions. Hanna was doubly grateful Karn held back from telling Biatach about her incident.

As they were finishing up their dinner, Yoshi came to their table.

"Hanna," she said, "Master Juro wishes to speak with you."

Hanna nodded to Yoshi. "I guess my bath will have to wait."

She turned to her companions and said, "I will catch up with you later."

Then she bowed to Karn and said slightly sarcastically, "Thanks for joining us Karn; it's been most...informative."

She said goodnight and followed Yoshi to Master Juro's domicile. Yoshi led her in, bowed and disappeared down a hallway. Hanna stood, not sure if should sit. She tucked her hair behind her ears and then crossed her arms.

"Please, have a seat," Master Juro said as he made his way from behind the gauzy curtains and down the steps to greet her. He motioned to the grouping of armchairs in front of the hearth that was cold from the lack of use over the last few weeks. Hanna bowed and sat in the closest chair. She had heard much talk about Master Juro since arriving, but had not seen him since their first meeting. As he walked across the room, Hanna thought he looked much less impressive when he wasn't floating. He chose a seat facing Hanna, crossed his legs and held his hands with his fingers spread out in a pyramid shape in front of him.

"How are you settling in Hanna?" he inquired.

"Fine, thank you," she replied.

He raised an eyebrow, "I thought perhaps you would be a little more detailed than that."

"Ok, um...what would you like to know, if I'm making friends? Whether or not I like my classes? If I like my room?"

Master Juro nodded. "Yes," he simply said.

Hanna chuckled, "All right, yes I'm making friends, everyone here is so easy to get along with. History class is fascinating. I especially enjoyed our field trip today. Physical training has been surprising; I didn't think I would do very well at it but I'm doing all right."

"More than all right I hear. Seems you have skills to rival your Jagare classmates."

He paused before he spoke again.

"I understand you went to a Demi Geode today..."

Hanna nodded in agreement.

"Tell me what you saw."

Hanna was sure he already knew what she saw, but went on to explain anyway. When she finished he leaned back in his chair and absently stroked his beard. He gazed at Hanna as if trying to decide something. Hanna became uncomfortable as he stared. Finally he spoke.

"Hanna, I would like you to spend the day with me tomorrow. I have another field trip planned for you. Meet me here first thing. I suggest you turn in early."

"Can I ask you something?"

He indicated she should continue.

"Tahtay Jillian said you'd explain what the Geode is?"

"The Geode is the source of the Essence. It makes up the core of the planet and everything from the grass to the trees and mountains are tapped into it. When animals die their Essence returns to The Geode."

"So there's a giant crystal in the middle of the planet?"

"I don't believe it to be so. I suspect it is Essence in some sort of liquid form, but that is only a theory. We've never discovered liquid Essence, most believe it is not capable of achieving this state."

"Why do you think its liquid?"

"I can sense it, they way it moves throughout the world."

"So why not dig a hole and find out?"

Master Juro shook his head. "For what purpose? Whether or not the core is a crystal or is liquid doesn't change anything. Besides, liquid Essence, if it truly exists, serves its purpose where it is so what is the point of digging it up?"

"I guess..." Hanna realized something still didn't make sense.

"Why would it be called a Geode if it might not even be a crystal then?"

"Essence in crystal form is the highest concentration we've encountered and so that led to the assumption the source would be crystallized. Even if it were to be discovered as a liquid it would continue to be called The Geode. It has been named this for hundreds of years and so it shall be. Regardless of what it is, it's what it represents that's important."

Hanna nodded remembering her favourite Shakespearean line, "I get it; a rose by any other name would smell as sweet."

Master Juro gave one of his rare smiles.

"Well put." He bowed. "Until tomorrow then."

Hanna understood she was being dismissed. She clumsily got up and bowed. She was surprised and grateful that Master Juro had explained so thoroughly – from what she had learned this wasn't typical. She turned when she got to the door.

"Thank you Master Juro."

* * *

Hanna managed to enjoy a quick bath before heading back to her room for the night. Now she stood waiting for Master Juro in the entrance of his home. Yoshi appeared and without a word directed Hanna back out to the gardens. She motioned for her to stay and then left in silence. Hanna chuckled at Yoshi's usual taciturn manner. Within moments of Yoshi's parting Master Juro arrived. Once again, he was floating but this time he had a long staff that he used to move himself along. The staff was similar to the one she had seen Leader Chieo use, but the orb that the wood fingers held in place was silver. He bid Hanna good morning, and then asked her to follow him.

They walked through the garden until they came to an area made mostly of sand and rocks.

"Hanna, look at the sand and the stones. Let me know when you see their Essence."

Hanna concentrated until finally she could just make out a hint of the pink.

"I see it...but just barely."

"Excellent. Now can you feel it?"

Hanna reached out, cupped her hands and filled them with sand. As the sand trickled through her fingers she tried to feel the energy she had when she touched the crystals in the Demi Geode.

"It just feels like sand," she conceded.

"Try the stone." Master Juro picked up a stone the size of a large grapefruit and placed it in Hanna's hands. The stone had a smooth glossy texture and felt cool to the touch. Hanna began turning it in her hands, but Master Juro reached out and stilled her movements.

"Close your eyes," he said "and just feel."

She did. She felt the cold on her palms and then suddenly she felt a warm spot. Just faintly warmer than the rest of the stone, but she knew it was the Essence. She opened her eyes.

"I can feel it! Just ever so slightly but it's there!"

Master Juro gave a tiny grin.

"Can you move it? Try focusing on the warm spot and moving it up in your mind."

Hanna gave him a puzzled look then turned her attention back to the stone. Move it up? She was not sure where he was going with this, but she wasn't about to argue. Okay, she thought, up. Come on up you go! Nothing happened. She was not surprised.

After a few minutes Master Juro moved her aside. He grabbed a handful of sand and tossed it in the air. Instead of sand raining down on them the granules just hung in the air not moving. Master Juro moved his hand and the sand spread out like a sheet of dust hanging before them. He grabbed one grain and dropped it into Hanna's hand.

"Everything contains the Essence," he said. "And what contains the Essence can be manipulated."

He moved his hand again and slowly the sand settled back onto the ground. Then he looked at the stone she still held. Slowly it rose into the air and glided over to sit on top of a larger stone.

Hanna was amazed. "That's a pretty good trick. Do you think I will be able to do that?"

"We shall see. Come. We have a long journey ahead of us."

He led Hanna through the gardens until they came to a door embedded into a grassy hillock far away from where they had entered the garden. He tinkered with an unusual locking mechanism and then swung the door open.

They entered a passage leading down a flight of stairs. The orb on top of Master Juro's staff illuminated their way. The passage was narrow enough that Hanna could reach out and touch both walls at the same time. Feeling a bit claustrophobic she was relieved when they reached the bottom of the stairs and the passage they followed widened. After a kilometre the corridor opened up to reveal a simple rowboat floating in a narrow canal of water. In the boat Hanna saw a basket that she hoped was full of food, as she hadn't eaten yet that morning.

Hanna sat in the front of the boat facing Master Juro, meaning she was backwards when they began moving. How they were moving was a bit of a mystery to her as the boat didn't appear to have any motor and Master Juro was not using the oars that lay on the floor. The water in the canal didn't seem to be moving as they exited the tunnel and headed outside. She figured Master Juro was using a similar method to move the boat that he used when he was floating. A short distance from the tunnel they passed a river stream that emptied into the waterway, the source of the canal they were travelling. Hanna noticed the rapidly moving river had been slowed by wooden planks that jutted into the stream; by the time it joined the canal it barely caused a ripple. Trees flanking the canal created a green canopy overhead. After they were well on their way Hanna could no longer contain her discomfort.

"Master Juro, is there food in the basket that I may eat?" she said pleadingly.

"But of course you would not have eaten yet! My apologies; please help yourself."

Hanna didn't need to be told twice. She pulled the basket towards herself, eager to discover what goodies might lie inside. The smell of freshly baked bread wafted through the air as she opened the lid. She unwrapped a towel to discover warm buns. She found a tiny jar of jam and proceeded to spread it generously on one.

"Would you like one?" she asked.

"No thank you."

"Is there something else I can get you? Looks like there is fruit and cheese and all sorts of stuff in here."

"I have already eaten," he said.

When he saw Hanna about to inquire further he added, "We have the morning meal earlier than the students."

Hanna knew the teachers ate somewhere other than the long hall, but had always assumed they ate at the same time as the students. She didn't envy the teacher's earlier mealtime; she tended to be more a night person. Getting up on time each day was challenging enough.

She began devouring the jam-covered bun. Once her hunger pains began to subside, Hanna's curiosity took over.

Between mouthfuls she sputtered, "Where are we going anyway?"

Master Juro's face was an unchanging mask of concentration yet when he spoke he was as smooth and cryptic as ever.

"We journey to a place to discover possibilities."

Obviously back to his vague self, Hanna understood he would not be as forthcoming as he was about the Geode so she let the matter drop and rooted through the basket some more. She found two water skins, each with a rope attached. She took a long drink from one and put it over her shoulder. Grabbing an apple, she closed the basket with her elbow. She would rather see where they were going rather than where they had been so she swung her legs over her seat to face the other way and enjoy the scenery.

The day was warm, not a cloud in the sky. Hanna calculated that she had been on Galenia for two months which would mean it was mid-July back home. She thought it was an amazing coincidence their seasons were the same, but then she had no idea if they even had different seasons. It was relatively quiet, just the sounds of birds in the trees and the water stirring as the boat glided over it. The trees cleared away as they approached another river. Instead of it joining the canal this time, it flowed below them as the waterway continued across it via a bridge.

Anticipating Hanna's reaction to the bridge Master Juro said, "It's called an aqueduct. Do you have these back home?"

Hanna nodded, "Yes but I've never seen one. I remember hearing that the Romans built them to move water to where they wanted it. I think it's what they used for their baths, but I'm not sure of the details."

Master Juro looked intrigued.

"We also use them for our bath houses. This one serves the extra purpose of continuing our canal across the river."

Hanna leaned over the boat to look at the water below the bridge. It was at least a twenty-foot drop and the river below was moving rapidly. Her grip tightened on the side of the boat; feeling a little dizzy she sat back. Once across the river, the landscape returned to one populated with trees. Hanna dipped into the basket for more food to munch on and contented herself with a mix of nuts and dried fruit. She reflected on what she had done and seen over the last few months when Master Juro stirred her from her reverie.

"Hanna, would you please give me your crystal?"

Hanna turned to face Master Juro, shock clearly evident on her face. The precious crystal that hung around her neck had never been removed since she had placed it there. It was her lifeline – without it she knew she would quickly become weakened, lose consciousness and eventually die.

Sensing her trepidation he said, "Trust me Hanna. What I ask is for your safety."

With hesitation, she grasped the crystal from beneath her shirt and lifted it over her head. Master Juro held out a box lined with soft fabric and as Hanna carefully placed the crystal in it, it sank within its folds. She trusted that Master Juro knew what he was doing. She made herself comfortable again and let her mind drift off, unconsciously pressing her hand where the crystal typically rested.

For the next hour, as they glided along, Hanna reflected on how similar this land was to her own. True the buildings and lifestyles of the people were old-fashioned, but the forest and surrounding land could have been anywhere back home. Aside from the Demi Geode she had seen, everything else was reasonably familiar.

There were times when walking through the gardens or in the woods, Hanna would forget she was on a different world.

This was not one of those times.

As the trees cleared they rounded a bend and Hanna was shocked. After the familiarity of the ride thus far she was quite unprepared for the sight before her.

At first, she thought she was seeing massive icebergs, but they were shaped more like mountains, although not as

225

high. Still the structures were enormous casting rainbows where the sunlight was reflected, revealing it to be something other than frozen water. Unlike icebergs, they were glossy pink with jagged tops and angled sides. They were still some distance from the awe-inspiring formations; Hanna wondered how big they would be when she was next to them.

"What are they?" she asked without taking her eyes from the view.

"Look deeper." Master Juro responded.

As ambiguous as his response was, Hanna understood what he meant. She gazed ahead trying to see more, and then she did. Once again she was met with a vision of objects popping out at her. The structures glowed brightly; brighter than anything she had yet encountered.

"Crystals?" she asked incredulously, tearing her eyes away to look at Master Juro.

He nodded.

"But they're so....big!"

With a wave of his hand he said, "Welcome to Crystal Valley."

* * *

As the canal began to slope downwards, Master Juro raised himself above the boat. Hanna watched in fascination as pink dust from the air seemed to be pulled toward him as he constructed a bubble around himself. This filled her with so many questions, but before she could decide what to ask first, Master Juro began to speak.

"This sphere is for my protection. The Essence is so prevalent here I would be quickly in over-abundance. I can use this sphere to prevent any more coming in contact with me, but the shield itself is made of Essence. I am limited to how long I can remain here. You, however, do not have the same disadvantage."

This is why I asked you to remove your crystal; you have no need of it here and I don't want to risk you receiving excessive amounts. Now, I want you to close your eyes."

He waited a moment, "Can you feel it?"

Steadying herself to compensate for the boats angle, she reached her hands out, but with disappointment she conceded that she felt nothing there. She opened her eyes expecting to see a disheartened look from Master Juro so she was surprised to see that the corner of his mouth twitch and he had a twinkle in his eye.

Master Juro, in his protective bubble, followed as the boat continued to glide, it's momentum slowing as the waterway leveled out and finally coming to rest against the shore. At first Hanna thought the beach was covered with a strange, but pretty colour of sand. On closer inspection she could tell it was more like a bank made of salt with smaller splinters of crystals lining it.

"Hanna, if you will, please pull the boat on shore a short ways."

Hanna got out of the boat and eased it onto the bank. She caught herself after she nearly fell as the shore proved to be slippery.

"While you are here you may explore a little, but I suggest not wandering too far. When you are ready, find a place where you can contemplate. See the Essence in the air and then try to feel it, and then try to move it. Don't worry if nothing happens, it would be miraculous if it did."

"Okay wait, what do you mean and aren't you staying?" Hanna asked a little nervously.

"I should explain to you that few people have ever come to this valley; in fact, most have never even heard of it. I trust you will help me keep it that way."

Hanna realized that statement was more of a request than a suggestion.

"I brought you here for...understanding. I will not be staying. It is not wise for me to linger here so I will go back down the canal a safe distance. I will leave you the boat; you can join me when it is time."

As Master Juro began to float away, Hanna called after him "and how will I know when it's time?"

He continued to drift off, heading back up the waterway.

"You'll know," he called.

"Cryptic guy," Hanna said to herself.

With little other choice, she began to explore for a little bit. The first crystal she came to was almost the same height as she was. She ran her hand over its surface. Although the flat surfaces were smooth and cool it felt more like a polished rock than the glass it resembled. She noticed there were smaller spires only a few inches high in amongst the taller ones. Navigating around the crystals proved difficult, as they tended to crisscross each other at varying angles. She made her way deeper into this odd crystal forest, ducking and twisting as she went. The crystals became wider and taller. When she reached one where the base was as wide as a bus was long she had to lean back to see the top, which was at least six-storey's high. Approaching the valley by boat, she had seen that further in there would be crystals twice as high as the one in front of her, but she realized they would be harder and harder to get to since they were closer together and the taller they were the longer it took to circumvent.

She began to head back in the direction she had come and was surprised to discover she was deep enough in not to be able to see the boat. As panic started to creep in she carefully, but quickly made her way until, with much relief, she could see the shore where she had landed. Now that she was confident she hadn't become turned around, she searched for a place where she might sit and be comfortable before trying to see and feel the Essence.

She picked a spot against a pillar wide enough for her to lean against without sharp crystal fragments that seemed to cover much of the ground. The angle of the tall, flat crystal did prove to be somewhat comfy, but it wouldn't be long before the hard unyielding stone-like surface would start to become less than desirable.

Once settled, she began the task at hand. It took only a moment for her to see the Essence in the air. One instant there was nothing and then, like when light shines through the dust in the air, she could see it. It was just a matter of changing her perception. It was denser here than anywhere she had been. Instead of floating dust particles it was more like steam. When she reached her hand out she could see it move around it, similar to how smoke would wrap around an object. She knew she hadn't moved it herself; it was more that she could perceive it moving. Using both hands she tried pushing the substance together. At first it just swirled around, but after a few minutes she managed to get it spiraling in a funnel cloud type shape; thickening as it did. Once enough had gathered she reached out to touch it and was surprised that it had more substance. It reminded her of cotton candy, but just as she tried to grab it, it once again became like smoke. After another twenty minutes of playing with it she hadn't come any closer to grasping it so she decided it was time to find Master Juro.

She made her way back to the boat and using the oars, rowed back up the canal. Master Juro was sitting beneath a tree just beyond the bend. Whether or not he heard her arrive, Hanna was unaware, as he didn't move so she slowed down to a stop, got out and once again pulled the boat to shore. It proved to be a bit more difficult this time, but at least on the grassy hill she felt much steadier on her feet. Before she moved away from the boat Master Juro spoke up.

"I think this will be a fine spot for our picnic if you will be so kind as to bring the basket?"

Hanna grabbed the basket and made her way to sit with Master Juro. When she was seated, but before she began emptying the contents of the basket, he opened his eyes and reached out to hold her hands.

"Tell me what you saw and of your experience."

Hanna explained how she felt the crystals, how they changed in size as she walked further in and how they got closer together. He looked eager as she explained and she realized he had never wandered that far; this was an experience unique to her. When she told him about how the Essence looked and felt, his eyes widened slightly, but otherwise his expression was unchanged. When she was finished, he released her hands and sat back.

"First let me say that you have absorbed enough Essence to last you the duration of the day, but I will return your crystal before we reach Kokoroe; by that point it won't do you any harm. Now, I want to explain something to you."

"If I were to bring a Jivan or Jagare to the valley, they would be able to see the Essence in the crystal spires. However, they would still not be able to see it in the air; it would be like trying to see the wind. If I were to ask them to move the Essence, it would be like asking them to catch the wind. For a young Juro it would be like grasping steam or smoke as you have said. For an advanced Juro, it's more like wool, but stretched very thin which is what I assume this cotton candy you refer to is." He paused. "What you managed to accomplish is somewhere in between a student and a Leader. To make you understand this more clearly let me explain. A Juro is a student for many years; they don't reach the level of a Leader for at least a century. What you have experienced in moments usually takes any Juro fifty years to behold."

His usual stoic manner shifted into one of amusement.

Hanna was still a little puzzled. Clearly she had another gift of the Juro and obviously at a much-accelerated rate, but she had no idea what the relevance of it was. And why did Master Juro find this so amusing. Instead of feeling reassured by his manner it made her nervous.

230

She asked, "So, what does this mean?"

"It means it is time to begin your Juro training."

Hanna replied, "I thought I was already doing Juro training."

Master Juro answered, "No, your current training is what the Juro did. Now you will learn what it is we do. What we did was learn how to survive; what we do now is study."

Hanna was still puzzled and was tiring of his riddles. She wanted answers and plain speech.

"I still don't think I understand" she said exasperated.

He tapped her on the knee. "You will, you will. For now let us eat!"

CHAPTER SEVENTEEN

Observation and Perception

The silence was broken.

Nandin woke to the sound of persistent knocking. He leaped out of bed and opened the door to find Hatooin waiting.

"Good morning sir. Master Mateo wishes to see you. I will wait for you to make yourself presentable and then lead you to him."

He turned and stood against the wall in the hallway. Closing the door again, Nandin quickly made his way to his sink where he splashed water on his face and gave his mouth a quick rinse to get rid of the taste that was thick in his mouth. He ran his wet hands through his dusty coloured hair and patted it down to stop it from sticking up. With haste he stripped and donned the grey training attire. He returned to the door and found Hatooin as he had left him.

Hatooin took him to the lift and they rode it down several floors. As they passed each door Nandin noted the numbers that were painted on each one. When they reached the door labelled four, Hatooin rang the bell. Nandin stiffened and his throat became dry as he walked into the lab where he had his treatment. He had to resist the urge to run. It's not like he regretted the treatment he had undergone, but he had no desire to repeat it. Hatooin noticed Nandin's discomfort.

"No need to fret sir, we won't be giving you any more injections."

Nandin relaxed a little at hearing this, but he still felt uneasy. The room was very much how he remembered it, full of glass jars of various sizes, plants and herbs, books and scrolls that dominated the shelves and tables. Mateo sat behind the desk in the corner hastily jotting down notes. He looked up as Hatooin and Nandin approached. He greeted Nandin with enthusiasm as he pushed his chair back and rose to meet him. He placed his hand on his shoulder.

"Nandin, good to see you, come let us sit."

He guided him over to the two chairs flanking the unlit fireplace and gestured to take a seat.

"Thank you Hatooin that will be all."

Hatooin bowed and exited the room. Mateo studied Nandin a moment as he took a seat in the other chair.

"How did the hunt go?" Mateo asked.

Nandin replied, "We managed to bring back enough game to last a while I think."

Mateo folded his hands together and said. "No, I mean how did the hunt go for you?"

Nandin shrugged. "I caught a few rabbits, nothing major. Truth to tell, I don't think hunting is my thing."

"Why do you suppose that is?"

"I guess I'm a little impatient. I get bored just waiting in the bushes. I'm also not fond of gutting the animals. Not that I'm sentimental or anything, I just don't like dealing with the blood and guts, it makes me a little queasy."

Mateo leaned his chin on his hand while he contemplated what Nandin had just said. Nandin didn't know if his honesty had disappointed Mateo and he wondered if he should have been a little less forthright.

After a few minutes Mateo spoke again.

"You are a man of action and I understand your impatience. I never was one for hunting either; however, patience will be imperative in your role as Yaru. I will send you on a few more expeditions, but I'm not concerned about your ability to butcher animals – you can leave that task to others. I want you to pay attention, learn to track, be stealthy. I know you possess skills with the bow and arrow so your ability in that area is not an issue. Once you have the stalking part down, you will be able to kill your prey without a problem. The next time you go out, concentrate on your surroundings. Be aware of the plants you see, the birds in the air or anything potentially out of place. Although you may need this skill more when you are among people, keep in mind there is a lot of wilderness between any given town or city."

There was a faint knock on the door.

"Enter." Mateo said.

Hatooin came in carrying a tray full of food. He placed it on a small table between Mateo and Nandin. He bowed and then left the room. Mateo poured hot tea into two mugs.

He grabbed a piece of cheese and popped it into his mouth.

"Help yourself," he said.

Nandin reached over and selected a warm biscuit and cheese. He picked up one of two bowls of porridge and ate it hastily. After a few more helpings of various fruits he grasped his tea mug and sat back.

"Today," Mateo began, "I have a few simple tests for you, nothing harmful I promise. I just want to test the absorption level of the Essence. Based on your skills, it is clear the treatments were successful."

Mateo put down his empty mug.

"Whenever you're ready."

Nandin indicated he was ready and Mateo stood and led him across the room.

"Please stand with your back against the wall. Let's see how tall you are now."

He made a mark, and then flipped through a book that was on a nearby table. Nandin watched him make some notes and then he looked up.

"Nandin you've grown more than I would have guessed! Look here."

He pointed to the markings on the wall.

"You were here before the treatment and now you're a hand-span taller. I think that's the biggest growth I've recorded!"

Nandin was surprised.

"I didn't even notice I was taller. I guess I didn't have clothes or anything to compare to, but it's weird I wasn't able to tell."

Mateo waved the comment away.

"Not really. Your whole environment is new and the people around you have also undergone some growth. The discomfort you felt during your recovery was related to this increase in height, but all the stretches and exercises you did helped you get accustomed to your taller stature. "

Nandin conceded the point. Mateo took him across the lab and into another room. A large window expanded across one wall which let in enough light for the whole area. There was a sizeable table in the centre of the room with two chairs, one on either side. The table was topped with a large box, a variety of plants and two smaller boxes. Mateo walked around to one side and sat in a chair motioning for Nandin to sit in the other.

"Take a look at these plants," Mateo said. "Obviously they are all different species, but there is more to them than that. Take a moment and then tell me if you can tell what it is."

Nandin observed the specimens in front of him. One was common to the forest floor and had green heart shaped leaves. There didn't seem to be anything particularly unique about it so he turned his attention to the next. It was a type of vine and had wrapped itself around several sticks that had been placed in the pot. The leaves were small, delicate green and purple; this plant was also common where he grew up. Nandin had never seen the following plant. It had large curled leaves that were pointy at its tips. What made it unique were the additional round spiky bulbs which were lime -coloured. The last plant had long thick, green leaves with tiny little barbs along its length. Nandin remembered his mother using the jelly like substance contained within this type of plant to treat his minor cuts and scrapes when he was a boy.

Nandin didn't know what he was looking for. He wasn't sure if it was supposed to be something he saw or something he surmised.

"Am I supposed to see something or try to figure something out?"

Mateo sagged a little. "So you don't see anything in particular?"

"No," he said.

"Very well, what can you deduce?"

Nandin thought for moment then said, "I would say that each of these plants contains a different amount of Essence."

Mateo brightened a little.

"What makes you say that?"

"It just seems to make sense." Nandin replied.

"Try to put them in the order of the least Essence to the most." Mateo sat back to watch.

Nandin shuffled them around until the order of the plants were: vine, heart shaped, spiky bulbs, then what he thought of as the jelly plant. He looked up to see Mateo smiling at him.

"You are correct. Tell me, how did you come to this conclusion?"

Nandin reached out to the vine and grasped the delicate leaves.

"Well this plant is so thin, even the stems are tiny, they can hardly contain much Essence in addition to all the other nutrients."

Then he reached for the last plant.

"This one contains a thick substance which works well to heal cuts and open wounds so my guess is that it contains much more Essence. I'm assuming that since this plant," he indicated the next one over, "which has a few spiky bulbs on it, would contain slightly less than the one with the thick leaves; if my guess is right, I would say the bulbs are also full of Essence. So that leaves just the heart-shaped plant."

"Well done. You've taught me something." Mateo admitted.

Nandin was taken caught off guard. He never thought he could teach Mateo anything and if he did he never thought Mateo would be the type to confess it.

"When I look at these plants, I see the Essence," Mateo said. "I can tell you which one has more simply by looking at which has the most intense aura around it. I never bothered to try to see it any other way. Let's move onto the next test."

Mateo slid his chair down the table until he was in front of the two small boxes. Nandin followed his example until he was across from Mateo. The boxes were each the size of a loaf of bread. They were a wooden construction with no apparent opening. Mateo turned the boxes around and Nandin saw a hole at the end of each box with some sort of material sealing it.

"Place your hands into the boxes."

Nandin slid one hand into each box. The fabric was tight and stretchy, but also cool and rubbery. With his hands completely immersed in the boxes he looked up at Mateo expectantly.

Mateo said, "One box contains Essence in its gas form the other contains a different gas. Can you feel the difference? Can you tell which is which?"

Nandin thought the pressure inside the boxes felt a little different than the room, but it was the same sensation to both his hands. He wiggled his fingers on one hand and then the other. Then he kept them perfectly still, palm up. He began to wonder if there really was anything in the boxes to begin with or if Mateo was just playing mind tricks on him. Finally he gave up.

"They feel the same to me." Nandin said.

"Remove your hands," Mateo said.

Mateo stood up and carried the small boxes over to the larger box at the other end of the table. He returned to Nandin with a small polished, wooden box with carvings. Placing it on the table, he opened it away from Nandin to conceal its' contents. When he closed the hinged lid, Mateo placed two plum-sized items in front of Nandin. The objects were wrapped in cloth and were roughly the same size and shape.

"Underneath the wrappings are crystals. One is full of Essence; the other is completely void of it. Hold one at a time and cup both hands around it with just enough pressure so you can feel the crystal with each hand."

Nandin gently grasped the crystal with the light tan wrappings and held onto it firmly. After a minute Mateo indicated he could switch so he grabbed the crystal wrapped in navy blue. After another minute he returned it to the table.

"So, which one has the Essence."

Nandin tapped the table in front of the crystal wrapped in blue.

"This one," he said.

Mateo said, "Open them."

Nandin carefully removed the cloth from both crystals to reveal that a bright pink one wrapped in the blue and a clear one in tan. He was pleased with himself.

Mateo squinted his eyes as if trying to read Nandin's mind.

"How did you figure it out? Could you feel it?"

Nandin replied, "No, I guessed. I thought that since the tan fabric was such a light colour perhaps you could see through it a bit if the light was right so it would make sense to put a coloured crystal in the darker fabric."

Mateo slapped the table.

"Ha! I like the way you think Nandin. You apparently don't have the Juro ability, but you are clever. You notice things using different skills than I do. The Juro are even more arrogant than I am with their use of their perception of Essence; you may be able to outsmart them without even having the ability to see or feel the Essence."

Nandin was intrigued as to what circumstance would lead him to try and outsmart a Juro, but thought this wasn't the time to ask. Instead, he chose to ask something that had been on his mind for a while.

"Master Mateo, remember back in the clearing when you made your offer to turn us into Yaru?"

Mateo nodded.

"How did you know?"

"Know what?" Mateo inquired.

Nandin struggled to recall the words. "You said we were unique and that we had something that was key to making us Yaru. What was it?"

Mateo was intrigued. It seemed Nandin had a knack for picking up little details. "It's rather interesting," Mateo replied. He pulled back Nandin's sleeve and pointed. "You see that?"

"My mole?" Nandin asked

"Yes. All potentials have moles – the more they have the better the treatment works."

"But," Nandin started, "how did you know that I had moles?"

"Well, it's not just moles. Freckles are also a sign. So we look for men with freckles, check that they have moles and study the kind of person they are before we ask them to join."

A look of concern furrowed Nandin's brow. Before he asked his next question Mateo continued.

"Yes, Nandin, we observed you. It wasn't mere coincidence that brought you here. You were special. You were chosen. But you had to make the choice to come here; all I could do was show you the way."

Mateo waited to see how Nandin would react. At first Nandin was a little uncomfortable with the idea that someone, Nean presumably, had been watching him. Then he realized that they had watched him and still, they chose him. The moles and freckles may have made him a candidate, but it was what they saw in him that got him the invite and that, he realized, made all the difference. He smiled and nodded his head. Mateo acknowledged that Nandin wasn't just showing his understanding but his acceptance of what had occurred.

Mateo came to a decision. "I'd like you to do me a favour. The men look up to you Nandin. You are great for morale around here. I want you to report to me every day, let me know how things are going. I value your perspective."

Nandin bowed his head slightly. He felt pride at being noticed and appreciated. He knew the men would be glad to hear that they had the ability to communicate their issues with Mateo without approaching him themselves – many of them still felt intimidated by him.

CHAPTER EIGHTEEN

Operations and Designations

Nandin became skilled at stalking.

Over the next few weeks all the Junior Yaru took turns learning how to hunt. They didn't always catch game, but often just practiced following animals, trying to see how close they could get before the creatures were alerted to their presence. Nandin found this challenge much more to his liking rather than the actual killing and dressing of an animal.

In addition to tracking, they also practiced running through the brush at top speed which required them to jump over bramble and logs, even partially climb trees and then jump to the next one to get past spots too thick with underbrush to navigate. It was slow going at first, but they learned to apply some of the climbing skills they had learned in the gym to good effect. To help them climb the trees, they wore barbed straps around their hands and spikes in the tips of their shoes. These enabled them to latch onto a tree without slipping off.

A particularly tricky exercise they worked on was scaling the walls. One method they learned used only the metal objects they threw at the walls for hand and foot holds. The first trick they had to get the hang of was how to throw the metal objects so they would actually sink into the wall and not just bounce off it. Once they were able to do that, they had to determine where the best place to throw them was; too far apart and you wouldn't be able to reach them, too close together and you didn't move much and wasted one of your hand holds. Nandin was fascinated when he watched the Yaru leaders throw them perfectly at the same time as another Yaru used them to climb. Their precision was impressive. Nandin knew he would practice a lot before even attempting that trick, as the thin triangular objects were sharp enough to sever a finger or even a hand if his aim was off. Another challenge with these items is that they only worked on certain structures. If the surface was too hard they would bounce off it and it would leave the metal dented so they used them strictly on wooden walls.

Another method they used to climb the walls was a grappling hook, which was a long rope with four claw-like barbs on the end. They would toss it over a wall and when it was securely in place, they would climb up it. They even practiced climbing walls that were too high to throw the hook over by climbing on each other's shoulders until the top man was high enough to throw the grappling hook.

In addition to all the training outside the castle, they also spent time with the Kameil community. Nandin particularly liked Feast day, the last day of the week where everyone gathered for a dinner and festivities. The people in the main city would get together in the open courtyard by the main wall. Mateo held his banquet in the main dining hall of the keep. He would invite all the Kameil that worked in the keep along with their families. In addition, he invited several of the Kameil families who were new to the city to join them as a way to get better acquainted. It reminded Nandin of back home. He noticed most the men felt the same way and it really helped them come to terms with the new direction their lives had taken. Nothing could make a greater impact for Mateo's cause than being part of this new community made up of a people who had been abandoned by the rest of the world.

It was early in the morning on their day off when Jon knocked on Nandin's door. Nandin groaned as he answered it.

"Ah Jon, it's my one day to sleep in, why are you dragging me out of bed?"

Jon was dressed and looked eager to start his day. "Come on Nandin, I want your help."

Nandin didn't budge. "With what, may I ask?"

Jon pushed his way into the room and went to Nandin's wardrobe. He pulled out the leather hunting gear that hung inside.

"I want to get a buck for tonight's feast."

Nandin waved to him as he stumbled back to bed.

"Well good luck with that."

Seeing that he was getting nowhere, Jon disappeared into the washing room. By the time he returned Nandin was lying back on his bed drifting off to sleep. Jon smirked, then preceded to dump a bucket of cold water over Nandin's head. Nandin yelped and jumped up.

"FOR CRYING OUT LOUD WHAT WAS THAT FOR?!" Nandin screamed.

"You're coming with me. Hurry up."

Jon threw a towel at him. Nandin knew there was no way to get back to sleep now; even if he could, his bed was soaked. Grudgingly he pulled off his wet clothes and replaced them with his hunter's garb.

"Why me?" he grumbled. "There are lots of people around here who are better hunters than I am and more to the point, there are some who even like it."

Jon shrugged. "I like your company. Besides, you could use the practice."

Nandin knew he was right. Maybe, he thought, if he put more effort in today he wouldn't have to do it anymore. When he finished getting ready, they headed to the lift and then off to the stables to get their horses.

"See," Jon said, "I'm not completely unreasonable. I've already gotten our gear and tacked the horses. I've been up for a few hours."

Nandin made note of the still emerging daylight and shook his head.

"You're really ambitious today aren't you?"

"This is the best time of day to go! Trust me."

Nandin rolled his eyes, but there was no point in complaining any further. Instead he turned his attention to more pressing concerns.

"I know this might put a damper on your plan, but don't you think we should eat before we head out?"

Jon tapped the side of his head with his finger. "Nope, I thought of that. I packed us some food. I even have some fresh bread from the kitchen – it was just coming out of the oven."

Nandin gave him a crooked smile. "That's great. Can we eat it?"

Jon chuckled. "Of course not, we need to get going. We'll have something when we get settled."

"Right, of course, what was I thinking?"

Nandin felt that this was the worst part of hunting. He'd rather be in bed than up at the crack of dawn to go creeping throughout the woods on an empty stomach. Remembering his plan to put in more effort today, he followed Jon's lead.

Later that afternoon Nandin and Jon arrived back at the castle grounds. They rode around to the kitchen to unload the buck that they had brought back. A few of the kitchen aids came out to help bring it in.

"He's a beauty Jon!" said one of the young men.

Jon nodded toward Nandin. "You can thank my good friend Nandin. He brought this big fellow down with one clean shot."

With his new determination to be focused, Nandin discovered he wasn't bad at this hunting venture. He had to admit he had enjoyed the time he spent with Jon even though for most of it they were communicating silently.

"Ah, gee, thanks Jon but I couldn't have done it without your great coaching skills."

Although Nandin had said it sarcastically he actually meant every word. Jon was the one who had first spotted the tracks and had also prevented Nandin from stepping on a twig, which would have certainly frightened the animal away.

Jon gave him a friendly cuff to the side of the head. "Come on, let's go get cleaned up. How are you going to impress any girls when you're all covered in blood?"

Nandin cringed. He hated having blood on him to begin with, but he sure didn't want to engage in conversation with any of the local ladies in this condition.

They quickly made their way back to the keep and up to their floor. Before they went into their respective rooms, Nandin turned to Jon.

"Thanks for today Jon, it wasn't so bad."

Jon winked and then disappeared into his room.

After Nandin had washed up he settled in for a quick nap before the evening meal. He woke a short time later feeling surprisingly refreshed. He finished getting dressed, knocked on Jon's door, but no one answered. He smiled to himself – no doubt Jon was already helping set up the tables while flirting with one of the local girls. Nandin knew he had his eye on Sarah but Jon would never admit it.

Everyone was gathering in the dining hall preparing for the evening meal. It was always such a jovial atmosphere with someone playing music and almost everyone singing as they set up extra tables and chairs and laid out the food they had brought to share. Hatooin took on the role of organizing everyone, but it was such a common affair his advice was hardly needed. Most people just patiently listened to his instructions and then went on about their business. Mateo usually made his entrance once everything was set up. He would engage in conversation or watch those who took up dancing, but Nandin thought he always looked somewhat apart – like his mind was somewhere else. During the evening's meal Jon made a toast in Nandin's honour for his successful hunt of the day. Nandin laughed as the Junior Yaru banged the table yelling "speech, speech" which was soon joined by everyone in attendance.

Finally Nandin stood and waved to everyone.

"Thank you, thank you. Yes, as poor as my hunting skills have proven to be, it is with much luck I provide you with such wonderful fare tonight..."

The Yaru hollered "you're too modest" and "hardly luck."

"Fortunately," he continued, "Jon was at my side if I should mess things up. My compliments to the cooks who turned a slab of meat into this delectable feast and cheers to all of you, my fellow companions whose company I have the honour of enjoying."

He bowed, then raised his goblet of wine and drank.

His speech was met with whoops and hollers and the musicians struck up another tune. Jon asked Sarah to dance; she gladly took his hand as he swung her around the hall. One of her friends approached Nandin and boldly grabbed his arm. He almost spilled his refilled goblet of ale as he stumbled to his feet to join in the dancing.

When things started to settle down, Mateo approached Nandin and subtly pulled him aside.

"Well done today son. I wonder if it was my advice or Jon's that brought you good fortune this day."

He tilted his head to look at him.

Nandin laughed, "A little of both I think. As determined as I was to heed your advice, Jon was the one who kept me from screwing it up." Mateo also chuckled at that.

"I do enjoy your candour. I hear Jon is quite the skilled hunter."

"He is," Nandin said. "I think even Plyral would have to agree that Jon's the best. He also really enjoys it; I'd wager he'd go out every day if he could."

"What about the other exercises, how does he fare with them?" Mateo asked.

"He's pretty good at them, but I think for the most part his heart just isn't in it. Even though he has the ability of a Yaru it seems he's still very much Jagare in spirit."

Mateo nodded. "I have had the same sense. Currently we've been relying on the outlying farms for most of our food. We haven't had a Huntmaster for some time...now that I have found a remedy that allows the Kameil to venture away from the Essence source they could learn to hunt. The Huntmaster would be responsible to teach them – do you think he'd be up for the job?"

Nandin nodded enthusiastically.

"Absolutely. I think you couldn't find a better fit."

Mateo squeezed Nandin's shoulder.

"Then I will make it so. I have another job opening...how would you feel about being my first commander?"

"Me?" Nandin asked. Mateo nodded his head.

"What about Nean or Mayon or any of the other senior Yaru? Wouldn't they be better qualified? I mean they've been around longer."

"They've already been given their roles. As my captains, they will be reorganizing the Yaru based on their skills as well as adding some of the Kameil men to their teams. I need you to be my intermediary, someone who is a link between the captains and myself. They won't always be inside these walls and I will need to get messages to them when they aren't here. Also, what they will be privy to concerns only their mission. But someone needs to know the overall plan; I want you to be that person. Besides," he smiled, "they recommended you."

As an afterthought he added, "Although, I would have asked you anyway."

Nandin wasn't sure what to say so he simply said, "I'm honoured sir."

Mateo asked, "Is that a yes?"

Nandin bowed. "Yes. Yes, I am at your service. When would you like me to begin?"

"Nandin, you already have."

Nandin gave him a quizzical look. Mateo just turned away and over his shoulder he said, "Tomorrow we will go over my plan and the missions."

CHAPTER NINETEEN

Divide and Conquer

Hanna was unable to relax.

The rest of the day, with Master Juro, had been uneventful. When they finished their lunch, they headed back to Kokoroe. Since arriving a few hours before the evening meal, Hanna took the opportunity to have a private bath and reflect on the day's events. She joined Kazi and her other classmates at dinner time with some hesitation as she hadn't figured out what she would tell them. She hoped she could be vague and they would be content with that, but sometimes Kazi could ask a lot of questions.

Avoiding talking about the details of her day turned out to be easier than she anticipated. They spent most the meal talking about their history class; Celine had made it her personal duty to fill Hanna in on all the details of the day's lessons. Compared to Hanna's day, the lesson on the lifestyle of the Juro who occupied the cave – women and children who never ventured out and the men who took on the role of hunting, seemed rather boring. Of course, Tahtay Jillian's delivery would have been far more engaging than Celine's prattling, but Hanna was glad to hear it nevertheless. As intrigued as she was to spend the day with Master Juro, part of her regretted missing out on her regular studies. Having heard what the day entailed, she was relieved that nothing particularly exciting had occurred. Even the fitness class was somewhat subdued after their action-packed adventures the day before. They had just spent more time in the field exercising and working on endurance. It did sound like they played some fun games as they ran around, but nothing topped her adventure to Crystal Valley.

Before they left the long hall for the night, Kazi finally got the chance to ask Hanna about her day. She simply replied that she spent the day with Master Juro who was trying to figure out what to do with her. Next week they would be splitting into additional lessons aimed at teaching the talents of each race. Kazi was a little disappointed at first when Hanna said she would be training with the Juro, but then realized that they could meet at the end of each day to share what they had learned. Hanna hadn't given it much thought, but Kazi was so enthusiastic about discovering what the Juro were taught that she too was anxious for the lessons to begin.

The next few days' history classes were spent studying the ancient symbols and learning how they had changed over time to make up the current writing system. Hanna was grateful for this approach because looking at their existing writing was very confusing; it just looked like random squiggles that would take a long time to memorize. Once she could see what the original picture looked like, it made much more sense. They practised making the simple drawings first and then when they did the "short hand" version it was much easier to remember.

Physical training included learning some team exercises and reminded Hanna of the gym classes she had had back home with the exception that they still did the warm up with the whole student body and everything took place outside. The weekend was spent doing their assigned chores and some much appreciated down time. The start of the next week, they were given their new schedule consisting of a morning divided between Tahtay Biatach's fitness class and Tahtay Jillian's history which was to become much more reading and writing based. The afternoons were when the students were separated. The Jagare would continue additional training with Tahtay

JOURNEY TO KOKOROE

Biatach in the areas of hunting, the Juro would receive instruction from Tahtay Sohil and Tahtay Etai and the Jivan would rotate throughout the school and therefore would have several instructors teaching them more life skills passed on by the Juro.

Hanna wondered why they were being split into their races especially since the school was supposedly based on the Juro. As they made their way to the morning meal she asked Kazi about it.

"Kazi, I don't get it. If this school is based on Juro knowledge why is everyone splitting up? I mean why would the Jagare learn to hunt at a Juro school?"

Kazi said, "I asked my dad the same question when he told me about the three schools. As you know, before the races came together they each had to survive independently which means the Juro had to learn how to hunt and raise their young and cook. Right?" Hanna nodded.

"Now these may not have been their strengths, but they had to learn a trick or two to survive. So at Kokoroe they pass on that knowledge which the other races can add to what they already know works. For example, the Jagare were great hunters. Being big and fast reflected the way they hunted. A Juro couldn't attack a Beast with a sword or staff; they'd be crushed, so they had to find a different way such as laying traps; likewise with the Jivan. The Jivan grew gardens and farmed, but the Juro didn't. They ate only what they caught and what was provided so they know which wild plants are edible and which are poisonous. Their skills in laying traps will be passed onto the Jagare and learning about which wild plants are safe to eat is what I'll be learning."

Hanna said, "I kind of like that. It's as if everyone is saying, 'even though you might not be the best at this we accept that what you know still matters.' I wonder what they'll teach me."

Kazi's eyes lit up.

251

"Me too. It always seemed so mysterious to me. Leader Chieo wasn't exactly into sharing and he's the only Juro I've spent any time with. All I know is that they spend years here. I think at some point they go to the other schools, but they always come back here and study until they become Leaders and that takes years."

Hanna nodded as she recalled what Master Juro said about taking a century to become a Leader.

When the afternoon finally arrived, Hanna joined the other Juro students outside the school. Tahtay Sohil, their Juro instructor, met them there and led them to a different room in the school. This room consisted only of cushions on the floor. There were no pictures on the walls, no plants and no desks. The cushions were arranged in a wide circle; a little more than an arm span apart. Tahtay Sohil walked to the centre and placed a dark wooden chest he had been carrying on the floor and then kneeled in front of it. The chest had ornate carvings on it; very reminiscent of the first ornately carved box she'd seen so long ago. Hanna noticed it had an interesting locking mechanism.

"Please be seated," he said.

Tahtay Sohil was the same height as the other Juro, measuring just a little over three feet tall. His long jet-black hair was tied loosely behind his back. His facial hair, which just reached his chest, was also black and was tied in the middle and bottom in a similar fashion as Master Juro's, creating a skinny pencil like beard. He wore a navy blue robe with a pearl white sash, the standard apparel the teachers wore.

The only student in the room Hanna knew was Chie as she was in her other classes. She had seen many of the others in the living quarters, the bathhouse or in the long hall, but had not spoken to any, save for a word in passing. Chie had explained to her over lunch that their class would be made up of many levels or ages of Juro. Hanna was glad she had prepared her somewhat or she would have thought she was in the wrong group. Most of the students in the room looked to be similar in age; Hanna found it difficult to tell how old any Juro was – for all she knew, the Juro sitting on her left could be fifty years old. She hoped not. She felt intimidated enough as it was to be included with this group; it would be easier if they were all awkward beginners like she was.

When they were all seated, Tahtay Sohil opened the chest and removed several small cloth bundles. He handed some to one student who had joined him in the centre and together they distributed the bundles. His helper then sat on the empty cushion on the perimeter of the circle.

Softly Tahtay Sohil spoke; "As you may have noticed we have two new students joining us today. Chie," Chie gave a slight bow, "and Hanna."

Hanna copied Chie's bow. He quickly introduced the other six students in the room.

"For their benefit I will explain the exercise. Place your bundle on the floor and unwrap it."

Hanna pulled back the fabric to reveal a pink crystal the size of a grape. She looked around and saw that everyone had a crystal, but all were various sizes. Only Chie had a crystal the same size as Hanna's.

Continuing in his quiet voice, he looked at Hanna and Chie and spoke. "At first you will place the crystal in your left hand. Start with a closed fist and feel the Essence. Let it warm your hand. Open your hand and hold onto that feeling."

He waited until they did this. Although the other students had obviously done this before they followed the instructions as well.

"Now hold your right hand above the crystal, keep it close for now but don't touch it. Try to feel the Essence with this hand. When you feel it, try to push the crystal to your fingertips with the right hand. What you want to do is push against the Essence not the crystal itself."

Hanna could see movement out of the corner of her eye and knew that the other students were already skilled at this task. Hanna could feel the stone with her left hand and she could feel its Essence, but with her right hand she felt nothing. Regardless of being able to feel it she tried to move the stone. Unsurprisingly, nothing happened.

Sohil watched her for a while then clapped his hands softly once.

"Okay," he said, "disperse."

Aside from Hanna and Chie everyone stood up, grabbed their cushion, crystal and wrappings and moved to random locations throughout the room. Tahtay Sohil approached Hanna and Chie and sat in front of them.

"Every student is at their own level," he told them, "they each have their own task known only to me. Manipulating the Essence is an art form and cannot be rushed or mastered by sheer will. It is unimportant what your neighbor is doing as it does not help you to reach your goal. The reason I had everyone do the first exercise together was not to make either of you feel incompetent but to show you two things. The first is that the task I gave you is possible – I know both of you noticed the other students moving their crystals. The second lesson was to demonstrate that you cannot be successful at the task before you if your mind is not focused and dedicated to that task. You must learn to block out everything around you when you are working with the Essence. Your attention must be on what's right in front of you. There will be times and places for you to perceive more, but not here and not now. Concentrate. Focus. I would like you two to turn back to back. Forget the others in the room – they are concentrating on their own task. I will be monitoring everyone at different times or I will be concentrating on my own task. At any time, on any day, if you have success at your given task, repeat it or try to do more. I will approach you and give you advice when needed or new challenges if required. Hold any questions or comments until that time or when class has been dismissed so that you do not break someone else's concentration, for that is a skill that everyone in this room is trying to master."

"Before you begin again, do you have any questions?"

Hanna wished she could come up with some question that would help her with the task, but nothing came to her so she just shook her head.

"Begin," he said.

Hanna tried again. Nothing happened. Over and over she tried and with each failure her frustration level rose. She wanted to chuck the crystal across the room. What was she doing here? She wasn't a Juro. She could feel the tears beginning to well up in her eyes and that made her even more frustrated. She stared at the crystal with pursed lips wishing the class would just end.

She gave a slight jump when Tahtay Sohil placed his hand on her shoulder. He proceeded to sit down in front of her; with legs crossed they sat knee to knee.

He leaned in and whispered, "That's good, you are concentrating on your task so well you didn't notice my approach."

Hanna tried to return his smile, but she was working too hard to prevent tears from falling; all she managed was a slight upturn of one side of her mouth.

He cupped his hands over both of Hanna's.

"Close your eyes."

As he said this he closed his eyes so Hanna did too.

"Breathe deeply through your nose and out your mouth, gently. Good. Again. Now release the tension in your shoulders every time you exhale. Feel the crystal that you wear, feel the Essence as it flows into your chest. Feel it move within you. Breathe. Remember your journey to the valley."

Hanna was somewhat surprised at Tahtay Sohil mentioning this, but was focusing on his words too much to give it any further thought.

"Remember how it felt as you ran your hands through the air. Feel the Essence."

Hanna remembered the cotton candy texture. She felt Tahtay Sohil remove his hands from hers.

"Feel the Essence and slowly move it to your fingertips. Excellent. Now move it back. And again. Continue and open your eyes."

When Hanna opened her eyes she was a little startled to see the crystal moving up and down her hand, but the Essence felt so tangible to her it seemed to only make sense that she could move it. It was almost like pulling a yo-yo on a string. She could pull it back and forth and like a yo-yo she thought she should be able to pull it up. As she did the crystal lifted ever so slightly off her hand. She pinched her fingers closer trying to grab the invisible string and managed to get it about an inch off her hand before her "thread" broke and it landed back in her palm. It wasn't until that happened that she realized what she had just done. She looked incredulously at the crystal and then up at Tahtay Sohil to see if what she just thought happened actually did.

"Again" he said enthusiastically.

He got up and walked around the room to observe the other students. Hanna was thrilled. She spent the remainder of the afternoon making her crystal roll and hop up and down her hand. She couldn't wait to tell Kazi.

* * *

Hanna spent every afternoon of the week moving crystals. Every day she was given a crystal slightly bigger. By the end of the week her crystal was the size of an apricot. Each day she was given a different task, each one a bit more difficult. She no longer held the crystal; instead it was to be placed on its wrappings, on the floor. The fabric had patterns that she would trace with the crystal or move it from one pattern to another by rolling it or sometimes hopping the crystal. The larger the crystal, the heavier it proved to be and therefore took a great deal more effort to move, but after the success of the first day she had the patience to work on it until she achieved her goal, even if it took her all class.

Keeping in mind what Tahtay Sohil had said about no one in the class knowing what anyone else was working on, Hanna made sure not to give Kazi the details of what she was doing even though she really wanted to. She was just itching to tell someone about her successes, small though they might be, but she understood the need for restraint. When she first saw that everyone else could move the stone and she couldn't, it really blocked her ability to concentrate. What if Chie was still using the first stone? If that were the case and their roles were reversed, Hanna knew she would just want to quit. For now, she would just have to accept the quiet suppressed praise she received from Tahtay Sohil. She knew he was impressed with her; she could tell by his eyes. She just wished he would say as much. Not that she always needed praise, but this was amazing! She just wanted to share it with someone.

CHAPTER TWENTY

Restricted and Afflicted

Hanna was intrigued.

The following week she did her morning classes as usual, but when she began making her way to Tahtay Sohil's class, Yoshi intercepted her. *What could Master Juro wish to see her about this time?* she wondered since, after her initial time at Kokoroe, the only time Yoshi approached her was when Master Juro requested a meeting.

"Hanna, come with me please."

Hanna shrugged when Chie looked at her questioningly and turned to follow Yoshi. They went into the school, but instead of going upstairs, Yoshi took her along a hallway that led around to the back of the school and down a staircase to the level below. Wall sconces lit up the way, yet Hanna still felt the gloom of going underground. At the end of the hall, they entered a room on the right. It was fairly plain and had the look of a reception area. There were a few chairs lined up against the wall and a desk facing them. Behind the desk, a Juro was busy studying a scroll. She was dressed as a student with just a bit of purple sash showing. Hanna knew beginner students wore white sashes and that purple symbolized a higher level. There were various other colours, red, blue, purple and black, that Hanna had not learned the relevance of. The student glanced up at Hanna as Yoshi directed her to take a seat. When Yoshi left, the student returned to her studies as Hanna continued to examine the room. Hanna wanted to know what this was a waiting room for and was just thinking of how to ask the student when another teacher entered. Surprised that it wasn't Master Juro she was meeting, Hanna was fairly certain this teacher was Tahtay Etai since she knew her other instructor would also be a Juro, and she wore the same navy robe with pearl sash that the other teachers. Her assumption was proved correct when the lady approached Hanna and bowed.

"Hanna, I am Tahtay Etai. I will be instructing you for the rest of this week. Please follow me."

Hanna stood feeling a little awkward, as she still hadn't become used to towering over her elders. Aside from Etai being a teacher, Hanna knew she must be quite old as her hair was silver and although friendly, her face had the folds of time. She wondered just how old that must have made Etai since Hanna had met Juro over fifty who looked no older than someone in their twenties. Master Juro was really the only one who looked truly aged and Hanna knew he was over six hundred. Tahtay Etai let her hair hang long down her back and it sparkled with miniature gems. Hanna hoped that when she was sixty she would look as elegant as Tahtay Etai.

Hanna followed her through a door that led to a hallway with even more doors on both sides of the hall. She walked part way down the hall and then stopped and turned to Hanna.

"I understand your progress with the crystals has been going very well. Tahtay Sohil has had many positive comments about you. He did mention though, that you were easily frustrated when first you began your task but overcame that once you had success."

When Hanna looked embarrassed at this Etai reached out her hand and grasped Hanna's.

She said, "Each of us has qualities that can hinder us and prevent us from being successful on our journey. If we have the courage to recognize these, and overcome them, then we are stronger for it. If we didn't struggle from time to time, what incentive would there be to grow and change? Only you have the power to make that change. It is a choice that lies with you."

Etai remained still as if waiting for something. After an extended silence, Hanna acknowledged Etai's point with a nod of her head.

Etai gave Hanna's hand a squeeze and said, "Good. This next task will challenge that quality. Here, patience is the key to success."

Hanna repressed a shudder as she thought she was about to face something more challenging than the wall she had feared. Patience was definitely not one of her strengths. She wasn't one for waiting around; her curiosity often got the best of her and she liked results. Already she could feel herself resisting the coming task.

Etai opened the door. Hanna looked in and was surprised to see nothing. It was a compact white, empty room. The walls were white. The floor was white. Even the ceiling was white. The only item in the room was a square cushion on the floor... and it was white. Tahtay Etai motioned for Hanna to enter. Hanna hesitated a moment then walked in.

"Please have a seat."

Even though Etai's voice was light and cheery Hanna felt like she was being punished. This resembled nothing more than a jail cell or what she imagined an isolation room in a psychiatric ward would look like. She went to the middle of the room and took a seat on the lone cushion facing her instructor.

Etai said, "Your task is simple. See the Essence in the room. Feel the Essence in the room."

Hanna tilted her head waiting for further instructions, but Etai just smiled at her, her eyes twinkling with merriment. Hanna wondered, what could possibly be amusing about this?

"So that's it? Just see it and feel it?"

"Oh there is one more thing," Etai said, "please remove your shoes."

Hanna did and Etai picked them up.

"Someone will come get you when the lesson is done for the day."

With that she closed the door.

The first thing Hanna noticed was that there was no doorknob. She felt around where the door handle should be, but she only felt a smooth surface. The door itself was so perfectly lined up with the wall it was difficult to tell where the edge of the door even was. Okay, she thought, this is just a test. They just want to see how I handle the situation. Tahtay Etai said that I get frustrated easily so this is just to help me get my Zen on. I can do this.

She went back to her cushion and sat down cross-legged. She looked around the bright white room. Bright white? She just realized there were none of the usual wall sconces or candle chandeliers that she had seen throughout the school and in the other buildings she'd been to. The ceiling was flat and white but it was somehow lit. She couldn't tell how. She stood up again and tried to reach it, but it was at least eight feet high and even if she jumped she would not be able to touch it. She leaned against the wall and tried to see if there was a crack between the ceiling and the wall that she might be able to see through. There wasn't. She ran her hand along the wall to feel the smooth surface. When she got to the corner she turned and continued walking. She spotted something out of the corner of her eye – her cushion. Oh, ya. I'm supposed to be sitting, looking for Essence – not lights.

Again she sat down. "Okay," she said out loud, "I can do this."

She closed her eyes and breathed deeply. Remembering Tahtay Sohil's advice, she relaxed her shoulders as she exhaled trying to calm herself. She opened her eyes and looked. She was in a big white box. She looked again. She was still in a big white box. Well, not that big. She stretched out her arms.

She could almost touch the walls. She lay down and stretched. The wall and door were just out of her reach. She sat up and looked around. This was going to be a very long afternoon.

Three hours later the door opened. The Juro student from behind the desk chuckled as she peered in on Hanna curled up on the floor using the cushion for a pillow. Hanna was sound asleep. The student cleared her throat and Hanna sat up with a jolt. She wiped the drool from her cheek.

"Oh, sorry." She said.

The student smiled, "Your lesson is done for today."

She handed Hanna her shoes, then Hanna followed her back down the hall to the waiting room and proceeded to go up the stairs to the main floor of the school. She wasn't sure what kind of consequences there might be for sleeping during her task. She hadn't meant to fall asleep she was just trying to get comfortable. She chuckled to herself when she thought what Kazi's reaction would be when she told him she had slept all afternoon.

* * *

"You what?" Kazi's jaw dropped.

"Well, I couldn't help it. I was in a small white room with a pillow! What else could I do?"

Kazi laughed, "How about look for Essence for starters? Isn't that what you were supposed to be doing?"

Hanna groaned. "Well ya, but IT WAS A SMALL WHITE ROOM WITH A PILLOW! I could only stare ahead for so long! Maybe it was some sort of punishment, you know, to remind me not to get frustrated so easily?"

Kazi shook his head.

"Since when is having a nap punishment? I think if you were going to get punished you'd know for sure. Karn has fond memories of not following instructions."

Hanna rolled her eyes.

"Don't remind me. I hope Tahtay Etai is more forgiving. Maybe that Juro student will be like Karn and refrain from telling on me."

Kazi grinned, "You can always hope."

* * *

The next day, Hanna prepared herself for another lesson. After lunch she made sure to go to the bathroom in case she was to be sealed in another isolation room for three hours. This time, Tahtay Etai met her in front of the school and led Hanna down into the basement again. She appeared quite pleased to see Hanna so she was sure Tahtay Etai didn't know that she had fallen asleep. Hanna made a mental note to thank the girl who had woken her.

When they entered the same waiting room, Tahtay Etai greeted the girl behind the desk.

"Good afternoon," Etai said.

Hanna also gave a slight bow as she said hello. The girl responded to their good wishes with a slight tilt of the head. Tahtay Etai entered down the same corridor that they had gone down the previous day and opened the same room. Hanna slipped off her shoes, handed them to Etai then quickly skipped into the room. She perched herself on the cushion, at full attention.

"Hanna, you seem eager to study today." Etai said in an inquisitive tone.

Hanna was feeling grateful that the 'receptionist' had not told Tahtay Etai about her nap, which meant she would not be facing a week of scrubbing pots and pans. Of course, she wasn't about to tell Tahtay Etai the reason for her somewhat chipper mood.

"Sometimes it's nice to have alone time I guess," was the best excuse Hanna could come up with.

"I think I understand." Etai replied. "Remember your task; see the Essence, feel the Essence."

She began closing the door then popped her head back in, "and try to do it while you are awake today."

Hanna cringed as Etai closed the door. Hanna felt the need to make up for lost time. She tried to get herself comfortable sitting with her legs crossed on the cushion in the middle of the floor. She sat up straight, closed her eyes and concentrated on her breathing. She relaxed her shoulders and then slowly opened her eyes. Alas, she was in a big white box. She sighed but she wasn't overly surprised. She tried to squint. It didn't help. She tilted her head. Nothing. She went cross-eyed. That just succeeded in making her eyes hurt. After twenty minutes of trying to see, she had to move. She needed to stretch or something. She stood up and did some jumping jacks and stretched her legs. She moved the cushion closer to the wall and sat back down. It wasn't much of an improvement, but at least she could lean against the wall. Her legs were extended and her hands rested in her lap. Leaning her head against the wall, she gazed up at the ceiling once again musing how they lit the room. She began twiddling her thumbs until it started to tickle. She regarded her thumb as she began to scratch it. She thought her hands undoubtedly looked pink in this plain white room. She held her hands out in front of her. The longer she looked at them, the pinker they appeared. In fact even the spaces between her fingers had a tint of colouring. Wait, she thought, the spaces between my fingers?

She stared between her index and middle finger then slowly lowered her hand without taking her eyes from where the spot where her hand once was. She could still see the tinge of pink in the air. She held her breath and tried not to blink; concerned she might not be able to see it again. Her eyes began to sting so she finally gave into the urge to blink, exhaling as she did. To her surprise, as the air rushed out of her mouth the tinge of pink darkened. As her breath dispersed into the air it lightened again. She inhaled deeply, and then emptied her lungs. She was rewarded with a pink haze. Hanna thought it was like being able to see her breath on a chilly winter day, but instead of a white mist this was pink. And then it was gone again.

Hanna was excited. She took a chance and looked around the room. The far side of the room was still pretty much white, but the air closer to Hanna had colour. It was clear to her that the main source of Essence in the room resided in her. When she breathed, she added Essence to the room; therefore, she reasoned, the longer she was in here the more Essence would be in here. That is unless of course the air could escape. She knew from her previous examination of the door that there was little chance of air escaping that way. There were no windows and no detectable cracks anywhere else. She wondered how intense the colour would be by the time she was let out of the room.

Now that she could see it, Hanna thought she would try to feel it. If she thought seeing it was difficult then feeling it proved to be almost impossible. She waved her hands around in front of her, but only felt the breeze she created. She stopped her movement and held her hand still. She became aware of tingling in her hand, like tons of tiny pinpricks. Every time she moved her hand the sensation would stop, but would return the moment she became still again. She leaned back against the wall and rested her hands palm up on her legs. She closed her eyes and paid attention to the tingling feeling. She didn't know if it was the Essence. She didn't even know if the feeling was caused from outside or inside her body. She thought about her time at Crystal Valley and how the Essence had felt tangible. It had been easy to feel though since there was so much in the air. *'That's it!* she thought, *I just need there to be more.'*

Keeping her eyes shut, she exhaled then tried to feel the Essence that she released. All she felt was the slight moisture from her breath. As she lowered her hand, she passed the crystal hanging around her neck and for a brief instance she felt the Essence. It suddenly dawned on her that she had a crystal full of Essence. She lifted it over her head and placed it on her palm. *'Okay,'* she thought, *'maybe this is a distraction, but it will keep me from getting bored.'*

This crystal was bigger than any she had worked with in Tahtay Sohil's class, but Hanna was up for the challenge, it's not like she had anything better to do, she reasoned. She easily managed to feel the Essence in the crystal and then began trying to make it move. Slowly at first, it jerked back and forth. Then she had it spinning. As she became more and more adapt at feeling it, the easier it was to move. She floated it up and then down not letting it get too high. She noticed that the farther away it was from her the less she could feel the Essence and therefore the less she could control it. Hovering it a few inches off the floor, she began moving it away from her. When it got too far, it would begin to sink. She found it easiest to control when she imagined she was pulling on a rope. If she sat still, she could make the stone hover, but it was hard to get it to move, especially the way she wanted it to. The more she practiced, the further she could move the crystal away before it began to drop.

She lost track of time. She was having so much fun playing with her crystal; she had forgotten what she was originally trying to do. As much as she was enjoying herself, she found her eyes becoming heavy. She blinked several times and gave herself a shake to try to stem off her sleepiness but was having little luck. She put her crystal back on because if she did drift off she definitely didn't want to be caught with her crystal on the floor. She replaced it and tucked it back under her shirt. She squeezed all her muscles then relaxed them again.

As she rested her head against the wall, she thought she should probably stand up and stretch to prevent herself from falling asleep, but she just couldn't bring herself to move. She realized that the room was now definitely pink. *'I was right'* was the last thought she had before succumbing to sleep.

The door opened. Hanna lifted her eyelids, first one then the other, desperately trying to appear awake. She was still leaning against the wall, but her head had lulled to the side. She jerked it upright feeling rather dizzy. Tahtay Etai came in the room and gave Hanna a hand getting up.

"That's better Hanna, I see you've made more progress."

Hanna felt fuzzy and wasn't thinking clearly. "How's that exactly?"

Etai said cheerfully, "You were sitting up."

Hanna asked, "Does this mean you won't give me extra dish duty for falling asleep?"

Etai looped her arm through Hanna's as she continued to give her assistance while they walked out of the room.

"Everyone falls asleep in this testing chamber, why would you be given dish duty for that?"

Hanna was relieved.

"You mean everyone gets bored and falls asleep and you're okay with that?"

Etai gave a warm melodic laugh.

"Not exactly. Regardless of boredom, you can only re-breathe your air for so long before you get sleepy. Even those completely engrossed with the task at hand would pass out if we left them in there too long. Tell me, how did you do today?"

Hanna was proud that she could tell Tahtay Etai that she was able to see the Essence, that it was subtle at first and she had deduced that it would darken the longer she was in the room. She felt she could tell her the struggles about trying to feel it, but would leave out the part where she had been playing with the crystal.

Etai listened with genuine interest. She was fascinated that Hanna, after only two days in the chamber, was able to see the Essence in the air. Most students would be able to see it within the last twenty minutes before they fell asleep or the door opened. More experienced students could perceive it after about an hour, but only a few had the ability to see it as quickly as Hanna had. Etai pondered what might transpire tomorrow.

* * *

Day three: Hanna found she wanted to go into the testing chamber. She thought it kind of odd that she wasn't pulling her hair out at being cooped up in a cell with no way to escape and knowing that she was going to pass out from lack of fresh air, but she felt like she was getting close to something. Now that she knew there was barely any Essence in the room before she arrived and that there would be little to see or feel to begin with so instead of wasting her time trying to feel the air, she planned on playing with her crystal. She had some tests she wanted to try and this was a great place to do it.

When Etai had left and the door was firmly shut, Hanna removed her pants. She placed them in a bundle in the middle of the room and then took off her crystal and placed it on top. She grabbed her cushion and sat on it, back against the wall. She reached out her hand and waited to feel the crystal's Essence. Once she did she pulled the imaginary string to raise the crystal up. She raised it higher and higher until it was past her ability to feel, then it began to fall. She tried to stop it, but only managed to slow it a little before it landed back on the pile of her pants. She crawled over to it to make sure she hadn't damaged it at all

268

and was gratified to see her "landing mat" had done its job perfectly. She sat back on her cushion and repeated the process, but this time she didn't let the crystal get as high before she dropped it on purpose and then tried to catch it again.

After about an hour of this, Hanna was able to get the crystal to the ceiling, hold it there and then drop it when she was ready. She was also able to slow its decent and stop it before it touched the ground. She was pleased with herself. She gave her invisible string a tug and the crystal flew towards her. She caught it and put it back around her neck. The Essence in the room was easy for her to see now. She raised her hands and was delighted when she discovered she could feel it. She wasn't sure why it was so easy today, but thought that maybe it had something to do with playing with the crystal. She had become so adept at manipulating the crystal that even slight traces of the Essence were detectable to her now. She pulled and gathered the Essence and formed it into a ball.

"That's cool," she said aloud, "now what do I do with it?"

She got an idea to try bouncing it off the wall and see what it would do. She gave it a mighty push and it hit the door causing it to burst open with a loud bang as the door crashed into the wall across the hall.

Hanna cringed. The Juro student came running into the hallway. She peaked in the room to see Hanna still a little stunned sitting on the floor against the wall without her pants on. She couldn't read the expression on the girl's face so she had no idea what to say.

"Oops." Hanna shrugged her shoulders.

"Come with me."

After pulling her pants back on, Hanna got up and followed her back to the waiting room. She asked Hanna to sit and then went through one of the other doors. Moments later she returned with Tahtay Etai.

Normally Tahtay Etai was all smiles and had much to say, but now she just motioned for Hanna to follow. Quietly they went back up the stairs and outside. As they approached Master Juro's domicile, Hanna started to panic. Was she in trouble? Was she about to get kicked out? Maybe it would be just a week of dishes...

Etai pointed to the chairs inside Master Juro's front room. "Please have a seat Hanna."

Hanna wanted to ask Tahtay Etai what was going on, but was afraid she wouldn't like the answer. A few minutes later Etai, returned with Master Juro at her side.

He nodded to Hanna then sat in the same chair he had the last time they were here. Etai took a seat in a chair beside him.

"I hear that you've had enough of the white testing chamber."

Hanna willed herself to speak and tried not to squeak in the process.

"I didn't mean to do it, I mean, I wasn't trying to blast the door open."

"No?" Master Juro said. "What then were you trying to do?"

"I was just trying to bounce the ball."

He furrowed his brows.

"Ball? Explain."

Hanna rushed on. "Well I gathered all the Essence up into a big ball and thought it would be fun to, well, play catch with it, so I was just trying to bounce it off the wall."

She looked pleadingly at him hoping he would understand. '*Oh please just give me dishes; I don't want to leave!*'

Master Juro sat back with a slight smile. Then his grin grew broader and broader. Hanna regarded Tahtay Etai who appeared as if she was going to burst with pride.

Master Juro said, "Well done Hanna, well done. Typically, by the time a student has the ability to collect the Essence, they use it to open the door, not usually with

270

such force though. Aside from the fact you weren't trying to do this, but were you just trying to amuse yourself, you did it in less than three days! This is...unexpected. It is not an easy process; however did you manage to do it and for what reason were you without your pants?"

Hanna flushed a little at this but now that she finally discovered she was not actually in trouble she relaxed and sat back in the chair. She tucked her legs up under herself and crossed her hands on her lap. She realized the truth was less embarrassing than any other reason she could think of for taking her pants off, so she confessed.

"Once I realized that I wouldn't be able to see or feel the Essence for the first while that I was in there I thought, I might as well keep myself amused while I waited."

In her defence she added, "I thought it would also help keep me awake. I decided I could practice moving my crystal, but I didn't want to risk damaging it so I used my pants as a landing mat."

Master Juro was intrigued. "Landing mat?" he inquired.

"Yeah. I was practising raising my crystal off the ground; I wanted to see how high it would go."

She continued to explain to them how she moved the crystal and eventually how she was able to control it.

"At that point," she said, "there was enough Essence in the room to see so I figured I'd work with it a bit. After practising with the crystal, I found it pretty easy to feel the Essence in the air. It didn't take me long to collect it and that's when I made the ball..."

Master Juro and Tahtay Etai exchanged glances. "Fascinating!" he said. "You combined both of your lessons. Etai, I think Hanna may have inadvertently caught on to something here."

"I think you're right," Etai said. "I wonder if this technique will help other students achieve this goal in less time..."

Hanna asked, "So how long does it normally take someone to collect the Essence? A week or so?" Tahtay Etai could hardly contain herself.

"No Hanna, years! Some may never be able to pull it out of the air like that. I'm still beside myself that you were able to achieve it."

Hanna was dumbfounded. Two things hit her at once. First, that she managed to complete a task in record time and second, that they gave her a task that normally took years to master. It was the latter that caused her concern.

With hesitation she prodded. "I thought I was only going to be here a few weeks. Just how long do you think I'm going to be here?"

Even Master Juro had to laugh at that.

"In all my years I have never thought that impatience would pay off. Are you able to learn so quickly because you are worried you will run out of time?"

"Yes." Hanna blurted out. "Well no."

She tried to gather her thoughts.

"Truthfully I never thought about it. I mean sometimes, like when we found out about going on that field trip to the cave, I hoped I wouldn't get sent home before the trip, but I haven't been trying to 'hurry up and learn' if that's what you mean."

Etai said, "Yet you do seem in a hurry to learn. Have you always been this impatient with your studies?"

"Wait," Hanna said softly, "you never answered my question. How long do you plan on keeping me here?"

Master Juro's expression became sombre.

"You are not a prisoner Hanna, you may leave whenever you wish."

Hanna blushed. "Well no, of course not. I just meant...are you any closer to finding out how to get me back home?"

"I was going to speak with you about this later today. Another tear has occurred not too far from here and I plan on going to see it myself. Would you care to join me?"

"Oh, yes sir! Not that I'm not enjoying myself here, but I really should be getting back."

Master Juro tilted his head and spoke softly.

"Don't get your hopes up yet child. We are just going to investigate – it may all come to nothing."

Hanna had slid to edge of her chair, hearing what Master Juro had said but obviously not really listening. Already she showed signs of a barely contained excitement at the prospect of going home.

"Do you think I should say goodbye to my friends? Just in case I mean?"

Etai and Master Juro exchanged worried looks.

"I don't think that will be necessary Hanna," Master Juro began.

Etai placed a hand on Master Juro's knee.

"Perhaps you can include Kazi on this little venture on the off chance something more comes of it?"

Seeing the light in Hanna's eyes, Master Juro consented to the offer.

"That is acceptable. Hanna do you think Kazi would be interested?"

"Are you kidding? He'll be thrilled! When do we leave?"

"First thing in the morning. Pack for an overnight trip, as it will take a few hours to get there. I would prefer to rest before the return trip."

Hanna looked fit to burst. Master Juro knew there was no point in detaining her any longer.

"Thank you Hanna. We will meet you by the main gate tomorrow morning."

Hanna jumped out of her chair and hurried out the door. As an afterthought she popped her head back in attempting to bow.

"Thank you Master Juro!"

When the door had shut, Master Juro sat back with a look of concern on his face.

Etai laughed. "I'll sure miss that girl when she's gone."

Master Juro sighed, "She's not going anywhere any time soon I'm afraid."

"What do you mean?"

"If there was a way back into her world, do you not think someone would have found it?"

"How so?" Etai asked a little puzzled.

"Even if it was by accident, someone would have crossed to her world. We have not heard of anyone disappearing, at least not in that way."

"Maybe that is what's happening. Maybe people aren't being kidnapped, but are slipping through this tear?"

Master Juro pondered for a moment.

"I have considered that; however, those who have gone missing were nowhere close to any reported tears."

"So are you saying you don't think she can ever go back?"

"I am not saying that...yet. It is what I believe though. Once I've investigated this tear myself I will have more answers."

Now Etai slumped back in her chair, unsure of the greater tragedy: Hanna's excitement of returning home, which was unlikely, or Mahou's conviction that she couldn't.

CHAPTER TWENTY-ONE

Fears and Tears

Hanna waited.

She and Kazi were so excited about the upcoming trip that they got up early and were anxiously waiting at the front gate where they discovered Karn waiting with four horses.

"Karn what are you doing here?" Kazi asked.

"I've been given the privilege to escort you on your journey," he explained with a bow.

"Great!" Kazi replied. "So you get to skip classes too?"

Master Juro arrived at that moment.

"Although Tahtay Biatach still refers to him as his student, young Karn here has completed his studies. He came back to Kokoroe as a leader-in-training. Modest as he may be he is a most talented Jagare and a welcome addition on our expedition."

Karn chuckled. "Yes, I think Tahtay Biatach will call me his student long after he retires. Master Juro, shall I ride ahead for a ways, then double back to report?"

"There's no real need while we are this close to Kokoroe. You can begin your scouting ahead in an hour or so."

"Very well."

Karn assisted Master Juro onto his horse and then helped Hanna and Kazi. After adjusting their stirrups, he hopped onto his horse and then led the group through the open gate, waving to Jaylin, the Gatekeeper as he passed by.

It took four hours to reach their destination. Hanna wasn't sure what to expect, but when they arrived at the inn, she was surprised. It looked very strange that a four-story building stood alone with no town surrounding it, just a stable in the back where they took their horses to be cared for. Hanna leaned over to whisper in Kazi's ear.

"Seems sort of odd to just have this one large building out in the middle of nowhere."

Kazi nodded his agreement. "Perhaps people prefer to stop for a break before continuing on to Korode."

As Master Juro leaped over the side of his horse and handed his reigns to the stable boy he said, "Oh this inn serves more than just travellers. Many different tradesmen meet here. They pass on their wares to Wagoneers who then take their goods to towns or cities."

Hanna was intrigued. "What sort of tradesmen?" she asked.

"The Ice Cutters have a trek they follow higher into the mountains that comes out near here. Many Loggers also go up the mountain and cut down trees, then load their wagons here."

"How do they get the trees here from where they cut them if they don't use wagons?"

"Yes, the wagons are far too cumbersome to take into the woods so they use horses or oxen to help drag the large boles, pile them up over there," he pointed across the road from the inn, "until there is enough for a wagon load."

"If there is so much traffic through here, how come a town hasn't sprung up?" Hanna asked.

Master Juro led the small group to the entrance of the inn. Karn had ridden ahead for the last part of the journey. Finding nothing of concern on the way, he stayed at the inn and prepared for their arrival as instructed by Master Juro. When they entered the inn, Karn was sitting at a table with drinks and food for all of them. Only two other patrons were currently sitting at tables in the inn, obviously travellers who just stopped for a pause in their journey before continuing onto their destinations. Master Juro continued to answer Hanna's questions as they made their way toward Karn.

"Well Hanna, our towns need to be close to a nesting ground and there isn't one close by. The few Jivan that work in the inn and the Jagare that hunt and secure the area around it, live in the inn. It's easier to protect and maintain than several smaller houses."

They greeted Karn, eagerly took their seats and began helping themselves to the bread and cold meats that had been set out for them. Hanna took a large gulp of chilled water.

"Is the place the tear occurred close by here?"

Master Juro said, "Yes, not too far. Just twenty or so minutes deeper into the woods."

Hanna looked puzzled. "Only a Juro would be able to detect it, right?"

Master Juro nodded.

"From everything I've learned so far, there wouldn't be a Juro Ice Cutter or a Logger. Would there?"

"No. Those would not be trades you would find a Juro working in."

"So then how would a Juro happen upon a tear way out here? Especially deeper into the woods."

"They would have found it while on their pilgrimage. There is very special place nearby where many Juro come to visit. I will take you there after we've had a chance to eat and rest a little."

* * *

The four of them made their way into the forest after their meal. Karn spoke with one of the local Jagare before leaving and was provided with a map of the surrounding area. Master Juro seemed confident about leading the group even though he said he hadn't been in the area for a hundred years. The oak, beech and maple trees grew close together, but the shrubbery gave way to a pathway making it fairly easy to navigate. Every now and then they would have to duck under a branch that reached across the path. Once Kazi attempted to pull the branch back, but after he released it and smacked Karn across his chest he refrained from doing it again.

The moss-covered rocks the path led to intrigued Hanna. So intent on admiring them, she didn't realize they formed a narrow stairway leading up until Kazi pointed up to the plateau at the top. Master Juro was the first to begin to climb followed by Hanna, Kazi and Karn who brought up the rear. Hanna thought Master Juro was surprisingly nimble for someone his age; she chuckled when she realized she had no idea how old he actually was. Kazi quietly counted the stairs as they went, but Hanna was concentrating on her footing; some of the rocks were quite narrow and she didn't want to risk slipping. When Hanna looked up, she was surprised that Master Juro had disappeared. Resisting the temptation to look back over her shoulder and speak with Kazi, she continued on until she found herself in a darkened entryway. She stopped and ran her hand over the stone bricks that made up the narrow doorway when Kazi bumped into her causing her to stumble, landing on her hands and knees inside the darkened space.

"Sorry Hanna. Here let me help you up."

"Ouch!" Hanna cried. "You're standing on my foot! I think I'll get up on my own thank you."

They heard a striking sound and light suddenly flooded the space. Master Juro was smiling as he lit a torch that hung on the wall. Karn, who had nimbly swept past Kazi, aided Hanna to her feet then continued further into the space.

"What is this place?" Hanna asked as she and Kazi joined Master Juro.

The walls were covered in hieroglyphs similar to the ones Hanna and Kazi had seen in the caves Tahtay Jillian had taken them to, but these were much more vivid. They looked as if they had been painted only a few years ago instead of a thousand.

"This, Hanna, is our most sacred place. It is thought to be the first shared living space between races over a thousand years ago. The pictures on the wall tell us how Juro and Jagare came together. They made the stairs leading up here and carved into this rock to make this cavern."

"The pictures look so new though." Hanna pointed out.

"Yes. When the Juro come here on their pilgrimage they spend days touching up any of the faded paintings. I remember when I came. Let me show you the pictures I worked on."

With torch in hand he led them deeper into the cavern. Karn was waiting only a few feet away, but had been swallowed by the darkness before they moved in his direction.

"Whatcha doing Karn?" Hanna asked.

His face still mostly in shadow, he turned to look at them.

"Just making sure we have no guests in here."

Kazi tried to peer around Karn as if he expected something to jump out from behind him.

"What kind of guests?" he asked.

Seeing Kazi's worried expression he replied, "Nothing big. There's no way a Wolcott or bear could fit through the doorway. I just wanted to check and make sure there were no Kameil stowing away in here or a badger family making a nest. Either of those scenarios wouldn't have ended well."

Karn grinned as if he had just made a joke, but Hanna could tell, even in the dim light, that Kazi had gone a shade paler.

Karn also noticed Kazi's reaction. "Don't worry Kazi, the coast is clear."

Kazi nodded and swallowed, his eyes still the size of saucers. Master Juro pointed to a section of the wall farther in.

"That looks like a picture of Essence crystals," Hanna said.

"Yes, exactly. According to this mural, this cavern used to have a small supply of crystals. They were used up many centuries ago. This is the section I had the pleasure of restoring."

Kazi said, "It looks really good. You did a great job."

Master Juro chuckled. "Thanks Kazi. I think it has been touched up a few times since then."

Kazi blushed and said under his breath, "I knew that."

Master Juro let out a sigh. "Well, thank you for your patience. I just wanted to stop in since we were so close by. We can go back outside now."

They returned to the doorway and exited one at a time starting with Karn, who was followed by Kazi. When Hanna went out Master Juro said, "Just pause there for a moment will you Hanna?"

Hanna slid over to the side as best she could to allow Master Juro space to stand on the narrow platform next to her.

"When my colleague first detected the tear, he had just come out of the cave. He stood here for a moment to allow his eyes to adjust to the change in light when he noticed something that looked a little off. Can you see what he was speaking of?"

Hanna shielded her eyes from the glare of the sun and began scanning the woods below. Slowly she turned her head being careful to not overlook any area. She was about to give up when she saw what he referred to on the far right, in the direction heading away from the road and the inn.

"There!" she pointed. "The trees are a bit different in colour and the air looks...well it had no colour, no pink."

Master Juro began descending the stairs.

"Then that would be our destination."

When he reached the path at the base of the stairway Master Juro led the group in the direction Hanna had indicated. There wasn't much of a pathway, but it was clear someone had gone this way before as the brush had been pushed aside, even cut away in places to allow easier passage. It only took them fifteen minutes to reach the tear. At some point, Hanna had grabbed Kazi's hand. She squeezed it as they approached feeling nervous about what they may or may not discover. Master Juro slowly walked around the area then stopped and knelt on the ground. Hanna released Kazi's hand and joined Master Juro. Hanna gasped at what she saw before them. Hearing Hanna, Kazi leaped forward to see what was the matter. All the bushes and saplings within a three-foot area looked as though all the life had been drained out of them. At the edge of the spot lay a dead squirrel.

"Whoa," Kazi said, "What do you suppose happened here?"

Master Juro sat in silence. Kazi was about to ask another question when Karn pulled him and Hanna back. After a few moments, Master Juro called Karn over. His voice was shaky.

"Karn would you be so kind as to escort young Kazi back to the inn. Hanna and I will be along shortly."

Karn bowed then took Kazi by the shoulders and turned him away as he began asking more questions. Master Juro waved Hanna over. She knelt to the ground next to him. When he looked up, gazing at the tree canopy above them, Hanna saw a trace of a tear at the corner of his eye.

"So Hanna, what do you suppose happened here?" he asked using Kazi's wording.

Hanna felt the ground and looked around.

"It's as if the Essence has been sucked out of everything in this area."

"Yes. My thoughts exactly." He stood up and made his way to the closest tree.

"Come. Do you feel that?" he asked as he held his hand on the large trunk.

Hanna placed her hands on the tree.

"Um, I'm not sure what I'm supposed to feel."

He took her by the hand and led her to a tree further out of the dead zone and placed it on the trunk.

"Feel," he said.

Hanna closed her eyes. She wasn't sure if it would help, but it seemed the natural thing to do. She could feel the breeze pushing against the tree causing the upper branches to sway ever so slightly.

"Oh!" she exclaimed. "I can feel...Essence, moving through the tree."

He nodded, then took her hand and led her back to the previous tree, once again placing her hand on the trunk. Again Hanna closed her eyes. Again she felt the breeze causing it to sway, but this time there was none of the energy movement she had felt before.

"There's nothing..." she said.

"That's right."

Hanna opened her eyes. She looked up at the tall tree and observed the lush green leaves still attached to its many branches.

"The tree looks healthy."

Master Juro sighed. "It won't for long, it is dying. Just like the bushes and grass below it. The Essence has been sucked away."

"Do you think it's because the tree is so big that it's not dead yet?"

"It's a reasonable theory. It contains more Essence to begin with so it may take longer to suffer from the withdrawal." He inched closer to the small, brown furry animal on the ground. "What do you think this is?"

"You mean the squirrel?" Hanna asked.

"Squirrel you say? Poor creature."

Hanna looked bemused. "You don't have squirrels here?"

Master Juro shook his head. "No. We do have picos, which look somewhat similar, but their tails are not bushy like this, they are thin and long. They use them to swing from tree to tree. And their fur is green." Master Juro spoke softly and seemed very distressed. Hanna felt a little uncomfortable, not sure what to say.

After an awkward silence, Master Juro spoke again. "This squirrel came from your world?"

Hanna nodded.

When he didn't continue, Hanna tentatively said, "This is where the tear is then, for sure?"

"Yes. Do you feel a...pulling sensation?"

Hanna stood perfectly still for a moment then began slowly walking away from the dead area. Once she was again among the living plants, she turned and walked back to Master Juro.

"Not really," she replied, "I can feel the difference between the area with the Essence and without. The air in the dead zone is drier or something."

Again Master Juro sat on the ground and closed his eyes. Time seemed to pass slowly. Hanna sat and joined Master Juro in his meditation like state. He spoke quietly after a while.

"I can feel where the world has been ripped. Something caused the Essence to be pushed out of the ground and whatever caused this seemed to have ripped into your world."

He looked around thoughtfully. "Imagine an immense wave crashing on the shore. It leaves behind water caught in pits in the sand and when it recedes, it brings back debris that was on the shore."

"The wave is the Essence?"

"Yes."

"Then the shore would be Earth and I am the debris?"

"Not quite. If we were to carry this analogy further, I would say that the shore was between two oceans. The wave from the Galenia *Ocean* crossed the shore and reached the Earth *Ocean.* When it receded, it brought you with it and left Essence behind."

He lifted a handful of dirt and dead leaves. "See this leaf here, this isn't from these woods. Is this leaf and that squirrel common on your world?"

Hanna looked at the items in Master Juro's hand.

"Yes. I've seen that plant all over my woods and there are lots of squirrels too."

Master Juro tilted his head. "Curious. I wonder if this tear opened close to the tear you came through."

Hanna was anxious. "That would be interesting to find out. So how do I get back through?"

Master Juro's eyebrow knit. "The tear is no longer open, the wave, as it were, is no longer crossing the shore."

"Well if there's another big wave, then the tear will open again, right?"

Master Juro looked concerned. "Yes, but we must not let that happen. Who knows how much damage could be done? There is not an endless supply of Essence. The more we lose, the more Galenia will suffer and die."

Hanna needed to ask. "But, but how will I get home?"

Master Juro shook his head. "I do not think you can. At this point, we have no idea what caused this "wave", no way of controlling where it will occur, and for that matter, we do not even know if it would push you back to your own world. You could end up somewhere, between. It is too dangerous to consider."

He began pacing around the area as he considered what he had learnt.

"This is not a natural event, someone caused this to happen. We must stop them for doing it again."

Suddenly he froze in his tracks. Master Juro eyed Hanna who had wrapped her arms around her knees and was rocking back and forth. Obviously this news had troubled her, but at the moment there were more immediate concerns.

"Hanna," he whispered.

Noticing the concern in his tone, Hanna's head snapped up.

"Run!" he said no longer trying to keep his voice low.

Hanna heard the Beast crashing through the trees before she saw it. Master Juro ran and leaped into the air pushing off trees like a pinball machine. Hanna jumped up and ran after him, hearing the Wolcott pursuing her. Master Juro yelled as he continued on.

"I will get some help. Just keep running!"

Hanna didn't bother responding, but concentrated all her energy on putting as much distance between herself and the Wolcott. The quick glimpse she had caught of it terrified her to the bone. It was even larger than she had imagined. Its boar-like body was the size of a bison she could imagine. The tusks were not overly long, but could still shred her as easily as it tore away the brush. The snarling grew louder as it gained on her. Weaving through the woods, she avoided any open clear paths to make it harder for the creature to follow her. She vaulted over bushes and branches continuing to run at full speed. Her lungs felt as if they would burst and her heart pounded. As she glanced over her shoulder, she tripped on a protruding tree root and rolled into a cavity under a large fallen tree. The animal was too close. If Hanna tried to get up and run it would be on her before she took two steps. She held her breath hoping the tree hid her well enough. The Beast snarled and barked. Running straight towards her, its' foot slipped under the tree. Its large body crashed into the tree preventing it from sliding into the hollow. Once the Wolcott pulled itself back, it tried to force its head under the tree. Hanna suppressed a scream as its jaws snapped mere inches from her chest. It tried to push the tree aside using its head. The tree barely moved. She heard the creature move away and was hopeful that it had given up when suddenly it charged. Hanna couldn't help but scream as it crashed into the tree causing the tree to jump a few inches. Now Hanna had two problems: if the Beast kept pushing the tree, it would be able to reach her, however, it would also cause the tree to move, crushing her in the process. The Wolcott began to charge again, but to Hanna's surprise instead of colliding with the fallen tree it leapt over it. Hanna's relief was quickly turned to a new terror.

She heard the Beast crashing through the trees along with terrified screaming. Without thinking, Hanna rolled out from under the tree and ran after the Wolcott. She saw, twenty yards away, a mother with a small child in her arms trying to run away from the approaching Wolcott – she knew they would never make it. Hanna grabbed a large stone that lay on the ground and threw it with all her might at the animal. It paused for only a moment and then continued its charge. Hanna ran forward picking up a larger stone as she went. She took a second longer to aim then launched the stone which smacked the Wolcott on the inside of its back thigh. It yelped in pain as its back leg buckled. As it spun to face its attacker, Hanna threw another rock and this time caught the Wolcott in the side of the head. It shook its head and then changed its attack back to Hanna.

All thoughts of the women and child forgotten, it sprang toward Hanna, covering the distance between them faster than Hanna imagined possible. It plowed ahead. Too late to turn and run, Hanna closed her eyes and held her hands in front of her to brace herself for the impact. She felt a great force press against her, but to her surprise it was not followed by pain. She opened her eyes and to her astonishment there was a large shield of Essence between her and the Beast. The stunned creature shook its head unsure of what had occurred. It clawed the ground and growled, its anger fuelled, and charged again. Now fully aware of the Essence she had pulled from the life around her, Hanna confidently braced herself for the next impact. Keeping her eyes open she saw how the Essence shield vibrated under the impact, but still it held. The Wolcott snarled, snapped and crashed again and again into Hanna's shield. After each strike Hanna was pushed back, finding it harder and harder to keep her balance. She felt her shield becoming weaker; she knew she couldn't take much more. The creature struck again sending Hanna to her knees, but instead of a victorious howl the animal yelped in pain again.

When it whirled around, Hanna saw an arrow protruding from its inner thigh. Shouts of men taunted the creature and more arrows were shot at it. Most bounced harmlessly off its tough hide, but one or two found a sensitive spot to penetrate. The arrows may not have caused the Beast any serious harm because its' hide was too thick, but they were very effective at frustrating it and drawing its attention away from Hanna. It charged towards the men who started to run. Every now and then, an archer would turn and send a few arrows towards the Beast to ensure it continued its pursuit. Exhausted and terrified, Hanna pulled herself back to her feet and followed the hunting party of Jagare; now sure she was out of immediate danger she was curious how they would go about killing this behemoth. It didn't take long to catch up to the group as they had finally stopped running and formed a semi-circle to confront the creature. Seeing the men turn, the creature slowed its approach, twisting its head left, then right, trying to ascertain where the next attack would come from. As one, all the men drew back their arrows and let fly, sending a dozen shafts through the air straight at the Wolcott. That was enough to enflame its fury and with a snarl it charged with all its speed. Hanna held her breath as she saw the great Beast trampling the underbrush, knowing in seconds its husks would tear into the hunters like a hot knife through butter. And then, it disappeared. A great shriek of pain and anguish filled the air as Hanna realized that the ground had given way. She slowly inched her way toward the edge and saw the Beast, twitching as it died, at the bottom of a fifteen-foot deep pit, impaled by several sharpened stakes that covered its base like a porcupine's quills.

As she looked at the Wolcott, she collapsed to her knees and began to shake. She bent over as the contents of her stomach made a quick and unwelcome exit, burning her throat along the way. One of the hunters rushed to Hanna's side.

"You're ghostly pale," he said with a note of concern in his voice.

Hanna was barely conscious of his presence as he swooped her up in his muscular arms and carried her back to the inn.

* * *

Hanna awoke to find she was lying on a soft bed in one of the rooms at the inn.

"Ah, you brave, brave child." Master Juro said as he took her hand.

Hanna sat up. "What happened? I don't remember getting here."

"You passed out from all the excitement I believe. I am so sorry I put you in danger. I should not have sent Karn away. It was unfortunate that I had to leave you, but I could have only detained the creature for a short time. It would have overtaken us before help came."

He handed her a glass of water with ice.

"Thank you," she said, "I am really thirsty. Is everyone okay?"

"Thanks to you. You saved that mother and child. If you had not distracted the Wolcott, they would surely have been killed."

Hanna shrugged. "I didn't really think about it, I just sort of, reacted."

"Yes. The same way you created that shield?"

Hanna smiled. "That was kind of neat, although, if those Jagare hadn't come along when they did I don't think I would be here to talk about it."

"Yes their timing was very good. I managed to find the hunting party just as they were returning to the inn for the day so, fortunately, they were already armed and ready. A little luck, some talent and a great deal of bravery saw you safely through the whole ordeal."

Kazi came into the room.

"Hanna! You're awake! I heard what happened. That was awesome! I wish I could have seen it."

Hanna shook her head. "No you don't. It was the scariest thing of my life! I could hear Tahtay Biatach telling me to run or the thing would bite my head off. I think that was the fastest I've run yet."

"Well I'm glad you're still here. I almost thought when Karn and I left I wouldn't see you again. Not only are you still here but I understand you're a hero!"

Hanna's eyes clouded over for a moment. She turned to Master Juro.

"Are you sure I won't be able to get back home?"

Master Juro sighed. "I'm sorry Hanna. I wish I could say differently, but you will not be able to go home."

Hanna sat very still. The ordeal with the Wolcott had definitely given her a new appreciation of life, but the thought of not going home left her crestfallen. While on

Galenia, she had been having the time of her life and had kept putting off the idea of going home, but not going back? That just hadn't occurred to her. As she thought about the implications of those words, images of her parents and brother flashed before her eyes. Her friends, as few and as superficial as they may be, also crossed her mind. She would never see them again. Ever. More than anything, at this very moment, she wanted to give her mom a hug. The room became a blur as tears formed in Hanna's eyes while the words "not be able to go home" kept repeating in her mind.

Desperately not wanting to cry in front of them she asked, "I'm sorry Master Juro, but do you think I could get some rest?"

He softly said, "Of course my dear, you have had a trying day. We will continue this discussion at a later time. Come Kazi, Hanna needs some sleep."

When they left the room, she immediately burst into tears. She collapsed back on the bed and buried her face in the pillow.

CHAPTER TWENTY-TWO

Honours and Bands

The room was quiet.

The morning following the feast the men gathered in the main hall, sitting at their usual places around the heavy oak tables. Their instructors for the last few months watched them; their expressions hinting at knowledge the new Yaru were not privy to. Jon's attention kept returning to Nandin who seemed to be struggling to maintain his stoic expression and looked as if he would break into a grin at any moment. Jon knew he could easily pry whatever it was that Nandin was trying to hold back except that Mateo stood at the head table gazing around the room waiting for the men's full attention before speaking.

When all eyes were unwavering on Mateo, he stretched out his arms and spoke.

"Thank you for joining me today my brothers. It has been a great privilege to watch you develop your skills; to see you become the Yaru I knew you could be. Of course your training has only just begun. I believe, as do your instructors, you have reached your potential here and it is time to take the next step. It is time for you to put what you have learned to use. To begin working towards the dream we all share. It is time for you to make this world a better place. Your missions will begin in one week. The Yaru captains have chosen their own teams based on each of your abilities. "

The men began to talk excitedly attempting to guess what team they would be on. Mateo allowed them a few

291

moments before he raised his hands again for their attention. Once they quieted down he continued.

"Each team will have its own missions, but may need to collaborate at times. You will be spread out across the countryside and will regroup at predetermined locations. I, however, must remain here as I have important work that needs to be done and I can't afford to be travelling at this time; therefore, I have decided to appoint a commander. He will be my eyes, ears and voice in the field. He will bring instructions from me and belay them to the Captains. Also, he will carry the Captains' reports to me. If a decision needs to be made immediately, he will make it on my behalf. With full support from the Captains, I am pleased to announce Nandin as my first commander."

At this point Hatooin and another Kameil hustled in the room with a large chair that appeared identical to Mateo's but slightly shorter.

"Commander Nandin..." Mateo gestured towards the newly placed seat.

As Nandin rose, the room exploded in applause. The men were sincerely excited for Nandin, not only because he was well-liked, but also because of the message it implied, for if one of their own could rise so quickly to sit at Mateo's right hand then they must truly be considered his equal. Even Jon clapped Nandin on the back as he made his way to his newly appointed seat; in Jon's mind this meant they were one step closer to righting any wrongs Mateo been part of and preventing any more from being made.

When Nandin finally made it to the head of the table, through all the hand shaking and back-slapping, he was caught off guard when Mateo embraced him. He presented Nandin a black armband, embroidered with a silver castle. Once seated, Nandin smiled and waved at his fellow Yarus and then gratefully took the glass of water that magically materialized in Hatooin's hand. He downed the mug, hoping when he finished his face would no longer be flushed as he had felt the heat rise the moment his name was announced.

As the room began to settle, Mateo continued with his announcements.

"It pleases me to see that Commander Nandin has all of your support. One other issue we need to discuss before we begin this lovely meal that Hatooin has so kindly arranged for us..."

With the appointment of Mateo's new commander, Hatooin couldn't help but feel like he was being replaced. At the mention of his name, he stood a little taller with the trace of a smile on his lips.

"With all of my Yaru departing from the valley, those of us left behind are in a bit of a predicament. We will be solely dependent once more on our farms, which will again become vulnerable to attack from Beasts without your protection. As you know, the Jagare hunting skills have been lost to us for many generations and only when your men brought your talents to us did we benefit from wild game. What we need is a Huntmaster to train the Kameil to hunt and protect our lands. Again, with the support of the captains, I humbly ask Jon if he would assume this position."

Since Nandin was well aware of Mateo's offer ahead of time, he had been watching for Jon's reaction. Nandin thought that the "humble" offer was a nice touch and would surely be an effective tactic to use when it came to Jon. If Jon had just been given the position he may have instinctively refused it. Describing the villages' need would also be a most convincing way to appeal to Jon.

Jon rose to his feet. "I would be honoured," he said in a strong, steady voice.

Hatooin stepped toward Jon and attached an armband with a green Mystic Flyer on it – a symbol known as the Huntmaster's.

As he sat down, Jon was still stunned by his new appointment. Huntmaster was the position he had always aspired to become back home. To be given the office at his young age was unheard of anywhere else on Galenia. Jon never thought Mateo would make any of his dreams come true, but more than that, being Huntmaster would allow Jon all sorts of freedoms and privileges he never thought Mateo would bestow upon him. Privileges such as coming and going out of the valley as he saw fit, as well as learning the surrounding landscape better than Mateo himself were two of the most prominent on his mind. Despite this newfound freedom, he already felt the burden his role would bestow upon him and began devising a better way to protect the farmlands from attack.

His concerns must have shown on his face as Mateo laughed, "Relax Jon. You will have plenty of time to plan your tactics. For today, let us enjoy our time together. When our meal is finished I request the audience of the Commander and the Captains in my study. Before we begin to eat, the Captains will hand out their teams armbands."

The Captains took turns calling out the names of the men on their perspective teams. The armbands had the symbols of each of the leaders specialty: swordsmanship, climbing, speed, combat and archery.

Mateo motioned to Hatooin who clapped his hands causing the entrance of several serving staff carrying platters of food. Once the food was laid out, the men, hungry as usual, but now filled with a fervour brought on by Mateo's news and appointments, devoured the meal hastily.

CHAPTER TWENTY-THREE

Apathy and Purpose

Hanna was numb.

She had spent the remainder of the evening holed up in her room at the inn. Kazi brought her dinner, but she barely touched it; she had no appetite. The journey back to Kokoroe was subdued despite Kazi's attempt to lighten the mood. Master Juro seemed lost in his thoughts, most likely trying to solve the problem with the tear; Karn was only ever with them briefly and when he was he also kept his thoughts to himself. As for Hanna, she seemed to be sinking into a deeper melancholy. Kazi understood why Hanna was upset; knowing that she would never see her family again must be devastating, but he couldn't help but be jubilant. Yesterday he thought he may never see Hanna again – that she would indeed find her way through the tear and be lost to Galenia forever. He had tried to keep his spirits up, but Hanna had become his closest friend. He felt he could talk to her about anything and she had a unique way of looking at things. Plus she was always making his life more interesting. Life without Hanna would feel empty.

Hanna was oblivious to those around her. The ride passed in a blur as she was immersed in the past. With each clop of the horses' hooves another image of her family would flash before her eyes; a birthday party, a summer at the beach, some random holiday dinner with various family members seated at the extended dining table filling the living room. She tried to remember the colour of her father's eyes, but for some reason that detail

295

was already lost to her or had she ever taken the time to notice?

The following days were filled with these thoughts. Excused from her lessons, she either spent her time huddled in bed or drifting through the quieter areas of Kokoroe. She teetered between depression and guilt. The depression was punctuated by her mourning the loss of her family as if they were dead. In fact, it was like everyone she had ever known before coming to Galenia was dead. She reasoned if there was no going home then she may as well get use to the thought they no longer existed. And this train of thought led to guilt. For her own family must be thinking the same thing. Hanna had disappeared off the face of the earth (they would be unaware how literal this was). They must be thinking of all the horrible things that could have happened to her and they would never know the truth. The truth being that Hanna had been having the time of her life. Horseback riding, making new friends, finding special skills, attending the best school she ever had. Guilt. They were worried and grief stricken and she hadn't given it a second thought once she arrived at Kokoroe. If Kazi didn't constantly show up with food she probably would have just forgotten to eat. It hardly seemed important to worry about herself anymore.

It was a warm afternoon when Tahtay Etai found Hanna sitting in the shade on one of the bridges connected to the gazebo, dangling her legs off the sides. The bridge was seldom used as it led off into the trees and was only chosen for quiet meanderings. Tahtay Etai approached silently.

"May I join you Hanna?" she asked. Without looking up, Hanna shrugged as if it didn't matter. Etai sat beside her and also hung her feet over the edge of the bridge.

"I see you are suffering," she stated.

Hanna's head was resting on a low rail of the bridge. Her hair fell to the side as she tilted her head to look at Etai.

After bottling up her feelings for the last few days, she finally felt the need to open up.

"I was having fun." Hanna sighed, "But now...I just feel empty inside. I never really thought I'd be here forever. I figured sooner or later I would go home. I just kept putting it to the back of my mind because I couldn't do anything about it anyway. Now the only thought that sticks in my head is 'I can't go home, I will never see my family again'."

Etai put her arm around Hanna. "You mustn't lose hope."

Hanna sat up.

"What do you mean? Master Juro said there was no going back. How can I still have hope?"

Etai looked up at the clear blue sky and smiled ever so slightly.

"Well, he doesn't know that. No one does. No one knows how you got here so how can anyone know whether or not you can go back?"

She glanced at Hanna who was mulling over what she had said.

With a little less anguish in her voice Hanna replied, "So then, why did he say that? Why did he sound so certain?"

Leaning in closer, Etai softly said, "I've known Master Juro for a very long time so I have a pretty good insight as to how he thinks. His main goal is to protect and preserve this world. His knowledge is vast and his interests are for the good of the people but, between you and me, sometimes this intense focus prevents him from seeing that which does not pertain to his goal."

Hanna dared to hope. "So are you saying that there may be a way for me to get home, he just doesn't see it?"

"Perhaps. I think it would be more accurate to say he isn't looking."

Etai noticed Hanna's face begin to flush.

"Before you get angry let me explain. The tear that brought you here is dangerous to our world. With every tear, Essence is lost, from what we can surmise. If that continues, every life form on this world is at risk. It is vital for us to understand what caused this so we can prevent any more damage occurring. Master Juro believes it is critical to determine what caused the tears and stop them from happening again."

Hanna bit her lip and her shoulders sagged. "So if they are working to prevent tears then any chance that I would be able to find one and slip through is unlikely."

Etai's eyes twinkled. "Not necessarily. Once we know what causes the tears perhaps we will be able to control them or contain them, enough so you could get back. Master Juro is tasked with the safe-keeping of our world, but there is no reason why your goal of going home need be dismissed simply because it is not his goal."

Hanna shook her head not sure she understood everything Tahtay Etai was trying to say.

"So, what do I do?"

Etai said knowingly, "I think you need to work together. Your paths are linked and I have a sneaking suspicion that you will both be able to achieve your goals with each other's help. I doubt there will be a quick resolution Hanna," she placed her hand on Hanna's cheek and turned her to look her in the eye, "But I believe, one day, you will return home."

Tears ran down Hanna's cheeks as she wrapped her arms around Etai. She believed Etai to be sincere and even though that one-day may be a long time coming, she was grateful for even that small sliver of hope.

* * *

Hanna and Etai made their way back through the grounds until they came to Master Juro's domicile. Hanna made herself comfortable in one of the chairs while Etai

298

went to find Master Juro and some refreshments. Hanna was grateful when she brought with her a tray, which included some cheese, fresh fruits and iced tea – after sulking for three days, Hanna finally felt hungry. Master Juro came in shortly after and took his usual seat across from Hanna.

Before he could begin, Hanna leaned forward and said plainly, "What can I do to help?"

Master Juro glanced at Etai who nodded. He leaned back and took a moment before he spoke.

"First, let me make clear the seriousness of the situation. What caused the tears cannot be a natural phenomenon. I've mentioned before that everything on Galenia is connected. This is not belief; it is a truth. If the trees and earth are losing their Essence, it will only be a matter of time before it affects the air, the water, and even our geodes. All living creatures will suffer. This is not something that would just happen - not this randomly and instantly. The only being I have known to be this reckless, as well as this skilled, is Kenzo, one of the Three and I know he is dead. That leaves Mateo, Kenzo's son, apprentice or who knows what."

"But how can you be so sure it's him? Couldn't another Juro have done it?"

"All other Juro are loyal to our ways and work in harmony with the world. Besides, these tears are a symptom. We still haven't found the cause of this destruction and at least one Juro would have detected it by now. There is only one place we can't go. One location hidden from our view, and that's behind that wall. That's where Mateo is."

"What about the Yaru, could it be one of them?"

"Until I meet one, I won't know if they have the skill to manipulate the Essence. Either way, from what we know, they are his men. What we need to know is what is happening on the other side of that wall. I have sent messages to the Sanctuary informing those there that we

299

need surveillance done on Mateo. For all these years we have left him to his own devices out in the far eastern quadrant, assuming if we left him alone he would return in kind. Apparently this was a mistake. My hope is that we will be able to collect enough intelligence to prevent any further incidents, however, that hope is not great. Even if we can find him or see what he is doing, I doubt it will be enough for us to stop him. These are dangerous and delicate forces he is dealing with. We need a clear understanding of what he is doing and how he is doing it. The only way that I think we will learn those answers is if he, or someone close to him, tells us. This is not likely."

Master Juro paused and studied Hanna. Finally Hanna broke the silence.

"So what can I do?" she asked.

"I have been considering something, a way you could help..."

Hanna tilted her head. "Go on."

Master Juro looked at Tahtay Etai and then quickly looked away.

"You are unique Hanna. You have the abilities of a Juro and, given proper training, I think you could have the strength and endurance of a Jagare. Yet, at any time you could pass as a Kameil."

Tahtay Etai sat a little straighter, tension visible on her face.

"If you were Kameil, there would be a chance you could meet those who have the answers we are looking for and bring this information back to us."

"Mahou," Tahtay Etai spoke in a hushed voice, "You aren't seriously considering sending Hanna right into the Kameil's arms? We may never see her again..."

Before Tahtay Etai could make further argument Hanna interrupted.

"You said yourself, I need to work with Master Juro."

Master Juro continued, "I have no intention of sending you unprepared or without more information. This

300

will take intense training and planning. You will learn to defend yourself, to survive. We will make sure to find the right Kameil to send you to and we will have a way to get you back. My first choice would be to apprehend Mateo and speak to him directly. That would require him leaving that fortress of his and I have no idea how likely that is. Therefore, my second choice would be to infiltrate his followers. Hanna if you are willing, this is the role I would ask of you."

Hanna closed her eyes. Home. That was all Hanna had been thinking about since the Wolcott attack. It's what she should have been concerned with since arriving on Galenia, how to get home. She barely had paused long enough to think how the tears were affecting anyone else, aside from her initial trip to Kokoroe when she used their concerns to ease any guilt or worry she had. Now Master Juro was talking about the survival of Galenia and Hanna could actually help. Going home was her ultimate goal, but at this moment she realized her problems were trivial compared to the destruction of an entire world. She could actually do something to make a difference and suddenly she knew, that's what really mattered.

She opened her eyes, locked them onto Master Juro's, and simply asked, "When do we start?"

ABOUT THE AUTHOR

Born in Alberta, Canada, LAURA L. COMFORT is a freelance writer whose works include fantasy novels, script writing and educational resources. She is a member of multiple online writing groups. Her passions include caving, horseback riding, tap-dancing and teaching; providing lots of material to help create her fantasy world. Her motivation to write page after page comes from her children's enthusiasm for the story and persistence for the next chapter. Expect the sequel soon!

Follow her on twitter:
https://twitter.com/LauraComfort2

Or join in on the Galenia Wikia:
http://galenia.wikia.com/wiki/Galenia_Wiki

Made in the USA
Charleston, SC
27 June 2014